# FAITH

THE GURU PART 2

MARK DAVID ABBOTT

Copyright © 2022 by Mark Abbott

All rights reserved.

No part of this book may be reproduced in any form or by any electronic or mechanical means, including information storage and retrieval systems, without written permission from the author, except for the use of brief quotations in a book review.

❦ Created with Vellum

*For Neil McKenzie*

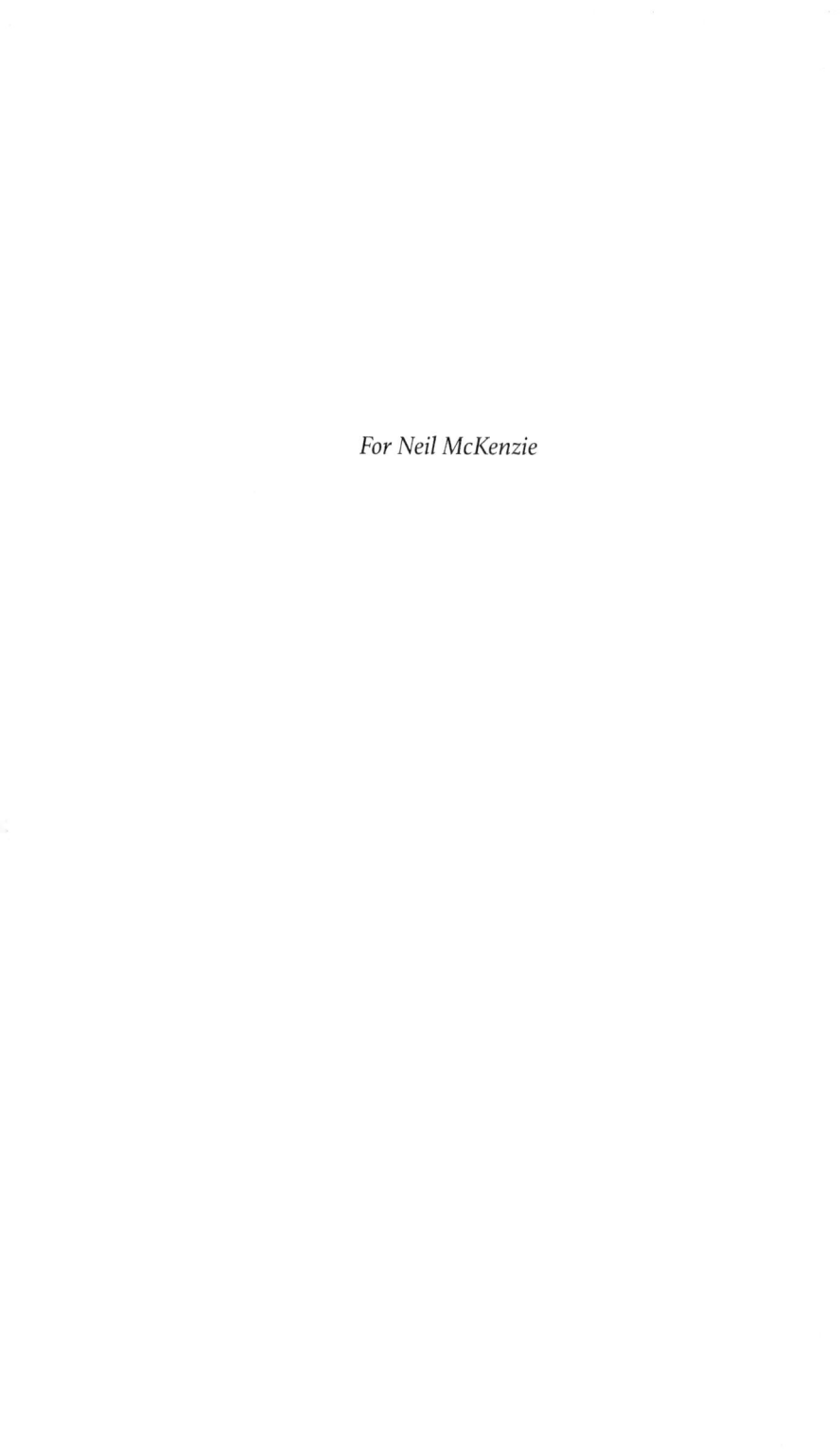

# DO YOU WANT ADVANCE NOTICE OF THE NEXT ADVENTURE?

The next book is currently being written, but if you sign up for my VIP newsletter I will let you know as soon as it is released.

Your email will be kept 100% private and you can unsubscribe at any time.

If you are interested, please join here:

**www.markdavidabbott.com**
(No Spam. Ever.)

*asato mā sadgamaya*
*tamasomā jyotir gamaya*
*mrityormāamritam gamaya*

Lead me from the unreal to the real, lead me from darkness to light, lead me from death to immortality.

# 1

Bablu Yadav wiped the sweat from his forehead with the end of the cotton towel draped over his shoulder. The humidity was debilitating and he couldn't wait to get back to the dry heat of his village in North India.

He'd be there soon. Just one more job.

He took a large mouthful of tepid water from a plastic water bottle, then tossed the empty bottle out the window of the truck. A passing motorcyclist shouted, raising a hand in protest, and Bablu sneered a reply.

Almost two hundred metres ahead, on the right-hand side of the road, sat his friend Ram, perched sideways on a stolen moped.

They'd been waiting for forty-five minutes and Bablu was getting anxious. The truck had been stolen earlier that day, and the longer he sat parked on the side of the road, the more chance a cop would pass and question him. They'd swapped the plates with another vehicle, just in case, but Bablu knew from experience that cops loved to hassle drivers like him. They always found a reason to extort money, whether it be incomplete documents, goods without the necessary permits and tax receipts, or a lack of maintenance.

The truck was a fifteen-year-old Ashok Leyland flat bed, and if the odometer was to be believed, had completed over two hundred and fifty-thousand kilometres. There were no bulbs in the rear lights and the tyres had barely any tread. No different to most goods vehicles on the road, but today Bablu didn't want to attract undue attention to himself.

"Come on, come on," he muttered, his eyes still on his friend up the road.

Bablu had to succeed, otherwise he wouldn't get the rest of the money. He'd taken five thousand rupees in advance and he'd get the balance of fifteen thousand when they completed the job. He'd have to split it with Ram, but with the money he'd saved over the last year, he had enough to pay off his family's debts and have a little left over for a small plot of land and even a cow or two. Bablu smiled. It had been a long time since he'd been back in the village, among his own people. Here, in the South, they didn't speak his language and looked down on people from the North.

A bead of sweat ran from his forehead into his left eye and he dabbed at it with the end of the cloth. The worst thing down here, though, was the weather. Back in his village, at least they had seasons. Here it was hot all the time, and he never stopped sweating. And the food didn't agree with him. They cooked everything with coconut oil and he just couldn't get used to the smell.

Ahead, Ram shifted on the moped and Bablu leaned forward to see better through the dirty, cracked windshield. A gate opened and out stepped a woman dressed in white. She looked unlike anyone else on the road. Her hair was a pale gold, and she was taller than most. Even from this distance, on a busy street, the way she moved, the way she carried herself, suggested she was a foreigner. It had to be her.

Ram removed his phone and stared at the screen, checking the photo that had been sent to them the previous day. Bablu saw him look up and nod in his direction.

It was her.

Bablu took a breath and reached forward for the ignition key. He turned it while pumping the accelerator until the tired old engine rumbled into life. Looking at the plastic figure of *Ganesha* glued to the dashboard, he said a small prayer, then touched his fingers to the statue of the elephant-headed god, and then his lips.

"*Jai Shri Ganeshaya Namaha*," he said out loud, glanced in the rear-view mirror, then hauled on the steering wheel and edged the truck out onto the road.

Ahead, Ram was now sitting astride the moped, revving the engine, clouds of blue smoke from the tiny two-stroke engine billowing from the exhaust. The foreign woman had walked ahead and as Bablu pulled onto the road, he saw her look both ways before hurrying across the road.

"*Accha hain*," Bablu muttered. "Good." She had just made his job a whole lot easier. He stamped his foot on the accelerator, sending clouds of thick black diesel smoke into the air behind him, and cursed as the truck took an age to respond. The speed slowly increased as he crunched through the gears, the woman appearing closer in the windshield.

He climbed another gear, swerving around a scooter that had stopped on the edge of the road, and kept his foot mashed to the floor, his eyes only on the woman. Fifty metres, forty, thirty....

He climbed another gear.

Twenty, ten... then he pulled left on the steering wheel.

There was an almost imperceptible bump as if the wheels had hit a pothole, but he didn't look in the mirror. He just kept on accelerating.

A smile spread across his face.

The job was done.

## 2

ONE DAY EARLIER.

"Come in," Manoj Shetty smiled from behind his desk and gestured toward the two chairs in front of him.

Sally gulped, forced a smile, then made her way inside and sat down. Wiping the palms of her hands on her loose cotton pants, she looked around the room. It was the first time she was meeting the ashram administrator alone.

Manoj closed a file on his desk with his short chubby fingers, adding it to a pile on his left. "The paperwork never ends," he shrugged, then sat back in his chair, steepling his fingers in front of him. "Now what can I do for you?" he frowned. "Sally isn't it?"

Sally swallowed again, her eyes darting from the gold rings on his fingers to his corpulent face. She nodded, but hesitated, still thinking of the best way to start the conversation. She hadn't spoken to him much before, but as manager he oversaw the day to day running of the ashram and had always been pleasant whenever their paths had crossed. Like Sally, he too was dressed in white, and had a mala of large *rudraksha* beads, the seeds commonly referred to as 'The Tears of Shiva,' around his neck.

"Umm, I... I don't know how to say this..."

The smile on Manoj's face faltered. He tilted his head to one side and sat forward. "Is something the matter? Are you unwell? I can get the Ayurvedic nurse to come and see you."

"No, no," Sally shook her head. "I'm fine. It's..." She sighed. There was no easy way to say it. She took a deep breath. "He has behaved inappropriately with me."

Manoj raised his eyebrows. "Who? One of the other students? Give me his name. I'll see that he is expelled immediately."

She shook her head.

"Then who?" His eyes widened. "No. You don't mean..."

Sally nodded.

"Guruji?" Manoj shook his head violently. "No, no... you must be mistaken."

Sally looked down at her hands in her lap. Her fingers were trembling, and she clasped her hands together to keep them steady. Looking up, she said, "He asked me to come see him last night. He said he wanted to discuss my progress." A tear formed in the corner of her eye. "So I went to his house." Her voice cracked, and she paused, looking down at her lap again as the memory came back. The tear trickled down the side of her cheek. "He told me to kneel in front of him... he said there were some psychic blocks holding me back, and he would help me remove them."

"Yes, yes, of course."

Sally looked up, tears now running from both eyes, and shook her head. "No, you don't understand. He told me to close my eyes..." She sniffed, and Manoj took a handkerchief from his pocket and handed it to her. She wiped her cheeks, then her nose, then sat staring at the folded white cloth in her hand.

"And then?"

Sally didn't look up. "I felt him move closer, and then... I don't know why... but I opened my eyes..." Her shoulders shook and she clenched the handkerchief in her hand.

"What happened, my child?"

"He was standing in front of me, and he had removed his..." She couldn't say it, the memory of what happened too awful to put into words and she broke down, her body shaking as she sobbed.

She heard Manoj push back his chair and stand up, then a moment later she felt his hand on her shoulder. She couldn't help herself, and flinched at his touch.

He stepped back, holding his hands in the air. "I'm sorry," Leaning back against the corner of the desk, he asked, "Was anyone else there?"

Sally shook her head and wiped her nose with the handkerchief, then dried her cheeks with her sleeve. "No."

She looked up and saw Manoj looking down at her, deep lines creasing his forehead. She searched his face, looking for reassurance.

"I'm so sorry, my child. Nothing like this has ever happened before."

Sally sniffed and looked down again.

"Have you spoken to anyone else about this?"

She shook her head. "I didn't know who to turn to. No-one else would believe me." She began to cry again. "I feel so ashamed."

"No, no, no, you have nothing to feel ashamed about, my dear. Nothing at all." She heard him sigh. "Look, are you sure about what happened? We can never hope to understand how... these things work. He is not like you or me."

Sally frowned and looked up. "You don't believe me?"

He held his hands up. "I'm not taking sides. I'm just trying to explain the facts." He took a breath. "Here's the thing. It may have happened, but when we come to his world, which is the opposite of all we know, we must try to understand it better.

"People like him get exposed to a different kind of energy. They work on a different level. They see things we cannot see."

Sally stared back, confused by what she was hearing "But what he did was wrong."

Manoj held both his hands up. "Yes, I agree, and I'll look into it. I'm just trying to see if there is a logical explanation for it."

Sally shook her head, anger growing inside her. "There is no logical explanation for this. How can you say that? What he did was wrong and should never happen. There is no explanation for this kind of behaviour. We should…" her voice became forceful, "we have to call the police."

"Yes, yes, I agree," Manoj nodded. "You are right." He smiled down at her. "But don't you worry anymore. I'll look into it immediately. We'll sort this out and ensure that it never happens again."

Sally nodded slowly, willing herself to calm down.

"Now, is there anything I can do for you right now? Shall I call the nurse? "

Sally shook her head. "No, it's okay. I… I don't want anyone else to know right now. I feel so embarrassed."

"Yes, yes, I understand. Don't worry, I will be discrete." He cleared his throat. "But would you like someone to be with you, so you're not alone? Are you staying in the ashram?"

"No," Sally shook her head. "I've got my own room in the village."

"Hmmm, okay. I will look into this, and Sally…"

Sally looked up.

"Thank you for coming to me. I appreciate it. Now let me call my driver and I'll get him to drop you back at your room."

"No, no, it's okay, I'll walk."

Manoj stood up and walked around his desk to pick up his phone. "I won't take no for an answer. It's the least I can do."

# 3

Manoj stood by the window and watched as the white Bolero drove out the ashram gate, then turned and sat back down in his chair.

Sitting forward, he leaned his elbows on the desk and massaged his eyes and temples with his fingertips. He didn't doubt Sally's story. It wasn't the first time he had heard something like this and probably wouldn't be the last. But it was an annoyance. Why didn't she keep quiet? Hardly any of the others took it any further. In fact, some of them welcomed it. He sighed, picked up his phone, and leaned back in his chair. It was nothing he couldn't deal with, though. He'd done it before.

Scrolling through the numbers on his phone, he found the one he wanted and pressed dial.

It rang for a while before it was answered and on hearing the voice at the other end, Manoj cleared his throat and sat up straight. "Good morning, sir. Sorry to bother you."

"What is it, Manoj?"

"Umm, sir... we have a problem."

Two minutes later, Manoj ended the call and placed the phone back on the desk. He stood, walked over to the filing cabinet, opened the middle drawer, and searched through the files until he found the one he wanted. He removed it, took it back to the desk, and opened it up. Inside was a single sheet of paper with a passport sized photo pinned to the top left corner. He picked up his phone, opened the camera and zoomed in on the photo until it filled the screen, clicked a photo, opened a secure messaging app and immediately shared it to the number he had called a moment before. After checking his message had been delivered, he deleted the photo and erased the message on his phone before returning the file to the cabinet.

Pausing for a moment, with both hands resting on the top of the cabinet, he closed his eyes and took a deep breath. He had done his duty, but whatever happened next was none of his business. Opening his eyes, he turned and gazed at the large framed photograph on the wall. Guruji would understand. Manoj walked over and picked up a packet of incense from the small table beneath the photo. He removed two sticks, lit them from the permanently burning oil lamp, then held them in front of him as he looked up at the photo. Thin tendrils of sweet smelling smoke spiralled up toward the ceiling as his lips moved in a silent prayer.

*I thank you for your blessings and for watching over me. Everything I do, I do for you. I surrender myself to you completely.*

# 4

John's eyes snapped open, a distinct feeling of unease threatening to engulf him. He frowned. He rarely felt like this after his meditation. In fact, quite the opposite.

Since his time in Sri Lanka, he'd made it a regular practice to start the day with an hour of seated meditation. It calmed him, prepared him for the day ahead, and he craved the deep sense of peace that sometimes filled his whole being when he sat. It didn't happen every time, but often enough that he had changed his morning routine, no longer beginning the day with a run, a habit he'd maintained for years. He was sleeping better, no longer troubled with dreams of events from his past, and Adriana had even commented that he seemed much happier.

But this morning was different. He glanced toward the window. It was still early, the sun only just making its presence known, the sky transitioning from black to a light grey.

He inhaled slowly through his nose, straightened his back, and closed his eyes again. As he exhaled, he scanned his body, looking for points of tension, relaxing body part by body part. He brought his attention to the sensation of the breath passing over his top lip, catching his thoughts every time his mind wandered, each time bringing his focus back to the breath.

He opened his eyes again. It wasn't working. Sighing, he unfolded his legs, shaking out the cramps, wincing slightly as the blood rushed back to his toes, the sensation of pins and needles making his leg twitch. There was no sense in fighting it. He'd learned the hard way that the more he forced himself to calm his mind, the more frustrated he became. Today seemed like one of those days. But he couldn't shake the sense of foreboding, the feeling that something bad was going to happen. Perhaps he did need to go for a run.

## 5

John slipped his shoes off by the door, punched in the code on the keyless lock, and walked into the apartment. The smell of freshly brewed coffee filled the air, and he eased the door closed, and padded silently across the apartment into the kitchen. Adriana stood with her back to him, a mug of coffee in her hand while she scrolled through the iPad on the countertop.

He moved in closer, slipped his arms around her from behind, and nuzzled her neck.

"*Bom dia.*"

Adriana leaned her head back against his. "Good morning." She placed her mug down and turned around, tilting her head back so John could kiss her on the lips.

"Oooh, you're all sweaty."

John tightened his embrace and moved his lips to her neck. "I can make you sweaty too," he murmured, pressing his body into hers.

"No, no," Adriana giggled, "not this morning. I have an early meeting."

"It won't take long," John protested.

"Ha," Adriana scoffed. "You know that's not true." She pushed him away. "But I won't say no tonight," she said with a wink.

John sighed loudly and let go of her. "I'll hold you to that." He removed a water glass from the cupboard, filled it from the tap, and drank half of it in one go before refilling it. Turning, he leaned back against the countertop and nodded toward Adriana's coffee mug.

"Is there more of that?"

"Yes, plenty. I just made it. Shall I pour you one?"

John shook his head and held up his glass. "No, I'll rehydrate first."

"How come you went for a run this morning?"

John shrugged. "I just felt like a change. The meditation wasn't happening."

Adriana frowned, "You're still enjoying it though?"

"Yeah... yeah," John shrugged again and made a face. "I just couldn't get into it today. It happens."

Adriana studied his face for a moment. "I know I've already said this, but I really think it's helped. You seem less troubled, more at peace with yourself. I like what it's done for you."

John grinned. "Well, that's good enough for me." He drained the glass and upended it on the draining board. "Can I make you some breakfast?"

Adriana glanced at the Cartier he'd bought her for her birthday. "No, I have to run. I'll get something in the office." She picked up the iPad, leaned toward John, and kissed him on the cheek. "I'll see you tonight."

John followed her as she picked up her bag and walked toward the door. "Let me know if you have time for lunch. I'll come in and see you."

Adriana turned in the doorway and flashed him a smile,

her eyes twinkling with amusement. "What and have the girls in reception swooning over you?"

John grinned. "I'll meet you outside."

Adriana placed a hand on his arm, "Joking aside, I don't think I'll get time today." She squeezed his bicep. "But tonight we have some unfinished business."

"I've not forgotten."

John watched her walk down the corridor and press the button for the lift. The lift doors opened, and she turned and waved before entering the lift. John stepped back inside the apartment, closed the door, and leaned back against it. The buzz from the run had subsided and once again, he had a feeling of unease.

# 6

Detective Inspector Rajiv Sampath returned the salute from the constable guarding the entrance to the Shivnagar Police Station.

"How's your wife doing?" He furrowed his brow. "Sujata, isn't it?"

The constable beamed. "Yes, sir. Thank you, sir. She is doing well."

"And the baby is at home now?"

"Yesterday, sir. My sister has come to help also."

"Good, good." Rajiv nodded and smiled at the proud young father. "If you need anything, come and tell me."

The constable's smile couldn't get any wider and he bobbed his head vigorously from side to side. "Thank you, sir. But everything is okay."

Rajiv nodded, patted the constable's shoulder, and entered the station. A labourer stinking of booze squatted on the floor, his hands clasped in front of him, while a chubby woman in a sari — his wife by the sound of it — harangued the senior constable at the desk.

The constable looked up as he entered, a pleading look

on his face, but Rajiv ducked his head, avoiding eye contact and scooted past and down the corridor toward his office. The last thing he wanted was to get involved in a domestic argument. Anyway, he wasn't sure why the woman had come to the station. She looked and sounded like she could sort her husband out herself. She had forearms like Popeye.

He removed his cap and tossed it onto his desk, running his fingers through his hair as he gazed out the window toward the *peepal* tree that shaded the police compound. He'd spent most of the day doing the rounds of the area, checking on his men, meeting informants, making sure they saw his face in the community. Good, honest policing. He enjoyed it but was now tired and thirsty and he welcomed the cool and relative quiet of his office. Walking over to the wall, he switched on the ceiling fan and turned the dial, increasing the speed to its maximum, the sudden movement of air setting the papers on his desk fluttering under the paperweight.

"Manjunath," he called out. He could murder a nice hot *chai*. The constable appeared in the doorway just as Rajiv rounded his desk and sat down. "Sir?"

"What's going on out there?" Rajiv could still hear the shrill voice of the disgruntled wife.

Manjunath grinned. "She wants us to lock him up. Say's he's a good-for-nothing who spends all his time drunk."

Rajiv sighed. "I'm glad I'm not out there. Bring me some *chai*, will you? I'm parched."

"Yes, sir. Oh, Sir, wants to see you immediately."

"Muniappa?"

Manjunath nodded.

Rajiv was about to make a face, but stopped himself in time. "Okay." He pushed himself to his feet and picked up his uniform cap.

"Don't forget the *chai*, and put lots of ginger."

"Right away, sir."

Rajiv placed the cap on his head and walked over to the small plastic mirror hanging on a nail by the door. He straightened it, then checked his cap in the reflection.

What the hell did Muniappa want? Rajiv had little respect for his boss, the superintendent of police. He was too political, always trying to suck up to the political leaders. It was never about policing for him. All he was interested in was career advancement and covering his back. They had clashed on many an occasion and Muniappa made little secret of his dislike for Rajiv. But the reflected glory of Rajiv's case record and performance made Muniappa look good, so they continued on in an uneasy atmosphere of mutual distrust and animosity.

With one last tug on his uniform shirt, he took a deep breath and walked the short distance down the corridor and paused outside the closed door of the SP's office. He knocked gently and leaned his head in toward the door, straining to hear a response over the continuing argument at the front desk.

"Enter."

Opening the door, he stepped inside, closed the door behind him and stood to attention in front of it, his eyes on a framed photo of Muniappa shaking hands with the Chief Minister, on the wall behind the desk.

Superintendent Basavraj Muniappa didn't bother to look up, simply gesturing with his left hand for Rajiv to take a seat.

Rajiv moved over, pulled out the chair, and sat down. He remained silent, waiting for Muniappa to acknowledge him. It was a power game, but Rajiv was content to allow the man his petty victories.

After a minute, Muniappa sat back in his chair. He looked Rajiv up and down as if inspecting his uniform, but finding nothing he could disagree with, closed the file on his desk and slid it toward Rajiv.

"I want you to take care of this."

Rajiv reached forward and picked up the file, opening it and scanning the sheet of paper inside. He frowned and looked up. "Security detail? For a... a god-man?"

Muniappa raised his hand as if to stop Rajiv saying anymore.

"The Chief Minister wants me to put my best man on the job, and..." he smirked. "You are my best man."

Rajiv ground his teeth together and tossed the file back on to the desk. "I have better things to do than babysit some..." he gestured at the file, "religious figure."

Muniappa frowned deeply and leaned forward, resting his forearms on the desk. "He is a very powerful guru, and it would do you good to show some respect."

Rajiv bit his tongue.

Muniappa continued. "The Chief Minister wants us to ensure his safety and to make sure that everything goes smoothly during his visit to Bangalore."

"Doesn't he have his own security?"

Muniappa nodded. "He does, and you will meet his head of security first thing in the morning. But he is a high-profile foreigner and you know how they're not used to the way things work here. So I want you in charge." He gestured at the file. "It's all in there. I suggest you familiarise yourself with the contents and prepare for tomorrow."

Rajiv mentally cursed his luck, but nodded agreement. "Will that be all, sir?"

Muniappa nodded and reached for his phone, the meeting clearly over.

Rajiv got to his feet and walked toward the door. As he opened it, he heard the SP's voice. "Make sure you don't make any mistakes."

"Sir." Rajiv replied without turning around and walked out.

The noise from the front desk had finally subsided, and he went back to his office and dropped the file on his desk before removing his cap and sitting down. Spotting his *chai*, he removed the saucer that covered it and took a sip.

"Dammit!" It was already cold. "Manju!"

# 7

"Tough day?"

"Yes," Adriana sighed, as she kicked her shoes off by the door and slipped her laptop bag off her shoulder.

John walked over, put his arm around her, and pulled her close. He kissed her on the forehead as she leaned her head against his shoulder. "I'm exhausted," she murmured into his neck.

"Drink?"

"Why not?"

John released his embrace, and with his fingertips under her chin, tilted her head upwards, kissing her on the lips, before stepping away.

"Gin?"

Adriana nodded and moved toward the sofa as John went to the drinks cabinet. He removed two Copa De Balon glasses as Adriana sat down and put her feet up.

"How was your day?"

John shrugged as he carried the two glasses in one hand and a bottle of Botanist in the other, toward the kitchen.

"Quiet. I went for a drive, had lunch down at BouBou's, nothing exciting."

"Hmmm."

John removed the ice tray from the freezer, filled both glasses with ice, then poured a generous measure of Botanist into each glass. He topped them up with cold tonic from the fridge and then added a slice of blood orange as a garnish.

Adriana was smiling as he carried both glasses into the living room. "No-one makes them as well as you."

"I've had plenty of practise," John winked as he handed the glass to her and then sat down at the other end of the couch. "*Chin chin.*" He raised his glass and Adriana did the same before taking a big sip and closing her eyes.

"Mmmm, I needed that," she murmured.

John sipped his own. He had to admit it was pretty good. "What's keeping you so busy?"

Adriana shook her head and took another sip before replying. "Nothing major. Just deadlines. But I got some interesting news today."

"Yeah?"

"An old friend has surfaced. You'll never guess who."

John raised an eyebrow.

"Go on, guess." Adriana urged.

John grinned and looked up at the ceiling as if giving it some thought. "Umm, Elvis?"

"Nooo," Adriana giggled. "Atman."

The smile disappeared from John's face as he looked back at her. "Where?"

"India."

"Huh." John shook his head. "Not surprising, I suppose. India has a long history of... gurus." He said the last word as if it left a nasty taste in his mouth. "How did you find out?"

"One of my interns. She knew I'd done the stories earlier this year. Apparently, Atman has an ashram there. He's doing some sort of tour."

John stared into his glass as he remembered the events in Sri Lanka over six months earlier. He'd suspected Atman would surface again somewhere in the world, but hadn't expected it to be so soon.

"Are you okay?"

"What?"

"Are you okay? You look a bit upset."

John looked back at Adriana, forced a smile, and shrugged at the same time. "Yeah." He sighed. "I'm just annoyed that these guys always get away with it. Even after all your hard work, your articles, the negative publicity."

"Hmmm." Adriana shrugged. "That's the world we live in, though."

John shook his head, then lifted his glass and drained the contents. The buzz he had felt had disappeared. He stood up and nodded toward Adriana's glass. "Do you want another one?"

Adriana frowned at him, then looked down at her glass. "Ah, no. I've just started."

John nodded and walked back to the kitchen, deep in thought. Why was he feeling so annoyed? Atman was no longer his business. He'd done what he could back in Sri Lanka. Driven him out of the country in disgrace, and Adriana's articles had exposed him for the fraud he was.

John refreshed his drink, then walked back to the sofa, conscious that Adriana was watching him with concern. He sat down and smiled. "I'm fine," he reassured her.

"Really?"

"Yes, really I'm fine. Now, do you feel like going out for something to eat or should we stay in?"

Adriana made an apologetic face. "Do you mind if we stay in? I just want a quiet evening. We can order something..."

"No problem." John smiled and took a sip of his drink, feeling the warmth of the fragrant spirit in the back of his throat as he swallowed. A thought popped into his head. Turning to Adriana, he asked, "Where in India exactly?"

"Bangalore."

## 8

"In here."

Rajiv Sampath waited as his driver pulled up in front of the entrance to the Vijaya Palace Hotel. Five waist-high stainless steel pillars blocked the way forward, and they waited as a security guard exited the guard booth to their left.

Rajiv had been to the hotel before. Not privately — it was too expensive. But he remembered coming here professionally. He watched the security guard record the Police vehicle registration number and time of entry on a clipboard and remembered that time.

He had been investigating the death of Surya Patil, the former Chief Minister of Karnataka, who had fallen to his death from his hotel room balcony. It had been explained away as an unfortunate accident, but deep down Rajiv was sure there had been more to it. He was also sure it had involved a man who, despite his methods, Rajiv had grudgingly come to respect. A man called John Hayes. *Where is he now?*

The security guard walked back into the booth and

pressed an unseen button. The five pillars slowly descended into the ground and Rajiv's driver edged the vehicle forward.

"Wait." Rajiv rolled down his window and beckoned to the security guard. The man hurried out of the booth and stood to attention beside the vehicle.

"Why didn't you check under the vehicle?"

"Sir?" The guard looked puzzled.

Rajiv nodded to the mirror on the end of a long pole, leaning against the wall of the guard booth. "You normally check under every vehicle before allowing entry, am I right?"

"Yes, sir." The guard swallowed. "But, sir, you are police."

"It doesn't matter." Rajiv growled, keeping his face stern.

The crestfallen guard wouldn't meet his eyes.

"I want you to check every vehicle. I don't care who it is. Police, government vehicles, staff, even Puneet Rajkumar."

The guard grinned at the mention of the famous movie actor's name.

"Everyone. Do you understand me?"

The grin slipped from the guard's face, and he bobbed his head. "Yes, sir."

"Good. I will check, and if I find you're not doing it, I'll have you removed from this post."

"Yes, sir. I will do it, sir."

Rajiv nodded and gestured for his driver to proceed. He'd been harsh, but the guards needed to take him seriously.

The police Bolero pulled into the *porte-cochere*, and Rajiv stepped out. "Wait in the vehicle," he instructed the driver, and then turned back to face the entrance. A doorman in a gold-embroidered calf-length tunic and sporting a luxurious handlebar moustache stood beside the door. To the left of the entrance, two more staff members stood beside a walk-through metal detector. He walked toward them and they stiffened, before one gestured toward the hotel entrance. "It's okay, sir."

"No!" Rajiv growled again. "It's not okay. Make sure everyone enters through the metal detector."

The staff member visibly paled. "Yes, sir. Sorry, sir."

Rajiv continued glaring at the young man, before switching his gaze to his colleague, who was suddenly finding the toes of his shoes very interesting. Feeling he had intimidated them enough, he stepped forward, removed his keys and a handful of coins from his pocket and placed them in a tray, then stepped through the detector. It beeped. He stopped and waited as the first young man stepped forward with a handheld detector. He avoided eye contact as he scanned Rajiv's body; the detector beeping again as it passed over Rajiv's uniform belt buckle. Satisfied, he stepped back and bobbed his head. "Okay, sir."

"What's your name?"

"Ramlal, sir."

"Ramlal, I want to make sure you do this every time. Don't allow anyone to get through without being checked. I don't care who they are."

"Yes, sir."

"I know some VIPs will object, but if anyone gives you trouble, you tell them to get in touch with me. Detective Inspector Rajiv Sampath. Shivnagar Police Station."

"Yes, sir."

"Good." Rajiv smiled for the first time, then walked toward the door. He nodded at the doorman's moustache and entered the hotel.

A massive flower arrangement twice Rajiv's height took pride of place on a table in the centre of the opulent three-story lobby. An Asian businessman, Korean or Japanese —

Rajiv wasn't sure — sat on a leather sofa to the right, and another couple stood in front of the reception counter, which took up the whole left side of the lobby.

A man looked up from behind the counter and spotted Rajiv in his uniform. He wasn't quick enough to hide his initial reaction, nor the nervous glance toward the guests checking in, but by the time he rounded the counter, a broad smile was plastered across his face.

"Inspector Sampath, welcome back. Anil Kripalani."

Rajiv shook the general manager's proffered hand. "You have an excellent memory, Anil."

Anil shrugged. "In my business, it pays to remember names." He lowered his voice. "And it's hard to forget the events of our last meeting."

Rajiv nodded in agreement.

"Can I get you something? Something to drink? Tea, coffee, perhaps something to eat?"

"No, thank you." Rajiv glanced around the lobby. "I'm here to see one of your guests. I believe he's expecting me."

"Yes, of course. What is his name?"

"Ahh... Mr... Atman."

At the mention of his name, a change came over the general manager. His face flushed and the fake smile he wore earlier turned into something more genuine, this time including his eyes. He held his hands together in front of his chest as if praying or about to say '*namaste.*'

"Oh yes. What a wonderful man. We are so honoured to have him stay with us. It is a true blessing."

"Hmmm. Perhaps you can tell me which room he is in?"

"I will do better than that, Inspector. I will take you up personally."

# 9

Rajiv remained silent as they rode the lift to the top level of the hotel. Unfortunately, the general manager didn't follow his lead, instead prattling on about how much power his guest had, how he felt so much at peace whenever he was in the same room, and how the hotel takings had increased since the god-man had checked in.

Rajiv struggled to keep his face neutral, focusing his attention on the numbers changing on the display as the lift climbed higher. Rajiv believed in God. He said a prayer every morning in front of the little altar in his house before leaving for work and joined his wife at the temple whenever he had time... which wasn't often. But he had an inbuilt suspicion of these men who surrounded themselves with followers and claimed a fast track to... God, heaven, enlightenment, wealth... whatever they promised. His country-folk put so much faith in them, but too often they were let down, even cheated by the men and women who, despite what they tried to portray, were often no holier than the average person. This Atman... huh... Rajiv scoffed internally... whatever his real name was... was staying in one of the most expensive hotels in Bangalore and seemed to have an inside connection with the Chief Minister, a man not known for his spiritual proclivities.

The lift chimed its arrival, putting an end to Rajiv's train of thought, and the doors glided silently open.

"This way, please." Anil led Rajiv left, down the luxuriously appointed corridor, and paused at the end. A door took up the entire width of the corridor and the words 'Presidential Suite' were engraved on a brass plaque in the middle.

Expensive, Rajiv thought as the GM pressed the bell.

A moment later Rajiv noticed the peephole darken, then heard a whirring of electronic locks and the door opened. Standing in the doorway was a large, well-built western man dressed in a white *kurta*. His hair was cropped close to his head, his face lean, and he looked Rajiv up and down with hard eyes, before forming a smile... of sorts.

"Please come in."

He had an accent Rajiv didn't recognise. Neither English nor American.

Rajiv stepped past the man and waited as Anil followed him in and the door closed behind them. A short hallway opened onto a broad living room with an expanse of floor to ceiling windows providing a stunning view across the city.

The large man moved past them and stood in front of Rajiv, holding out his hand. "I am Georges," he introduced himself, pronouncing the g like a j. "Atman's head of security."

Rajiv took his hand. A firm grip and Rajiv matched it, not breaking eye contact. "Detective Inspector Rajiv Sampath."

"A pleasure to meet you. Siddarth told me you would look after our security while we are here in the city."

Rajiv blinked at the mention of the Chief Minister's name. *First-name terms.* He stored the information away for later.

"Yes."

"Please come in, take a seat."

Georges led the way into the lounge area and gestured toward a couple of sofas, set at right angles to each other and facing a large armchair. Of Atman, there was no sign, although, after a quick glance around the room, Rajiv noticed a couple of closed doors. He sat down and removed his cap, while Anil hovered nearby.

Georges moved to the other sofa and gave the general manager a smile that didn't reach his eyes. "That will be all. Thank you, Anil."

"Oh." Anil's gaze flicked toward one of the closed doors. "Yes, of course. Umm..."

Rajiv watched his expression change from eager anticipation to disappointment.

"Do you need anything?"

Georges glanced at Rajiv. "Coffee, tea?"

Rajiv shook his head, and Georges turned back and looked at the now visibly uncomfortable manager.

"I ah... guess I should go then."

Georges said nothing.

Anil nodded to Rajiv, took a couple of steps backwards, then turned and hurried to the door.

Rajiv noticed Georges watching him leave, his face still expressionless, but once the door closed, he turned back to Rajiv. His mouth was smiling, but his steel-blue eyes seemed to bore right through him. Rajiv had seen eyes like that before, but couldn't remember where.

"So, Detective Inspector, or can I call you Rajiv? Seeing as we will be working closely together."

Rajiv nodded and smiled at the same time.

"Rajiv, what would you like to know?"

"Your program for the next... two days, is it?"

"Yes, two days." Georges shrugged, "For now."

Rajiv raised an eyebrow. "For now?"

Georges hesitated and glanced out the window as a brown kite swooped past the window at eye level. "Atman doesn't like to plan too much in advance." Turning back, he fixed Rajiv in his gaze again, "He prefers to be led by the universe."

Rajiv frowned. "What does that mean, exactly?"

Georges made a face as if he was explaining something to a child. "Atman operates at a different level to you and I. His understanding of how the world works is beyond our comprehension. He tells us there is always a greater power at work and that guides him. If it guides him to stay more than two days, then he will do so."

Rajiv nodded as if it made sense, looked down at the cap on the seat beside him and adjusted its position, while he put his thoughts in order. "Okay."

Looking back up, he studied Georges' face, his build, those eyes. "I'm guessing you're ex-military, Georges?"

Georges blinked in surprise but recovered quickly, the corner of his mouth twitching in the hint of a smile. He gave a slight nod.

It had been a guess, but Rajiv's intuition rarely let him down. "So, I'm sure you will understand that for me to do my job properly, I need something more... definite. I need to plan routes, I need to study venues, I need to know timings. In a city like this... a city with a population of over twelve million people, it's not something that can be done at the drop of a hat."

Georges stared back for what seemed like an eon, then nodded. "I can see why the universe has chosen you to be here right now. You're obviously the right man for the job."

Rajiv kept his expression blank. It wasn't the universe who had chosen him. It was his idiot boss Muniappa who wanted him out of the station.

Georges leaned forward and picked up a sheet of paper from the low table in front of him, holding it out for Rajiv. "I've printed out our program for the next two days."

Rajiv took it and scanned down the page as Georges continued, "But as I mentioned earlier, sometimes Atman is guided to do something off-program. I realise this may make your job a little more difficult, but please have faith that if Atman does something, it is for a good reason and that nothing will go wrong."

Rajiv looked up. "I don't mean any disrespect, but I prefer to put my faith in planning and forethought."

George dipped his head in acknowledgment.

"I see there's nothing for today?" Rajiv queried.

"No. We've had a long journey and Atman prefers to spend the day in meditation and reflection."

"Good. It will give me time to plan for tomorrow, so it's for the best." Rajiv paused. He had to ask. "Where have you come from?"

Georges dismissed the question with a wave of his hand. "It's not important."

Rajiv waited for him to elaborate, but Georges matched his gaze without saying anymore.

Giving up, Rajiv continued, "I'll need photographs and ID copies of everyone in your party. Is it just you and Atman?"

"There's one more."

"Okay, photos and ID, passport will be sufficient, as well as the details of the vehicle you will travel in." Rajiv removed a card from the breast pocket of his uniform. "You can have them emailed here."

Georges took the card, studied it for a moment, then slipped it into the breast pocket of his *kurta*.

"Do you expect any trouble at all? Is there any threat I should know about?"

Georges shook his head, the familiar half-smile returning to his face. "None whatsoever. It's more for... how shall I say this... crowd control? When people know he's around, crowds quickly gather."

Rajiv smiled. "Well, one thing about India is we can always guarantee a crowd."

"I'm sure."

Rajiv picked up his cap. "I have all I need right now. I'll be back with my men at," he glanced at the sheet of paper, "0930 tomorrow." He stood up and held out his hand. "I would have liked to have met Mr... ahh... Atman, so I know who I'm protecting, but as he is resting, that will have to wait for tomorrow."

"Why wait 'til tomorrow?"

## 10

Rajiv jumped at the voice behind him. He had heard no one enter the room, and he turned, surprised to see a man standing behind him. He was a similar height to Rajiv, tanned and fit, his medium length hair swept back away from his face. Like Georges, he too was dressed in white, a linen shirt open to mid-chest, and a pair of loose cotton pants. But unlike Georges, he smiled warmly, white teeth flashing against tanned skin, dark brown eyes twinkling with amusement.

"I am Atman."

Rajiv regathered his wits, smiled and reached out a hand, "Detective Inspector Rajiv Sampath."

Atman didn't take his hand, instead placing his right hand on his chest and dipping his head. "A pleasure to meet you, Rajiv."

Rajiv looked down at his outstretched hand and then let it fall to his side.

"I believe I will be in your capable hands for the next few days?"

"Yes... sir."

"Please, call me Atman."

Rajiv nodded. For some reason, he couldn't stop smiling.

Atman walked around the sofa and stood in front of him.

Rajiv noticed he was barefoot.

"Is there anything I can do to make your job easier?"

Rajiv, still smiling, shook his head. "No, thank you. Georges has given me a copy of your program. I will make arrangements and be back tomorrow in time for your first appointment."

Atman reached out with both hands, and to Rajiv's surprise, gripped his shoulders. He leaned forward and looked straight into Rajiv's eyes, as if staring straight into his soul. An unusual sensation rippled down his spine, and Rajiv realised he was holding his breath, but he couldn't look away. It was as if his eyes were locked in place.

A moment later Atman blinked, and the spell was broken. He smiled, still gripping Rajiv by the shoulders, and said, "You are a good man, Rajiv. An honest man. Everything is going to be okay." Only then did he release his grip and step away.

Rajiv exhaled, feeling lighter... relaxed.

"If you'll excuse me, Rajiv, I have some calls to make." He smiled in Georges' direction. "Georges here is my right-hand man. He will see to it that you have everything you need."

Rajiv opened his mouth to say something, but no sound came out. He cleared his throat and tried again. "Thank you."

"This way, please."

Rajiv turned to look at Georges, who was gesturing toward the door. When he looked back, Atman was already halfway toward the bedroom.

Rajiv checked he had left nothing behind, then followed

Georges toward the door and waited while the large man opened it and stood aside for Rajiv to leave.

Rajiv stepped out, placed his cap on his head, then turned to say goodbye, just as the door clicked shut behind him.

## 11

It wasn't until the evening that Rajiv had time to go through the documents Georges had sent over.

He'd forwarded the emailed documents to Manjunath, who had printed them out and placed them in a file on his desk.

He went first to the passports. There were three of them. The first two were Israeli passports for Georges Haddad and Maxim Klein.

Maxim's photo showed a young, tanned and lean face, with a close cropped haircut. Rajiv studied it for a moment and guessed he was probably ex-military like Georges.

He put the two passport copies to one side and picked up the third.

A passport issued by the government of Ukraine, for an Adam Melnyk. Atman's face smiled at the camera.

"So that's your real name." Rajiv turned his chair, moved the mouse to waken his computer terminal, opened the browser, and then typed the name into the search bar. Nothing came up.

He tried again with Georges Haddad. The search was

more successful this time, bringing up several articles linking him to Atman.

Rajiv clicked on the first one and skimmed down the page, frowned, then went back to the top and began to read it properly. The article alleged wrong-doings in an ashram in Sri Lanka. An ashram headed by Atman, and where Georges was head of security. Apparently Atman and Georges had disappeared in the middle of the night amid allegations of sexual assault and money laundering. The article was brief and gave little detail. Rajiv scrolled back to the top of the article and read the date. It had been published about six months ago. Rajiv frowned and sat back in his chair, staring at the passport copy lying on his desk. Was it true? The man seemed decent enough when he met him in the hotel. Perhaps it was just a smear campaign? He sat forward and clicked on the next article. This was much longer but written in a language he didn't recognise. A pop-up at the top of the browser offered to translate the article from Portuguese to English, and he moved the cursor and clicked on it.

Almost immediately, the article transformed into something he could read. It was clear it had been written by someone who had access to firsthand knowledge of the events, and the more he read, the more fascinated he became. It was the stuff of a fiction novel. Missing persons, grooming of students, sexual assault, piles of cash in desk drawers, weapons, special-forces bodyguards, and fleeing the authorities under the cover of darkness in dirt buggies.

Rajiv scrolled back up and clicked on the journalist's name. A bio page opened up with a photo of a very attractive olive-skinned woman with a thick mane of black hair. She could have passed for Indian, but for her eyes, which were a striking mix of brown and green. He dragged his gaze away from her photo and read her list of accomplishments. Several journalism awards, and many articles republished in international publications. Rajiv nodded. She was a serious journalist, not someone pushing a smear campaign. He read her name again. Adriana D'Silva. Somewhere in the back of his mind, the name rang a bell. Where had he heard it before?

Sitting back, he rubbed his face, then swivelled in his chair and gazed out the window. It was already getting dark, the branches of the *peepal* tree silhouetted against the twilit sky. A black shape flitted past the window as a tiny bat hunted insects drawn to the light from his office.

He thought back to the meeting earlier in the hotel room. He could imagine Georges having a shady past, but the man who called himself Atman? Rajiv shook his head. No. He usually had good instincts about people, and Atman had given him nothing but good vibes. Turning in his chair again, he stared at the computer screen and chewed his lip. But what if that journalist was right? What if he was protecting someone who, based on the allegations in the article, should actually be behind bars?

Rajeev's frown deepened. The fact the Chief Minister vouched for the man didn't fill him with confidence. Rajiv had never met a politician he could trust. He sighed and shook his head again. What had he been thrown into?

Leaning forward, he moused over the email address listed for Adriana D'Silva, copied it, then pasted it into his email program. He thought for a minute, his index finger tapping a rhythm on the side of the keyboard, then began to type. Forewarned was forearmed.

## 12

It was after eight by the time Rajiv walked in the door and dropped his uniform cap and keys on the side table. The welcoming fragrance of incense and spice filled the air and he could hear Aarthi moving around in the kitchen. He slipped off his shoes without unlacing them and walked in his socks through the living room into the kitchen.

"Mmmm, that smells good," he said as he leaned over the two-burner gas cooker and took a deep breath of the steam rising from the pot.

Aarthi grinned and gently pushed him aside as she sprinkled freshly cut coriander into the pot and turned off the flame. "Your favourite. Mangalore style chicken curry."

Rajiv leaned in and kissed her on the forehead. "Great, I'm starving."

Aarthi half-heartedly pushed him away, her eyes sparkling, "Hurry up and freshen up then."

Rajiv grinned and pulled her back, both arms holding her in a tight embrace. Aarthi giggled as he gazed down into her large brown eyes. "Have I ever told you how beautiful you are?"

Aarthi pretended to break free from his embrace, but her smile broadened. "Every day, like a scratched record."

"And I will continue to tell you every day, because every day you get more beautiful."

"Have you been drinking?"

Rajiv raised his eyebrows in mock surprise. "What? You think I have to be drunk to say this?" He leaned down and kissed her on the lips. She kissed him back, then pushed him away. "Hurry up, dinner is getting cold."

He released his hold on her, winked, then moved toward the kitchen door. "Give me five minutes." As he crossed the living room toward the stairs, he heard her singing and he grinned. It was always good to be home.

By the time he came downstairs, the table was set, and Aarthi was standing in front of the small altar attached to the wall. Her hands were clasped in front of her, her eyes closed, and her body swayed gently from side to side as she prayed. A small string of jasmine flowers was tucked into the long neat plait of her hair, falling two-thirds of the way down her back. In front of her on the altar, two incense sticks in a little brass stand sent twin spirals of fragrant smoke into the air. He stood and watched, a warm feeling filling his chest, and a moment later, as if sensing his presence, her eyes opened and she turned her head to look back at him. She flashed him a smile, then turned back to the altar, placed her fingertips to her lips, then touched the small brass idol of the goddess Durga. Only then did she turn around and speak.

"Come, let's eat."

Rajiv smiled, moved over to the table and pulled out a

chair, as Aarthi picked up his plate and spooned a big pile of steaming rice onto it.

"It's okay, I'll serve myself," Rajiv protested, knowing full well she wouldn't let him.

Aarthi ignored him, adding a generous helping of chicken curry before passing him the plate. It was a routine they went through every night. Rajiv never followed the so-called traditions. The male dominated customs that dictated a wife should wait on her husband hand and foot, but he knew that Aarthi felt happy to serve him his food.

His stomach growled, and he took a mouthful of curry and rice, and closed his eyes. "Mmmm, so good." Opening his eyes, he glanced at Aarthi who was helping herself to food, a satisfied look on her face.

"Not only beautiful, but an incredible cook."

"I think you've definitely been drinking," she giggled.

"No, I mean it. It's superb." Rajiv made a ball of rice and curry with his fingers. "And I'm so hungry. Actually, I didn't even get time for lunch today."

Aarthi looked up with concern. "Rajiv, you have to eat regularly. Work can wait."

Rajiv nodded, his mouth full.

"Why were you so busy today? Did something happen?"

Rajiv swallowed, then shrugged. "Nothing really. It's just been busy." He mixed the food on his plate, allowing the rice to soak up the curry. "Muniappa has got me doing protection duty from tomorrow, too."

"Oh." Aarthi knew how frustrated he got when he was prevented from doing his job properly. "Who is it this time? An actor?"

Rajiv grinned, his hand halfway to his mouth. "No. A holy man."

Aarthi's face lit up, and she leaned forward. "Really? Who?"

Rajiv waited until his mouth was empty before replying. "A foreigner. He calls himself Atman."

"Oh yes. I've heard about him. I'm going to see him tomorrow."

Rajiv looked up from his plate and frowned. "What do you mean?"

"You remember Meenu? Sudarshan's wife? She told me about him. He has a talk tomorrow, and she asked me to go with her."

Rajiv played with his food while he thought of a suitable response. Aarthi was much more interested in the spiritual aspect of life than he was. She prayed every day, went to the temple regularly, and often visited spiritual teachers. Rajiv didn't have time, and after the things he had seen in his job, he often wondered whether God actually existed. Of course, he never discussed this with Aarthi, sometimes accompanying her to the temple on one of his rare days off, and she never let him leave the house in the morning without saying a prayer in front of the altar. It made her happy, so he went along with it.

Religion was everywhere in India. His parents had brought him up to pray twice a day, rarely cooked non-vegetarian food, and had dragged him around the country on one pilgrimage after another. But now, as an adult, practicality had won over, and he took a more pragmatic view of life. Do good and be good, and let the rest look after itself.

He made an encouraging noise and popped another handful of food into his mouth to avoid saying anything.

"Apparently he is very powerful," Aarthi continued. "People talk about miracles and spontaneous healings. You're so lucky to be chosen for this."

"Hmmm," Rajiv swallowed. "Is that right?" He thought about what he had read earlier. But he didn't have proof yet, and he didn't want to fill her mind with negativity. "What time are you going?"

"Four o'clock."

Rajiv nodded, remembering the schedule he had memorised. "At Chowdaiah Hall."

"Yes."

He nodded thoughtfully. Attending a talk wouldn't do any harm. He smiled. "I'll keep an eye out for you."

## 13

"I got an email from the police in Bangalore today."

John looked up, instantly on alert. His heart began to race, and he felt an uneasy feeling in the pit of his stomach. He had a murky history with the Indian city, and the last thing he wanted was to hear from the police. But maybe he was jumping to conclusions.

"What about?" he asked, attempting to keep his voice calm.

"What do you think? Our friend Atman, of course."

John took a deep breath and exhaled slowly, feeling the tension immediately melt away. He reached for his wineglass and took a sip. A passing waiter, noting that his glass was almost empty, removed the bottle from the ice bucket and topped it up. He glanced toward Adriana's, but hers was relatively untouched and she smiled at him and shook her head. "*Obrigada.*"

John waited until the waiter had moved away, then asked, "What did they want?"

"Well, they wanted some more detail on what happened in Sri Lanka."

"Really?" John raised his eyebrows and smiled. "Hopefully, his past is catching up with him."

"Maybe." Adrian shrugged and glanced around the restaurant. They were in a small bistro John had discovered recently, run by a husband and wife team. The restaurant only sat ten people and was already full despite the relatively early hour. It had taken John two weeks to get a reservation. "This place is popular. The food must be really good."

"I know. It took me long enough to get us a reservation." John took another sip of wine. The bottle had been recommended by the waiter, a *Muros Antigos Alvarinho* from the *Vinho Verde* region of northern Portugal. It was dry and slightly fizzy, and John licked his lips with satisfaction. "If the food is as good as the wine, we have nothing to worry about."

Adriana smiled briefly and took a sip from her own glass before setting it down and staring at the table.

"Is something the matter?"

She shook her head.

"I know something is bothering you."

She looked up and studied his face. In the candlelight, her eyes looked darker than usual, more brown than green, and the soft light accentuated the contours of her face. She still took his breath away, as beautiful as the day he first saw her in that cafe in Bangkok.

She half smiled. "You're right, Mr Hayes. I can't hide anything from you, can I?"

John grinned. "No."

Adriana sighed. "It's what you said yesterday. Despite all we've done, the articles I've written, the evidence I presented, a man like Atman is still roaming around free. There doesn't seem to be any justice in the world."

John nodded thoughtfully as he played with the stem of his wineglass. He agreed, but didn't want to ruin the mood. "It seems like that sometimes." He looked up. "But we did our best. The rest is not up to us."

Adriana made a face, not satisfied with the answer.

John continued. "Have you replied to the email yet?"

Adriana shook her head. "Not yet."

"Then present all the facts to the Bangalore Police. Leave it up to them. The fact they are asking means they must have some suspicion."

Adriana nodded. She took a sip from her glass, her eyes on something unseen over John's shoulder, her mind elsewhere.

Refocusing on John, she smiled. "You're right. That's all I can do from here. The more people know about the real..." she let go of her glass and made quotation marks with her fingers, "'Atman,' the less chance he has to take advantage of others."

The waiter appeared beside the table, a plate in each hand, and placed them down in front of them.

*"Bom apetite."*

*"Obrigado,"* John replied and smiled at Adriana. "It looks and smells good."

"It does."

A thought popped into John's head as he watched Adriana pick up her knife and fork.

"What was the name of the policeman in Bangalore? The one who emailed you?"

## 14

Rajiv checked his watch and scowled. They were thirty minutes behind schedule and hadn't even left the hotel yet. He glanced over toward the gate where a large crowd had gathered and were noisily making their presence known. But unlike most crowds gathered to glimpse a VIP, they were well behaved. They weren't pushing, no-one was climbing the boundary wall attempting to gain entry to the hotel, and he doubted anyone would be drunk. The thought made him smile. Highly unlikely. Most were dressed in white, many with malas, strings of prayer beads draped ostentatiously around their necks, the women with flowers in their hair, the men with broad splashes of vermillion powder applied to their foreheads. They were vocal though, keeping up a constant chant of mantras or singing *bhajans*, the religious songs in praise of God. Rajiv doubted any of them would cause trouble, but he knew from experience that whenever a crowd gathered, the odds of things going wrong were multiplied.

He glanced back at the motorcade parked in front of the hotel entrance, engines idling, drivers hovering around near the front of their vehicles, waiting eagerly for the spiritual leader to appear. His own vehicle was at the front, the trusty Mahindra Bolero, its flashing red and blue lights reflecting off the glass facade of the hotel. Behind it was Atman's vehicle, a black Range Rover Sport with tinted windows, sleek and expensive looking, its powerful engine purring away in contrast to the noisy rattle of his own diesel-engined vehicle. Another police Bolero took up the rear, piloted by one of the better drivers from the station and accompanied by two armed constables, as was his vehicle in the front. The driver caught his eye and stood to attention. Rajiv nodded an acknowledgement, then walked over to the Range Rover. The driver's side window slid down as he approached, and the driver smiled back at him.

He was the young, fit looking Israeli whose passport he'd had checked the day before. Maxim. Rajiv had spoken to him earlier, and unlike with Georges, had taken an instant liking to the young man. He too held himself like an ex-soldier, but was more approachable than his colleague, polite, respectful, and had a ready smile.

"Do you know how much longer?"

Maxim shook his head and smiled. "I'm sorry. It's often like this. Atman works to his own schedule," he replied in accented English.

Rajiv frowned and glanced toward the hotel entrance.

"You are not expecting any trouble, are you?"

Rajiv turned back to Maxim and gave him a reassuring smile. "No, not at all, Maxim." He took a breath. "I just prefer things to run as planned. To keep to the schedule we have planned for."

Maxim nodded. "I understand. But as they say, man proposes, God disposes."

Rajiv nodded and sighed. "Yes. Look, if anything goes

wrong while we are in transit... I don't think it will... but if it does, my men are armed and they will deal with it. I'll ride with you. Just follow my instructions. In the worst-case scenario, we'll head straight back here to the hotel." He made a face. "Unfortunately Maxim, my vehicles won't be able to keep up with this, but I'll guide you on the best possible route."

Maxim nodded, no longer smiling. "I understand. And please call me Max. Maxim is too formal."

At that moment, a loud cheer went up from the gate and Rajiv looked up. The crowd was waving at the hotel and he turned back to see Atman walking out, Georges at his right shoulder and Anil, the general manager, following deferentially a few paces behind. Rajiv nodded at Max and hurried around the vehicle as Atman approached.

"Detective Inspector Sampath, good morning." Atman beamed at Rajiv and reached out for his hand, taking it in both of his. "I'm sorry to keep you and your men waiting." He shrugged apologetically. "There are so many calls for my time."

Rajiv couldn't help but return his smile. "It's okay. I understand. Are you ready to go?"

"I am. I put myself in your very capable hands." He was still holding Rajiv's hand and Rajiv stood uncomfortably, until his hand was released, then turned and nodded toward the lead vehicle. His men climbed in and he turned to look at the chase vehicle, where the two constables were already seated inside.

"Let's go."

He watched as Georges opened the rear passenger door for Atman, who paused and raised a hand toward the gate, setting the crowd cheering, before climbing inside. Georges closed the door, then ran round the vehicle to the other side as Rajiv opened the front door. He stood waiting for Georges to climb in and close the door. As the large man slid onto the seat, his white linen shirt hiked up, exposing the unmistakable black shape of a holster. Rajiv frowned, then climbed in and closed the door. No-one had said anything about Georges being armed. How did he have a weapon? It was hard enough for an Indian citizen to have a weapons permit, and virtually impossible for a foreigner, especially one who had just arrived in the country a day earlier. Rajiv bit his lip as the Range Rover rolled smoothly toward the hotel exit. He would deal with it later. Right now, he had a job to do.

## 15

Rajiv glowered as the motorcade pulled up in front of the entrance of the Chowdaiah Hall. Thirty minutes behind schedule had become an hour and a half.

He hated things not running to plan, but had to accept it came with the territory. Since ten that morning, he and his men had been criss-crossing Bangalore from one venue to another as Atman appeared before his followers. Bangalore's notorious traffic had been responsible for part of the delay, the roads so snarled that even with the use of the police siren and flashing lights, they had often struggled to make headway. The clincher had been the long lunch at the Chief Minister's residence, a lunch Rajiv hadn't been invited to, instead having to cool his heels outside with the rest of the men. What the Chief Minister had to discuss with a foreign 'Holy Man,' Rajiv had no idea, but the cynical side of him doubted it had anything to do with spirituality. Besides, India had enough god-men of their own, and with the Government's push to become more self sufficient, the Chief Minister should concentrate on people closer to home.

And then there were the bags. Three carry-on size bags were brought out of the Chief Minister's residence by Max and one of the staff and loaded into the back of the Range Rover. They were heavy, and it wasn't a stretch of the imagination to guess what was inside them. Rajiv had seen bags like that before. Usually around election time, when favours were being called in, or promises made in exchange for votes.

Rajiv's stomach gurgled threateningly as the Range Rover pulled to a stop. The food sent out by the Chief Minister's kitchen wasn't agreeing with him. The *dal* had been watery, and the rice had been undercooked. He glanced quickly at Max sitting beside him. His stomach seemed to be okay. The food eaten by the guests no doubt much better than that provided for the serving class.

Rajiv pulled his attention back to the present as he opened the door and stepped out, quickly scanning the environment. His men had fanned out around the vehicles, their service pistols holstered, but a *lathi,* the short length of bamboo used for crowd control, in each of their hands. There were several people gathered around in the street, more curious than anything else, wondering who was turning up in an expensive foreign car with a police escort. The hall was well known for featuring concerts and plays, and they must have thought they might be lucky enough to get a glimpse of a local celebrity.

Two women and a man, all dressed in white, stood on the top step of the hall, each of them with a garland of orange and yellow marigolds clutched nervously in their hands.

Georges had climbed out and was holding the door open, and as Atman stepped out, Rajiv tensed as the three rushed forward to greet him. He relaxed as Atman placed his right hand on his chest and gave them a big smile. One by one they placed a garland over his head and around his neck, bending down to touch his feet afterwards and then the man gestured toward the entrance. "Please, this way Guruji."

Atman turned and winked at Rajiv, then removed the garlands and handed them to Georges. Georges passed them over to Max, who had climbed out of the Range Rover, then hurried after Atman, who was already making his way up the steps.

At the top, Atman stopped and turned around. He beckoned for Rajiv to join him and waited as Rajiv jogged up the steps. "Come inside, Rajiv. Your men will be okay without you."

He frowned suddenly, then reached out and placed his fingertips on Rajeev's stomach. He closed his eyes for a couple of seconds, then when he opened them, he fixed Rajiv with that laser-like stare he had experienced the day before. "Your stomach won't trouble you now."

Rajiv blinked in surprise, glanced at Georges, whose expression hadn't changed, then back at Atman. But Atman had already turned toward the entrance.

The double width entrance doors opened as one, and as Atman stepped forward, the crowd inside erupted in applause.

## 16

Rajiv scanned the packed hall. Somewhere amongst the sea of white was Aarthi. But from his position at the back of the hall, all he could see were the backs of people's heads.

He leaned against the rear wall and turned his attention toward the stage. Atman sat in a large armchair in the centre. To his right were several musicians seated cross-legged on the stage, quiet now, unlike when he had entered, the tabla, harmonium, and flute accompanying the crowd as they had burst into song. To Atman's left was an altar, bedecked with flowers and sticks of incense, filling the hall with the smell of sandalwood. Georges and Max had taken up position at the foot of the steps leading up to each side of the stage, their eyes constantly moving, watching the massed ranks of devotees. Rajiv nodded approval. No-one would get past them.

He thought back to the weapon he had seen on Georges' hip. Was Max armed as well? Both men looked physically capable of dealing with a threat without resorting to weapons, but the fact they were carrying still troubled him.

Aside from the legality, why did a spiritual teacher need armed body guards? Who would want to attack him?

Rajiv looked around the hall again. Everyone's attention was fixed on the stage, and the faces he could see, those standing around the edges unable to get a seat, were filled with rapture, gazing with adoration at the man on the stage. Rajiv tuned into what Atman was saying, but after a minute, tuned out again. It was nothing he hadn't heard before... love for all, judge no-one, look inside yourself, happiness comes from within... etc, etc. All good advice, but something parroted by others of Atman's type.

His mind wandered to his experience outside the entrance. How on earth had Atman known his stomach was upset? A guess? Were others experiencing the same thing? But... he ran his hand over his stomach... it seemed to have worked. Perhaps it was psychological?

The crowd stirred, and Rajiv brought his attention back to the figure on the stage. Atman was telling everyone to get comfortable, to relax, and to close their eyes. Rajiv watched as the predominantly female crowd adjusted their positions and quietened down.

"Those of you standing, please find a place to sit if you can. It's important to be comfortable," Atman instructed. "I know there aren't enough seats, but please find a place on the floor. You don't need to see me for the meditation."

It took a couple of minutes until everyone settled, and the only one still standing was Rajiv. He felt a little self-conscious, but he was on duty and he wasn't about to sit on the floor and close his eyes when he was responsible for the safety of Atman. As if hearing his thoughts, Atman looked directly at Rajiv, and even at that distance, Rajiv could see a faint smile tugging at the corners of his mouth. He gave Rajiv a slight nod, then closed his eyes.

"Take a deep inhalation through your nostrils, filling your lungs completely, then slowly exhale, feeling all the tension leaving your body." Atman's voice filled the hall, deep, commanding, but also somehow comforting.

Rajiv felt his own eyelids drooping, and he shook his head. He needed to stay alert. A nice hot cup of *chai* would do the trick. He raised his wrist and glanced at his watch. Maybe he could sneak out and send one of his men to find some? There had to be a *chai* stand somewhere on the street.

"Whenever your attention wanders…"

Rajiv looked back at the stage.

"Bring your awareness back to your breath, the sensation of air flowing across your top lip…"

Atman raised his right hand above his head, his palm facing the crowd. His eyes were open, but only the whites of his eyes were visible, his eyeballs rolled back into his head.

Rajiv felt a shiver run down his spine, a tingling sensation in his fingertips. He blinked and shook his head, then his arms. A feeling of warmth spread through his body and once again his eyes threatened to close. He had to move, otherwise he would fall asleep. Glancing toward Georges and Max seated at either end of the stage, both with their eyes closed, Rajiv hesitated, then made a decision. Atman was safe enough.

He crept toward the entrance door and eased it open before slipping outside. His eyes blinked rapidly as they adjusted to the bright light, then he focused on the scene outside. There was no sign of the curious onlookers from their arrival and his vehicles had moved to block the entrance and exit gates while the Range Rover remained directly in front of the entrance door. His men were gathered around the lead vehicle chatting, and he shook his head in frustration. So much for security.

"Manjunath" he barked, and the men stiffened at the sound of his voice. Manjunath hurried over.

"You are not here to chitchat. Make sure the men are alert and watching the street."

Manjunath snapped to attention. "Yes, sir. Sorry, sir."

"Oh, and Manju. See if you can find me some *chai*."

"Of course, sir."

Rajiv watched from the top step as Manjunath hurried back and his men dispersed to take up position at each gate. At that moment, his phone buzzed in his pocket.

## 17

John waited as the phone connected and began to ring. Would he be busy? Would he accept a call from an unknown number?

"Hello?"

"Rajiv?"

"Yes... Who's this?"

John grinned. "It's John. John Hayes. How are you, my old friend?"

Rajiv's voice was hesitant, "John? I'm... um... I'm okay. Where are you? I don't recognise the dialling code."

"Don't worry," John chuckled. "I'm not in Bangalore."

"That makes me feel a little better."

"I'm hurt, Rajiv."

He heard Rajiv sigh. "Well, every time I hear from you, people seem to lose their lives."

John grimaced and rubbed his face with his free hand. Leaning up against the window frame, he gazed out across the street at the buildings opposite his apartment. On the roof of one building, an elderly lady was hanging clothes on a washing line. He glanced up at the sky, at the dark clouds looming on the horizon. Probably not the best weather to be drying clothes.

"Nothing to do with me, Rajiv."

"Hmmm."

"Anyway, I wanted to give you a warning."

"A warning?"

"Yes." John thought for a moment. He had rehearsed the conversation in his head, but now it came to it, he wondered about the best way to start. "You emailed Adriana D'Silva about Atman."

There was silence for a while and John glanced at the screen to make sure the line hadn't been cut.

"How do you know that?"

"Adriana D'Silva is my partner."

"Partner?"

"My girlfriend."

"You're kidding."

John shook his head as if Rajiv could see him. "No, I'm not. It appears our paths are destined to cross again."

"So... you are in... Lisbon?"

"Yes."

"Oh... okay."

"Yeah, I've been here for a while."

"And you're happy?"

"I am Rajiv," John smiled. "Very happy. Thank you."

"That's good. I'm pleased for you. We all need to find happiness."

"Yeah." John lapsed into silence, his thoughts running back to the events of their first meeting. When his wife Charlotte had been brutally attacked and killed in Bangalore. A time when John thought he would never find love or happiness again.

"So..." Rajiv interrupted his thoughts, "What are you

warning me about? I'm tempted to guess, but I'd rather hear it from you."

"Adriana told me you had enquired about Atman. Specifically, the events in Sri Lanka."

"Yes."

"Well, I was there."

Again, John had to wait for Rajiv's response.

"Somehow that doesn't surprise me, John," Rajiv replied after a while. "You seem to have a... what's the word... a talent for finding trouble."

John nodded to himself. "Believe me, Rajiv, I wasn't looking for it. I was on a meditation retreat... but you know me. I can't look the other way when something wrong is happening."

Rajiv sighed. "Yes, I know that. So are you saying that everything in the article was true?"

"One hundred percent. He's not a good man, Rajiv, and I thought you should know."

"Hmmm, thank you."

There was silence again for a while, and John watched the old lady pick up her empty washing basket and head for the stairs.

"I don't know that there is anything I can do, but thank you for the warning."

"Can't you lock him up, or deport him?"

"Not without evidence, John. What he's done in Sri Lanka has no relevance here."

"So he can continue taking advantage of young women? Sexually assaulting them," John's voice was rising, "with no repercussions?"

"I'm not saying that, John." John heard Rajiv exhale loudly. "But we have to catch him, and so far he hasn't done anything. In fact, he seems like a nice guy. People here love him."

John tightened his grip on the phone and closed his eyes. "Rajiv, I'm telling you, he's not what he seems. He's taking advantage of people and not just the sexual molestation, but I believe he's killed or had people killed."

"Okay, okay, don't get angry with me, John, but I'm a policeman. Things have to be done by the book. I need evidence. I can't go on hearsay. To build a case, I need to find proof. I can't just take matters into my own hands. There are procedures to follow."

John clenched his left hand into a fist and banged the window frame. "Rajiv, we both know following procedure doesn't always bring justice. Especially in..." John trailed off.

"India, that's what you're trying to say."

John grimaced, but didn't comment.

"Look, John, I know our system isn't perfect. But we do have laws, which I'm sworn to follow. There's no place for... vigilante justice."

John remained silent. Technically, Rajiv was right, but being right hadn't helped John when his wife was killed.

"John, I appreciate the warning, and knowing you were behind the events in Sri Lanka, believe it or not, gives me some confidence. I know you don't take things lightly and I believe you. But to an extent my hands are tied. I'll keep an eye on things, and believe me, if any laws are broken, I will come down on him with all the tools available to me."

John nodded again and relaxed his grip on the phone. "Yeah." He sighed loudly. "I know you will. Thank you, Rajiv."

"Look, I have to go. You look after yourself."

"You too, Rajiv. Keep safe."

"Always."

A thought struck John.

"Oh, one more thing, Rajiv."

"Yes?"

"Given our past history..."

"I don't think I'm going to like this question," Rajiv interrupted.

John made a face. "If I were to come to India, would I... have any difficulties?"

## 18

Rajiv ended the call and slipped the phone back into his pocket.

He turned and looked back toward the hall entrance. What had he got himself into? Before he could come up with an answer, he felt someone approaching and turned to see his driver with a paper cup in his hand.

"*Chai*, sir."

"Ah, good, well done." Rajiv took it from him and sniffed at the steam rising from the cup. Ginger and cardamom. "It smells good. Where did you find it?"

Manjunath gestured up the road. "There's a *chai* stand just up the road."

Rajiv fished for change in his pocket. "How much is it?"

Manjunath took a step back. "No, sir, it's okay."

Rajiv pulled a crumpled note from his pocket. "Here, take this."

"No sir, it..." Manjunath looked down at his feet. "It was free."

Rajiv raised a finger and shook his head. "I've told you this before. We pay for everything." He thrust the note into

Manjunath's hand. "Now go and give him this. I'll check, so don't think about putting it in your pocket."

"Oh no, sir. Of course not, sir."

"Hurry."

His men taking advantage of their uniform and getting things for free was something he hated. He knew it went on all over the city, but he wouldn't let it happen while he was on duty.

Rajiv turned away and took a sip. It was good *chai*, just what he needed.

He took another sip, feeling the hot, sweet liquid slide down the back of his throat. The call from John had disturbed him. Whilst he had had his suspicions after reading Adriana's article, to have someone like John Hayes confirm it for him only made it seem more real.

John Hayes.

A man he hadn't thought about for a long time. A tough, resourceful man who, despite the circumstances that had brought them together, he couldn't help but admire.

John was right. Getting justice in a country like India was hard. Especially if you weren't rich and powerful, or had connections that were. He glanced again toward the hall. Atman seemed to be connected. Not everyone got treated to a lunch at the Chief Minister's residence. Not everyone had access to handguns like the one he'd seen on Georges' waist.

His eyes wandered to the Range Rover. Who actually owned the Range Rover? He made a mental note to find out. A car like that cost twice as much as it did overseas once you factored in the import and customs duties.

Rajiv sniffed and took another mouthful of tea. He wouldn't be at all surprised if it was owned by a shell company linked to the Chief Minister. Which begged the question. If Atman had such high-level connections, was there anything Rajiv could do? He thought for a moment, then drained the cup of tea before crumpling the paper cup in his hand. Looking around for a garbage bin, he reassured himself. Atman had done nothing wrong so far, so there was no need to be concerned. Giving up on his search for a trash can, he tossed the crumpled cup onto a pile of litter that had been swept up earlier in the day. Until then, he would watch the man like a hawk.

# 19

It was nine-thirty in the evening by the time Rajiv and the motorcade returned to the hotel. He was tired and hungry and so were his men. It had been a long day with hardly a break and he was looking forward to getting home, kicking off his shoes and sitting back on the sofa next to his wife, Aarthi.

Rajiv jumped out of the Range Rover and opened the rear door to allow Atman to climb out. Georges hurried around to join them and then escorted Atman as he crossed the forecourt toward the hotel entrance. The door staff had formed up in a line in front of the door, standing with their hands held in *namaste*, their expressions betraying their eagerness to be noticed by the spiritual teacher.

Rajiv closed the passenger door and stood watching as Atman paused in front of each one and said a few words, the staff responding with broad smiles and, in some cases, reaching down to touch his feet.

Rajiv sensed a movement beside him and turned to see Max standing beside him.

"Is it like this overseas, too?" Rajiv asked.

Max nodded. "Everywhere he goes."

Rajiv turned back and watched Atman and Georges disappear inside, and the staff gather in groups talking excitedly amongst themselves. "It's amazing how one person can have such an effect on others," he said, almost to himself.

"He helps many people."

Rajiv turned and studied the young man beside him. "Has he helped you?"

Max didn't meet his gaze, still looking toward the hotel entrance, a distant look in his eyes. "He has," he said after a moment.

"How did you meet him?"

Max suddenly turned his head to face Rajiv, as if he had just broken free from a trance. "Through Georges. Georges and I... served together..."

"In Israel?"

"Yes," he nodded, his eyes becoming distant again. "He was my senior. We..." His eyes refocused, "I don't know if you are aware, but in Israel, it's compulsory to serve in the army."

Rajiv nodded.

"I saw things... I did things that..." He took a deep breath, then shook his head. "He's helped me get my mind in order. Given me peace."

Rajiv narrowed his eyes. He would have loved to have probed more, but Max was already moving away, back around to the driver's side of the Range Rover. "Same time tomorrow." He called out without turning around and raised a hand in farewell. Rajiv nodded even though Max couldn't see him and glanced at his watch. If they left now, his men would get a reasonable amount of rest before coming back on duty. He stepped aside as the Range Rover swung out and around the lead Bolero, heading for the underground parking, then beckoned to his driver.

"Manjunath, give me the keys. I'll take the vehicle from here. You go back to the station with the others. Get cleaned up, have a good night's sleep, and be back here at 0930 tomorrow morning."

"Yes, sir."

"Sharp." Rajiv gave Manjunath a stern look. "I want you all here on time."

"Yes, sir. Of course, sir."

"Good. On your way then."

Rajiv watched his men climb into the remaining vehicle, then walked over to his. Pausing beside the driver's door, he glanced up at the hotel facade, toward the suite level right at the top. The edge of a full moon peaked out from the top of the hotel, its light illuminating the margins of a bank of white cloud. Was the man up there in the luxury suite, the great spiritual teacher everyone thought he was? Was he a fraud? How on earth had he fixed his upset stomach?

Rajiv shrugged, then climbed into the vehicle and started it up. The diesel engine rattled into life, in marked contrast to the smooth hum of the Range Rover he'd been sitting in all day. He smiled. What would Aarthi say if he drove up in a Range Rover? He slipped the vehicle into gear and headed toward the hotel exit. He guessed he'd never find out.

## 20

"I'm going to India."

"What? Why?" Adriana had only just walked in the door. She dropped her keys on the side table and kicked off her shoes. "Atman?"

John nodded and waited for her to cross the living room. She stood in front of him as he leaned his butt on the back of the sofa. She stared at him for a moment and then leaned in and kissed him on the cheek. "Why don't you fix me a drink first and we'll talk about it?"

"There's nothing to talk about. I'm going."

Adriana sighed and placed a hand on each of his shoulders. "A gin and tonic will do nicely, thank you."

John stood up and walked over to the drinks cabinet. He'd been thinking about it ever since he came off the call with Rajiv and his mind was set. There was nothing Adriana could say that would convince him otherwise. He fixed two generous gin and tonics, then carried them over to the sofa where Adriana was now sitting, her legs tucked up beneath her, one arm resting along the back of the sofa. She smiled as he approached and took her drink from him.

"Why don't you start from the beginning? Why you've suddenly come to this decision?" She took a sip of her drink and nodded her approval. "Very good."

John sat at the other end of the couch, turning sideways so he could face her, and took a long pull of his drink, enjoying the instant sensation of warmth filling his body as he swallowed, his drink more gin than tonic.

"I phoned Rajiv, the policeman who emailed you."

Adriana's eyebrows raised.

"You remember when I told you everything about Bangalore? The things I had to do?"

Adriana nodded, a deep frown on her forehead.

"Well, he was in charge of the case... the cases, each time I was there."

"Small world. Why didn't you tell me yesterday?"

John made a face and took another sip of his drink to give him time to reply. "Well, I wasn't sure what I was going to do."

"Okay."

"But then I called him and it became clear."

"And?"

John looked away, turning his attention to the full height window and the view across the city lights. "I'm going to stop him once and for all."

Adriana didn't reply for a while, but he could see her reflection in the window, watching him.

"John."

He turned back to look at her. She had put her drink down and was tying her hair up in a loose bun, exposing the long slim line of her neck.

"Why do you want to get involved? Leave it to the authorities. We did what we could in Sri Lanka."

"And where did it get us? He's up and about as if nothing ever happened. It's only six months later."

Adriana sighed and picked up her drink from the side table. "I know." She swirled the glass around, watching the ice move around in the glass. "But maybe people will think twice now about believing in him." When she looked back at John, he was shaking his head.

"No, that's not what's happening. I went online. I checked some local news channels in Bangalore. He's got huge crowds attending his talks, as if nothing ever happened."

Adriana said nothing.

John continued. "How many other people are going to get hurt by him? How many lives ruined?"

Adriana took a drink, then gazed out the window. Both sat in silence, deep in thought, until eventually Adriana spoke up again. "What did the policeman, ah... Detective Sampath, say?"

"He said he appreciated my warning and that he would keep an eye on him."

"Then why don't you leave it to him?"

John drained his glass, then stared at it, surprised it was already empty. "Because for someone like Atman, in a country like India, it's unlikely there will be any repercussions." He turned to look at Adriana. "Do you know how many so-called spiritual teachers there are in India? How many of them are frauds and get away literally with murder for years and years?"

Adriana shook her head.

"Too many to count. And just like in Sri Lanka, he will have connections. Connections that will protect him, cover up for him, and see that he never has to face the consequences of his actions. Even if he doesn't have connections, the system moves so slowly it would be years before he ended up in court."

"But John, okay, I understand all that... But why you? Are you sure it's not just your ego? You're angry because he got away?"

John blinked. He hadn't expected that. He was about to respond with an angry retort, when he stopped himself. Was it his ego? Frowning, he stood up and walked with his empty glass toward the kitchen. He placed it down on the bench top and stared at it. Why him indeed? What was it that was driving him on?

But deep down, he knew. He'd just never put it into words. Taking a deep breath, he turned back to face Adriana and replied, "You know what happened to Charlotte."

Adriana nodded.

"And what happened to Amira in Bangkok... and to the Yazidi women in Syria." John took another breath, his motivations becoming more clear as he spoke. "No-one stood up for them until the damage was already done. If I can stop things like that happening again... even if I only help one person... in my own small way... then that's what I'm going to do."

## 21

"Wasn't he fantastic?"

Rajiv paused in the doorway, keys still in one hand, his cap in the other. It took a millisecond for his brain to work out what Aarthi was talking about. Then he nodded, smiled at her, and placed the cap and keys on the side table.

"I didn't see you there," he said finally as he removed his shoes and pushed them together with the toe of his right foot.

"I got to sit right in front." She gestured with her hands, "He was this close."

Aarthi's face was glowing, her cheeks flushed, eyes wide, as she stood in the doorway to the kitchen, drying her hands with a small towel. He smiled, but deep down, he was worried. If what John had told him was true... and he was pretty sure it was, then the last thing he wanted was his wife falling under Atman's spell. But he had to handle it carefully. She often complained he was too cynical, and if he didn't play it right, she might not believe him.

Aarthi continued. "I had such a wonderful meditation. So deep, and I could feel his power."

"Is that right?"

Aarthi's disappointment at his response was all over her face, so he broadened his smile. "So you enjoyed it. I'm happy." It was unlikely she would see Atman again, so he may as well humour her. No point in ruining her happiness. Looking over her shoulder into the kitchen, he changed the subject. "Is dinner ready? I'm starving. I had some awful food at the Chief Minister's house." He shook his head. "Terrible. Gave me stomach ache."

A look of concern passed across Aarthi's face. "Are you okay now?"

Rajiv hesitated. How much should he tell her? "Yes, fine now." Not wanting to discuss it further, he added, "I'll just freshen up."

"Yes, hurry up. I've got so much to talk about."

Rajiv groaned inwardly, but kept the smile fixed on his face. He winked and then made his way upstairs. She was happy, that was the main thing.

He was splashing water on his face when he heard his phone ring.

"Oh, come on.," he complained and looked at his watch. After so many years in the police, he was used to getting calls at all hours. But that didn't mean he liked it. Once, just once, he wanted a quiet evening at home, undisturbed. He sighed, dabbed his face dry, then walked barefoot out into the bedroom and picked his phone up off the bed. Glancing at the screen, he cursed, then straightened up, fixed a fake smile on his face, and answered the call.

"Sir."

"Rajiv, I'm hearing good things about you from Atman's man, Georges."

"Okay, sir." Rajiv frowned. It wasn't like his boss to call and share positive feedback. He usually only complained. Perhaps Atman was having a positive effect on him?

"The day after tomorrow, they will drive to their ashram on the coast near Mangalore..."

"Yes, sir."

"Don't interrupt..."

Rajiv rolled his eyes. Muniappa never missed an opportunity to put him in his place.

"It seems he is so confident in your abilities that he wants you to accompany him and oversee his security."

Rajiv jerked his head back in surprise. "What?" He thought fast. "Sir, that's not our jurisdiction... and I'm needed here. I've got work to do here, cases to follow up. Leads to pursue. I can't be heading off to the other side of the state just because some foreign... dignitary requests it."

"This is not up for discussion." Muniappa's tone was forceful, but Rajiv detected a hint of satisfaction in his boss' tone.

He pushed on, "It's a seven-hour drive. A complete waste of my time."

"Detective Sampath, I told you this is not up for discussion. Your work can wait. Besides, the CM has approved it."

Rajiv rubbed his head in frustration. He might have worn Muniappa down eventually, but he couldn't go against the Chief Minister. That was a career destroyer. "The CM?"

"Yes. He's even instructed the SP of Udupi district to provide any resources you may need."

Rajiv cursed inwardly. He wasn't getting out of this one. "Are any of the men coming with me?"

"No. You can take your driver, but otherwise you're on your own."

Again, Rajiv detected a hint of glee in Muniappa's tone.

"And remember, this is not a holiday. I'm sure I don't need to remind you that if anything goes wrong, the CM will not look kindly upon you."

"Yes, sir." Rajiv closed his eyes and shook his head.

Muniappa continued sticking the knife in. "It will not reflect well on your career."

"I understand," Rajiv responded a little too forcefully.

"Good."

The phone went dead before Rajiv could say anymore. He wasn't prone to swearing, but this time he couldn't help himself. "Shit," he growled and tossed his phone back on the bed. He was about to say more, but stopped himself.

"Rajiv?" Aarthi called from downstairs.

"Coming." He took a deep breath and exhaled slowly, then composing a smile, he walked out of the bedroom.

## 22

"You are so lucky."

Rajiv smiled. His mouth was full, so he replied with a, "hmmm."

"So much better than dealing with criminals." Aarthi sighed. "I wish I could come with you."

Rajiv stopped chewing for a second, gave a non-committal nod, then continued eating.

"Actually, Meenu was saying we should visit the ashram. He's starting a meditation retreat there this weekend."

Rajiv swallowed his food, then reached for his water glass and took a sip. He needed to nip this idea in the bud. "Why do you want to go so far? It's such a long journey. You can meditate at home."

Aarthi gave him a look as if he had said something stupid. "It's not the same. When the guru is there to guide you, your meditation is so much deeper and you make faster progress."

"Really?"

Aarthi smiled. "You are too cynical, Rajiv. All this dealing with bad people has stopped you from believing in miracles and blessings."

She was right. All he saw was the desperation and hardship people went through. Striving to get by in a city that was becoming more expensive by the day, and the things they did out of desperation. Sitting around with one's eyes closed, imagining the divine, was something only the comfortable could indulge in.

"I really think I should join you."

Rajiv shook his head. "I'm not going on holiday. I have work to do."

"Yes, I know, and I will be on the retreat. But at least we'll be in the same place and you will have lots of time off. It's not like you will have to stop anything bad from happening. It's an ashram."

Rajiv studied her for a moment. She looked so happy and he knew from experience that once she set her mind on something, it was nigh on impossible to convince her otherwise. But he should at least try.

"You do know that these ah... god-men... are not always what they claim to be?"

"Oh, Rajiv," she made a dismissive gesture with her hand. "There you go again. Always assuming people are bad."

"No, I'm not. I'm just pointing out that so many have been caught doing things they shouldn't. Look at Asharam Bapu. In prison for murder. Ram Rahim, the guy in Punjab. Hundreds of thousands of followers. Rape, murder, unexplained wealth."

He could see from her expression that a wall had gone up between them. He tried to salvage the situation. "I'm just saying I want you to be safe. I care about you."

"Rajiv, you can't stop me from doing things because you

think everyone is a criminal. Those are just two people. They are not all like that."

He could list more, but Aarthi was still talking.

"There are so many teachers out there who are good and honest. Gurus who have helped millions of people. Who have performed miracles. You were probably too busy today, but I spoke to so many people who have experienced miracles since meeting Atman. Healings, business success, children getting scholarships. Don't be so negative all the time. People are good."

"I'm not being negative, I just—"

"I don't want to talk about it anymore. If Meenu and I decide to go, then we'll go." She pushed back her chair and walked into the kitchen.

Rajiv stared down at his plate. Well, that had gone well.

## 23

John stared blankly at the ceiling, listening to Adriana's long slow breaths as she slept beside him. He just couldn't sleep, a million thoughts racing around his head.

Adriana hadn't argued with him, and he respected her for that. She was worried; he knew that, but she hadn't told him he shouldn't go because she was worried about his safety. Instead, she had come up with several pertinent points why it wasn't a good idea to get involved. Points he could not counter immediately, and it was those that were keeping him awake.

He knew from experience that once he decided to do something, he would find a way no matter what difficulties arose. But if he vacillated, he would become mired in self-doubt and not do a thing. Firm, decisive action was always the best way, but he also had no intention of going into something without preparation.

Rajiv had assured him that if he came to India, he wouldn't be arrested on arrival. He said there were no outstanding cases against him or even any suspicion that he had done anything. John had laughed on the phone, maintaining he had done nothing to be suspicious of, but they both knew the fact he was asking if it was safe to return suggested otherwise.

Could he trust Rajiv? Was he just reassuring him so he could arrest John when he saw him? John didn't think so. Although he had experienced the worst in people, he had also experienced the opposite. Rajiv had always been honest with him and, deep down, John knew he was a good man constrained by the environment he worked in. It was a risk, but John figured a low one. One he could reduce even further by not flying directly into Bangalore.

Which brought him onto the next thing. Adriana had already emailed Rajiv with copies of the documentation and research she had based her articles on, but John knew that wouldn't be of any more use to Rajiv than background information. There was nothing he could build a case on, especially in a country other than where the crimes occurred.

Adriana had suggested telling the Sri Lankan government where Atman was, but after the initial attention when her articles had come out, the government had shown little interest. It was potentially too embarrassing for them to bring it back into the public eye. There were too many powerful people with their fingers in the cookie jar.

So that raised the question of what John could actually do. On the face of it, possibly nothing. But he knew if he sat around in Lisbon, there was no chance of getting any justice. If he was there, on the ground, maybe, just maybe, an opportunity would present itself.

Besides, what was he doing with his day, anyway? He didn't need to work. His shareholding in Ronald Yu's

Pegasus Land provided him with more money than he would ever need, and even racing his classic Porsche around the country roads of Portugal was only going so far to fill his days with excitement. No, he needed to get some excitement back in his life, and if that meant going to India and potentially saving people from harm, then that's what he was going to do, no matter how much risk it was to him personally. At least he would feel alive instead of dying a slow death, whiling away the hours in cafes and bars.

A sound escaped Adriana's lips, and she changed position, rolling from her side onto her back. In the faint light filtering through the blinds, he could see her thick mane of hair framing her head in a dark halo against the white pillow. He wouldn't be happy leaving her behind, but then he wouldn't be happy staying, and to give Adriana credit, she knew he would be happier if he got involved.

Giving up on sleep, he carefully eased himself out from under the duvet and slipped out of bed. He padded silently across the room, eased the door open, and walked out into the living room. He had so many questions he couldn't find the answer to and if he stayed in bed, he would spend the entire night tossing and turning. In the kitchen, he poured himself a glass of water and then carried it over to the sofa, where he sat down facing the window. The sky was clear, but the light pollution from the city prevented him from seeing anything other than the moon alone in the blackness above.

Grabbing a cushion, he wedged it between his spine and the sofa-back and then pulled his legs up and crossed them in front of him. He took a long deep breath and then as he exhaled, felt his body relax as if melting into the sofa and he let his eyes close naturally. Focusing only on the breath, he allowed his thoughts to slow down on their own, not running after them like a hamster on a wheel.

There was no point in worrying about how he would do it. The answers would come to him in their own time.

## 24

Rajiv was up and out of the house long before Aarthi woke up. He wasn't due at the Vijaya Palace until nine-thirty, but had a pile of files on his desk that needed seeing to before he went away.

The sun was just making its appearance, the sky above steadily lightening, and the streets were relatively empty as he drove to the station.

A group of taxi drivers gathered around a *chai-wallah's* moped, sipping hot sweet tea or coffee from tiny paper cups, watching him with idle interest as he drove past. He braked suddenly to avoid a stray dog and swerved around a large pothole. The roads never seemed to get any better, despite the promises of whichever politician was in power.

His thoughts ran to the Chief Minister. What was his interest in Atman? It had to be nefarious. The CM did nothing unless it benefited his bank balance, and he certainly wasn't associating with Atman for spiritual reasons. Rajiv doubted the man had a single spiritual bone in his body.

Money laundering was his guess. Syphoning the

massive quantities of cash collected by party minions, through Atman's organisation as donations. That had to be it. But how was he getting it back? Rajiv pursed his lips. All that financial stuff was beyond him. He never really understood how it was done. All he saw were the big houses and fleets of exotic foreign cars driven by the men and women who were supposed to have the interests of the citizens at heart.

He slowed for the turning into the station compound, then eased the vehicle up over the broken footpath and into the rutted dirt compound that served as parking. They should spend at least some of the money on the police facilities. The Bolero he was driving had almost three hundred thousand kilometres on the clock and there wasn't a single body panel that wasn't scarred or dented. He turned the engine off and climbed out, glancing back toward the station building. The once cream painted walls were stained black with mould and soot. A banyan tree seedling had taken root on one corner, its roots spreading across the cracked concrete surface, searching for the ground. The rusting hulks of several impounded vehicles decayed into the ground beside a pile of abandoned motorbikes and scooters, and a rat the size of a small dog scurried across the parking area before disappearing behind the station.

In less than two hours, he would be standing outside one of the best hotels in Bangalore, protecting someone who was paying more per night for a suite than his constables earned in a month. He sighed and made his way toward the entrance. There was no point in thinking about it. He couldn't change the system by himself.

The night-duty constable dozed in his chair at the front desk, not even aware of Rajiv coming in, but he left him alone, walking past and down the hallway to his office.

Dropping his cap onto the desk, he walked around, pulled his chair out, and sat down. He looked at the pile of files on the right side of the desk, then at the dusty computer monitor on the left. Sitting forward, he switched the monitor on and waited for the system to start up. The files could wait. He wanted to do some research first.

## 25

John woke early and, despite his earlier trouble sleeping, felt refreshed. He had sat for a while on the sofa, at first his mind racing but eventually a deep feeling of peace coming over him, his mind emptying of all thought, and although his subconscious hadn't given him answers, he felt deep down that everything would become clear in time.

After almost an hour, he moved back into the bedroom and slipped into a deep dreamless sleep.

It was dark outside when he woke and Adriana still slept deeply beside him. He eased himself out of bed, then with a quick glance at Adriana, to make sure he hadn't disturbed her, left the bedroom, clicking the door shut softly behind him.

In the kitchen he fixed himself a French press, then carried it to the dining table and opened up his laptop.

While the coffee brewed, he pulled up a map of India and zoomed in on the southern part of the massive country. He had already decided not to fly directly into Bangalore, just in case Rajiv hadn't been entirely truthful. He doubted that was the case, but it was always better to be careful. After a quick scan of the map, he chose the city of Chennai on the East Coast. It had a large international airport and, although a six to seven-hour drive to Bangalore, was a much better option than flying into Goa, or Kochi in Kerala.

He pressed the plunger on the French press and poured himself a cup of coffee, took a sip, then switched to searching for flights. The shortest flight was via Dubai on Emirates and he was just about to make a booking when the germ of an idea began to form. Sitting back in his chair, the cup of coffee held in both hands, he stared out the window, watching the dawn sky lighten, allowing the idea to take shape in his mind.

After a minute, he smiled. It was perfect. He sat forward, put down the coffee cup, did another quick search, then picked up his phone. Scrolling through the phone book, he selected a number and dialled.

According to the website he had just checked, Dubai was four hours ahead of Lisbon, which meant he wouldn't be disturbing his old friend.

"Bloody hell, mate, what time is it there?"

John grinned. "Good morning to you too, Steve."

"Always good to hear your voice, mate, but... is everything okay? It's pretty early there, isn't it?"

"Almost six, but yeah, everything's good. How are things with you? How's Maadhavi doing?"

"All good, mate. All good. She's away right now. Shooting for a film in Europe."

"Europe?" John raised his eyebrows. Although now based in Dubai, Steve's partner, Maadhavi Rao, continued to be a popular actress in the Southern Indian film industry.

"Yeah, you know how they like to do those song and dance numbers in the middle of the film? Suddenly jumping from India to somewhere in Paris or the Swiss Alps. Bloody weird if you ask me, but hey I'm not the one watching them."

John had watched one of Maadhavi's films once, on a flight. He knew what Steve meant. "Plenty of people are, though. But what about you? How's business for Dubai's best private eye?"

"I don't know about best, mate, but business is good. Busy as always. Never a shortage of affairs or fraud in this city."

"I'm sure."

"How's Adriana?"

"She's good, asleep right now, otherwise I'd put her on."

"Say hi from me. You guys should come over once Maadhavi is back. It's been awhile."

John nodded to himself. It had. The last time he'd seen the big Australian who had become his friend was when they illegally entered Syria to rescue Steve's niece. It hadn't been a relaxing visit. "We will. Which brings me to the reason for my call."

"So you weren't just checking in on an old friend? I'm offended."

John chuckled. "You'll get over it. Look... ahhh... are you still using that guy who helped us with the documentation for Syria?"

"Yes, why?" Steve asked slowly, clearly intrigued. "What are you up to now?"

"I need his help again."

"Sure... but what for?"

"I'll tell you in person. I'm coming there tomorrow."

## 26

The first thing Rajiv checked was his email. Adriana D'Silva had replied, and he skimmed the email, then downloaded the attachments and saved them to a file on his desktop. He had a quick look through, a sinking feeling steadily taking over. There was enough well researched information there to remove any doubts as to the type of man Atman was beneath his public facade. Rajiv hadn't really doubted John, but to see it now in black and white made it much more real.

He clicked out of the folder, opened Google maps and searched for Atman's ashram location in Mangalore.

It was actually north of the coastal city, closer in fact to the famous temple town of Udupi, famous for its Krishna temple and a pilgrimage spot for millions of Hindus. The *Anandsagar,* Sea of Bliss, ashram occupied a large compound on several acres bounded by the Kapu beach to the west and the Kapu village road to the east. Rajiv switched to satellite view. There was a large hall, what looked like several accommodation blocks, and an administration building near the front. A large wall surrounded the compound on all four sides, and the main building appeared to have several satellite dishes amongst the array of solar panels that covered the roof. There was an adjoining compound that housed a single building, but apart from that there wasn't much around it, mainly the houses of fisherfolk, a few stores, and several larger homes that looked like holiday homes for wealthy city people. Rajiv clicked out of maps and, on a hunch, searched for any news about the ashram.

He scanned down the results, nothing in particular catching his eye. Mainly reports from the local paper regarding charitable work performed by the ashramites; tree planting, beach cleanups, welfare programs for the local fisher-folk. Nothing out of the ordinary. There was an article about the local politician being guest of honour at a recent festival, again nothing surprising. It was always good practice to stoke the egos of local leaders. You never knew when you might need them.

It was near the bottom of the first page of search results that something caught Rajiv's eye. He frowned and clicked on the link.

*Australian woman killed by rogue truck driver.*

He read on. *Sally Hughes, a student of the Anandsagar Ashram, was killed yesterday when she was mowed down by a speeding lorry in Kapu. The accident happened at eleven-thirty am when Sally Hughes was leaving her accommodation. Inspector Prakash Rao of the Udupi district police reported that there had been several eyewitnesses, but by the time the police arrived, Hughes was already deceased. The lorry was later found abandoned and had been impounded pending further investigation. A case has been registered and local police are making enquiries. However, sources confirm the vehicle had been reported stolen earlier and there is no sign of the driver.*

Rajiv sat back in his chair and stared at the screen. Coincidence? Possibly. But Rajiv wasn't prepared to dismiss it so easily. The missing driver was normal. No-one wanted to be subjected to the creaky Indian legal system even if it had been a genuine accident, but the fact the truck had been stolen didn't point too kindly toward coincidence. Running someone over in a truck was a tried-and-true assassination method perfected by many a dirty businessman or corrupt politician in the past. But... if it wasn't an accident, why on earth would someone want to kill a foreign student of the ashram?

Rajiv sat forward, reached for his notepad, and jotted down the name of the victim, the name of the investigating officer and the date of the incident, then tore off the page, folded it in two and tucked it into his wallet. It was something he would look into when he was there on the ground.

## 27

Atman stood beside him, his eyes closed, a beatific smile on his face, as if conversing with the divine. Rajiv watched him, trying to balance the appearance of the man before him with that mentioned in Adriana D'Silva's article, the man John Hayes had warned him about. Right now, it seemed as if they were two different people. Rajiv had observed him all day, his interactions with those around him, the way he worked the crowds, his energy that filled the venues when he conducted a guided meditation. He had watched him with the eyes of a hawk, his mind filled with suspicion, looking for any sign that he wasn't the other-worldly spiritual being that people believed he was. But there had been nothing. Nothing to even hint at improper behaviour or deception. He seemed to be everything they thought he was. Even when talking to the women who fell at his feet, seeking his blessings. There was nothing at all to suggest he would take advantage of his position, or abuse his power. Perhaps John and Adriana had got it all wrong?

As if reading Rajiv's mind, Atman's eyes opened, locking with Rajiv's. He tried to look away, his face colouring as if caught speaking his thoughts aloud, but he couldn't move as a heat spread through his body.

A moment later, the spell was broken as Atman smiled. "You are doing a good job, Rajiv. I am grateful."

Rajiv blinked, not sure what to say.

"You're probably wondering why I asked you to join me on my trip to the ashram. I know it's highly irregular and I'm sure you have a lot of work to do here." He reached out and took Rajiv's hand in both of his. "But I trust you, Rajiv. I... sense a great power within you. An overwhelming urge to do the right thing."

Rajiv tried to slip his hand free, embarrassed at the close contact with the man, but Atman wouldn't let go.

"I feel safe with you around."

The grip on Rajiv's hand finally relaxed as Rajiv tried to compute what the man was telling him. Safe? Why would he not feel safe? If he truly was guided by the universe?

Rajiv frowned and cleared his throat. "What... do you have to be worried about?"

Atman's eyes twinkled with amusement. "You misunderstand. I'm not worried about anything." He gestured toward the ceiling at the same time as looking upwards. "The Supreme will always look after me and guide me. No..." he looked down at Rajiv again. "What I am talking about is a feeling. A feeling you get when you are around people you trust implicitly. Like I do with Georges and Max."

Rajiv nodded as if he understood, and half smiled. But before he could say anything in reply, the double doors they were standing beside opened up, revealing the function room of a five-star hotel filled with seated devotees. Georges stood in the doorway as an excited murmur rippled through the crowd. His eyes flicked to Rajiv, then he turned to Atman and nodded.

Atman winked at Rajiv. "Showtime."

## 28

Rajiv peered over the stone wall on the edge of the road, the ground falling away on the other side toward the river deep in the valley below. Close to the wall, the slope was littered with discarded beer bottles and plastic bags. He shook his head in disgust. People. Why did they come to a beautiful place and destroy it? Opposite him, across the valley, a steep jungle clad slope rose toward the sky, the top hidden in a cloud. The air was cool, with a hint of moisture, and Rajiv shivered at the unfamiliar cold.

It had been four hours since they had left the concrete jungle of Bangalore, leaving early to beat the traffic, and journeyed westward across the broad expanse of sun scorched farmland. Eventually they had started the climb up into the hills of the Western Ghats, the Range Rover looming large in the rearview mirrors of the police Bolero, the powerful three litre engine of the luxury SUV easily able to keep up with the asthmatic underpowered engine of the Bolero. Near the top of the Ghats, Rajiv's driver, Manjunath, was forced to pull over, to give the well-used engine a chance to cool down.

They had parked the two vehicles in one of the rutted and muddy lay-bys constructed at regular intervals along the route. The road here was narrow, the surface pitted and broken, scarred by the passage of overladen goods vehicles and regular rainfall.

It was quiet, just the sound of a car horn in the distance and the steady roar from the rapids far below.

Rajiv pulled out his phone and looked at the screen. No missed calls or messages. Should he call her?

The previous night he had tried once more to talk Aarthi out of coming to the ashram, but she wouldn't budge. He tried everything, stopping just short of explaining his misgivings. What if he was wrong? What if it was all a misunderstanding? He saw how her eyes lit up when talking about her experience during the guided meditation, and he didn't want to take that away from her. In the end, he changed the subject, knowing he wouldn't get any further, but they had gone to bed with a lingering tension between them.

This morning, despite the early hour she had risen to give him breakfast before leaving, and he avoided the subject altogether, thinking that if he couldn't stop her, at least he could keep an eye on her.

He should check if she had left yet and where she had reached. He dialled her number from memory and held the phone to his ear.

Waiting for the phone to make a connection, he glanced back toward the Range Rover. Georges stood to the rear of the vehicle, speaking in hushed tones on what looked like a satellite phone, while Atman leaned his butt against the stone wall, his face angled toward the sky, his eyes closed. Manjunath, Rajiv's driver, stood a respectful distance away, puffing on a hand-rolled cigarette, while Max had disappeared into the undergrowth.

The journey so far had been uneventful. Rajiv content to stare out the window, watching the fields and villages flash by, remembering his own childhood growing up in the village. It all seemed so long ago. Part of him longed for a quieter, simpler life amongst the fields, but deep down, he knew that would never happen. At least not until he finally retired.

The phone call had still not connected, and he frowned at the screen. No signal. He heard the scuff of a foot against stone and he turned to see Max returning from answering the call of nature. Slipping the phone into his pocket, he took a deep breath of the fresh, cool air.

"I love it up here."

Rajiv glanced in surprise at Max, now standing beside him.

"You've been here before?"

Max nodded. "A couple of times. Whenever we come to Bangalore, we take this route to the ashram." He nodded toward Atman and Georges. "Atman likes it too."

Rajiv nodded slowly, returning his attention to the view in front of him. "I thought this was your first time here."

"No, but we've not been back here for some time."

Rajiv kept his tone casual, but turned to see Max's face. "Why is that?"

The young man shrugged, his eyes following the path of an eagle as it rode the up-draughts in the valley. "Just this and that. Other commitments. Travel."

"Where?"

Max glanced at him, then returned his attention to the view. "Europe, mainly."

Rajiv waited for him to elaborate, but when no further

comment was forthcoming, he tried another tack. "How long have you been with Atman?"

"About three years." Max stepped closer to the wall and looked over. "It's a long way down."

Rajiv nodded and leaned forward to look over, as if seeing it for the first time. "It's a good job this wall is here."

"Sure is. There wouldn't be much left of us if we went over."

"No... so... you mentioned you were in the army? Before Atman? "

Max nodded slowly, his hands still on the top of the wall, staring into the valley.

"How long?"

"Five years."

Rajiv turned his back on the valley and leaned up against the wall, crossing his arms in front of him. Atman was still in the same position, but Georges had wandered further away, no doubt wanting to empty his bladder. "It's mandatory, right, in Israel?"

"Yeah."

Rajiv frowned and turned his head to look at Max. "But five years? That's mandatory?"

"No. Three years. I stayed longer."

"You enjoyed it?"

Max stayed silent for a while and Rajiv wondered if he hadn't heard him. When Max finally spoke, his voice was quiet. "I did at first... not in the end."

Rajiv studied his face. The young man looked troubled, as if reliving unpleasant memories. He couldn't resist probing further. "Something happened?"

Max turned to look at him, his forehead creased, a muscle in his jaw pulsing. He locked eyes with Rajiv, but it was as if he wasn't seeing him, his attention somehow elsewhere.

A vehicle honked as it swept around the corner, and Max blinked, turning to watch the car disappear down the hill. He smiled and shrugged. "That's all in the past now."

## 29

John spotted him as soon as he walked into the arrivals hall at Dubai International Airport. The stocky Australian was leaning up against a pillar, a takeaway coffee in his hand, peering over the top of his Ray-Bans at a group of female aircrew walking past.

"Don't let me interrupt you."

Steve Jones grinned, tossed his cup into the garbage bin beside him, and threw his arms around John in a welcoming embrace.

"John bloody Hayes." He pushed him away, holding him at arm's length, a big grin still on his face. "Good to see you again, mate."

"You too," John grinned back. The two had been through a lot, risking their lives for each other, and it had formed a bond that no amount of time or distance would break.

Steve released his grip on his shoulders and looked down at the single bag by John's feet. "Is that it?"

"I like to travel light."

"Good, let's get going then. We have a lot to talk about."

Steve gestured toward the exit and started walking.

"How long are you here for?"

"A day. Two, tops."

Steve threw him a quick look but didn't break stride. He led John outside to a double-parked white Pajero. "Jump in, mate."

He walked around to the driver's side, stopping briefly to remove a ticket from under the windscreen wiper, then climbed in as John tossed his bag onto the rear seat and climbed in beside him. Steve stuffed the ticket into the cup holder, joining what looked to John like several others, started the engine, and pulled away from the curb.

"So, are you going to tell me what's brought you to Dubai, because I get the feeling it's not just to see me?"

John nodded and thought about where to start. "First, can you take me to your hacker guy? I'll explain on the way."

It was a thirty-minute journey from the airport to the dusty streets of Bur Dubai, the glitzy steel and glass skyscrapers making way for the sand coloured clutter of the Old Town. Steve listened quietly as John explained why he was there, interrupting occasionally when something wasn't clear and by the time they reached their destination, John had told him all about the events in Sri Lanka and how Atman had resurfaced in Bangalore.

Steve turned off the engine and turned slightly to face John, leaning his body against the side door. "So I'm guessing you want a new set of ID, given your history with Bangalore."

John nodded. "I can see why you're a private investigator."

Steve didn't laugh, his face serious. "You're still taking a risk."

John shrugged. "I've taken risks before. Look at what we did in Syria."

Steve half smiled. "I'll give you that." His smile disappeared as he studied John's face. "But is it worth it? You have a good life now, a beautiful partner... Syria was different. I called in a favour. It was for someone in my family. But this? What's the point? What difference is it going to make?"

"It makes a difference to me, Steve."

"Okay. Explain how."

"Because I know he's a fraud."

"So?" Steve gestured out the windshield. "Most people out there are frauds."

"Yes, but this one takes advantage of the vulnerable when they need him most. Those who need love, who need support, who look to..." John searched for the word, then made quotation marks with his fingers, "'The Divine,' for succour. Because their lives are broken."

"That sounds like all religions."

John nodded, conceding the point. "Yes, but..." he sighed. "Maybe I can do something about this one. Look Steve, I don't expect you to understand, but you should understand better than most. Remember why we went to Syria? Your niece had been brainwashed into changing her religion and then followed some idiot into a war zone where she was kept as a second-class citizen. You know what these guys can do."

"I know, mate. I'm not saying you're wrong. I'm just trying to understand it, and this isn't exactly the same thing. He's not sending them on a..." he paused, glanced around the exterior of the car and lowered his voice, "*jihad*. He's not convincing them to strap on a vest and blow themselves up so they can go to heaven to receive however many virgins he's promised them."

"No. But he's using his position of power to manipulate women into having sex with him, telling them they are receiving a special blessing or a fast track to divinity or whatever else he promises." John took a breath, feeling himself getting angry. "And these women go to him thinking he is helping them, improving their lives, repairing their damaged psyches. These are someone's daughters, sisters, nieces. To be honest, Steve, I don't really give a shit about the other stuff, the money laundering, the corruption, the political influence. That's going on in every government office in every country in the world. But this pretending to be better than everyone else and offering a fast track to God while manipulating people when they are vulnerable really makes me angry." John ran out of steam, lapsing into silence, his eyes on the street outside.

An elderly man in a dirty white *dishdasha* and a wispy grey beard that reached his chest, crossed the street in front of them and glanced idly at the two men in the car.

Steve waited until he passed behind the vehicle, watching his progress in the side mirror before speaking again.

"I get it. Anything you need from me, mate, don't hesitate."

John exhaled, not realising until now that he had tensed up. "Thanks, Steve. But I should be okay. But what I do need is a new passport."

Steve slapped his palm on the rim of the steering wheel. "Lets go get you one then."

## 30

They climbed out of the car and John followed Steve across the road and into the loading bay of a dingy, four storey commercial building. John had been here before and nothing had changed. Apart from a pile of garbage in one corner, there was no sign that anyone occupied the building.

"You know he owns the entire building, right? Who says crime doesn't pay?" Steve winked at John, then raised his fist and pounded on the unmarked door which led inside. He then turned and faced a security camera set in the ceiling, made a gun sign with his finger and mimed firing at the camera. There was the sound of an electronic buzzer, then the door clicked open. Steve turned and grinned at John. "He's made a few changes since you last came here. Automated the door. He hates leaving his computer."

John nodded and followed Steve inside. Lights flickered on in the corridor as they entered, the bright white fluorescents only highlighting the scarred and marked walls and the peeling and cracked linoleum underfoot.

"I like what he's done with the place," John quipped, his nostrils twitching at the dust and the stale air.

"As I said, he never leaves his computer."

They walked down the corridor to another unmarked door and Steve pushed it open without knocking.

"Well, Ramesh, I'd like to say it's a pleasure, but then I'd be lying."

"What do you want, Steve?" the thin young Indian man grumbled as he swivelled around in his chair. His eyes moved to John and his eyebrows lifted in surprise. He pointed his index finger at John, hesitated for a brief moment, then said, "John Hayes."

John gave him a broad smile. "Good to see you again, Ramesh. You have an excellent memory."

The corners of Ramesh's mouth twitched. He glanced at Steve, who had taken a seat on the edge of Ramesh's workstation, scowled, then looked back at John. "If Steve has brought you here, I assume you need something from me."

John nodded and moved further inside the room, allowing the door to swing shut behind him. The windowless room instantly darkened, lit only by the glow from the multiple computer monitors arrayed on the desk in front of Ramesh.

"Put some bloody light on, Ramesh," Steve growled. "What are you, The Hobbit?"

Ramesh didn't move for a moment, then reached behind him, picked up a remote from the desk and pressed a button. Instantly, the room was bathed in a warm yellow light from strips of LEDs that ran around the tops of the walls.

"Oooh, romantic."

Ramesh ignored Steve's comment, his focus still on John. "What do you need?"

"A new passport."

"British?"

"Yes, and an Indian visa."

"India?" Ramesh's eyebrows did a little jump again. "Why...?" he saw the look on John's face and stopped. "Of course, it's none of my business."

John nodded.

"When do you need it?"

"Yesterday."

Ramesh shook his head and raised his hands in the air. "Why doesn't anyone understand that an artist needs time?"

John replied before Steve could say anything, "I'm sorry, Ramesh, but I have faith in you. You did a fantastic job last time, and I'll pay whatever it costs."

The praise and the unlimited budget had the desired effect. "Tomorrow morning, okay?"

"Perfect." John reached into his back pocket and removed a small envelope. "Passport photos, multiple sizes."

"Where are you staying?"

John nodded in Steve's direction. "With Steve."

"I'll send them over."

"Payment?"

Ramesh dismissed the question with a wave of his hand, "I trust you. You can pay once it's done."

"What? Bloody Madrasi! You always make me pay in advance!" Steve protested.

Ramesh shrugged, his eyes still on John, the trace of a smile on his face. "What can I say?"

John reached out and shook his hand. "Thank you, Ramesh."

The young man smiled and handed John a card. It was blank apart from a single phone number. "If you need anything else, just call me. No need to go through the Aussie next time."

John smiled, turned to Steve, and nodded. "I'm done."

Steve stood up, placed a hand on Ramesh's shoulder, and gave it a squeeze. "You should get out more, mate. All this time indoors, and you're getting whiter than me."

"Maybe I'll come over tomorrow, with the passport."

"You do that, mate."

"I'll bring some of Mom's samosas."

"Don't you dare," Steve growled over his shoulder as he walked out the door. "I had the shits for three days last time," he added under his breath.

## 31

Just over seven hours after leaving Bangalore, the Range Rover, now in the lead, slowed and pulled up in front of a large steel gate set in a wall which stretched for at least a hundred metres on each side. Although Rajiv had an idea how the ashram looked from the satellite pictures, the size surprised him. The walls and gate must have been eight feet high, the walls topped with barbed wire, and security cameras on both sides of the gate. If it wasn't for the name *Anandsagar* painted on the gate, it could easily be mistaken for a top security government compound.

Max gave a quick toot on the horn and after a moment, the gates swung inward and the Range Rover rolled inside into a large gravel parking area lined with coconut palms and tropical plants. A uniformed security guard stood to attention beside the guardroom to the right of the entrance and to the left, in the corner of the parking area was another low building and a well. Max guided the Range Rover in a semi-circle, and pulled up in front of a stone archway, Manjunath parking the police vehicle just behind it.

Rajiv opened his door and climbed out as the doors opened on the Range Rover.

The air was warm, humid, and flavoured with salt. A crow cawed from its perch high in a coconut palm and in the background, Rajiv could hear waves crashing on the beach.

He turned at the sound of hurried footsteps and saw a middle-aged man hurrying toward them, down the path toward the archway. Another man, of similar age, but thinner, and with long greasy hair that hung to his shoulders, followed a respectable distance behind. The first man ignored Rajiv, moving straight to Atman, who was now out of the vehicle.

"Guruji," he exclaimed and bent over as if to touch Atman's feet. He only made it halfway before Atman held him by the shoulders and stopped him.

"Manoj. It's good to see you again."

Manoj stood in front of him, his hands clasped together in *namaste*, a broad smile on his face. "Guruji, I'm so sorry. I wasn't expecting you for another hour at least."

Atman smiled. "It's okay. We made very good time." He let go of Manoj's shoulders and nodded toward Rajiv. "Manoj, this is Detective Inspector Rajiv Sampath of the Bangalore Police. Officially, he will oversee our security while we are here," Atman turned and gave a warm smile to Rajiv, "but actually he is my guest."

Manoj shot a quick glance at Georges, his smile faltering a little. It was brief, but not brief enough for Rajiv to miss it. He then reached out a hand and grasped Rajiv's, his smile restored, and shook it vigorously. "Welcome, sir. I am Manoj Shetty. I have the honour of running the ashram here for Guruji. If there is anything you need, please come to me."

Rajiv returned his smile. "Thank you, Manoj. Please call me Rajiv."

"Manoj, please ensure Rajiv has one of the rooms on the top floor overlooking the beach." Atman added.

"Yes, of course, Guruji."

"Good, now it's been a long journey. I want to rest for a while before the evening meditation." Atman turned to Rajiv. "Please make yourself at home." He smiled, "And don't worry about my safety. I want you to relax. Nothing will happen here. We will meet again at six-thirty in the main hall. If there is anything you need, Manoj here will see to it."

Rajiv nodded. "Thank you."

Atman reached out and squeezed his shoulder, then set off with Georges through the archway, Manoj following, his hands still clasped together.

Rajiv watched him go, then turned back to the vehicles. Manoj's long haired assistant was helping the security guard unload the bags from the rear of the Range Rover, while Max looked on. Amongst the luggage, Rajiv recognised the three carry-on bags from the Chief Minister's residence and he watched as they were separated out from the rest of the luggage and wheeled away by Long Hair and Max.

Rajiv frowned. He had an idea what was going on, but there was nothing he could do about it.

## 32

"Do you know where we are staying?"

The security guard, a thin elderly man with skin burnt black by the sun, shook his head and wouldn't make eye contact. He continued to remove bags from the rear of the Range Rover, stacking them to one side.

"What's your name?"

"Mani, sir." He stood to attention as he said this, but still would not look at Rajiv.

Rajiv was used to this, people often having an instinctive wariness of the police. He didn't like it. He wanted people to trust him and if he was to oversee Atman's security, he needed to have Mani on his side. Stepping forward, he took one bag from Mani's hand. "Let me help you, Mani."

Mani seemed to relax a little, but still protested, "No, it's okay, sir."

Rajiv gave him a broad smile and took the bag, placing it next to the others. "How long have you worked here, Mani?"

"For two years, sir."

"And before that?"

Mani paused beside the rear of the tailgate. "I had a boat, sir. A fishing boat."

"You don't fish anymore?"

Mani shook his head, his smile fading. "No, sir. See my age. Fishing is for young men."

"You still look strong and fit to me, Mani." It was a lie. The years of hard physical labour obviously hadn't been kind to the man, but Rajiv's flattery had a purpose.

The old man smiled shyly, but straightened even more and pulled his shoulders back.

"Do you enjoy working here?"

"Yes, sir. It is a great blessing to work for Guruji."

"I'm sure. Is he here often?"

Mani shook his head. "Not very often." Then he smiled. "He's a great Master. People all over the world want to see him."

"When was he here last?"

Mani looked up at the sky as if the answer would come from there. After a moment, he said, "Three or four months ago."

Rajiv remembered the article about the foreign woman being hit by a truck. That was about three months ago. But before he could ask any more, he heard footsteps and looked up to see Manoj returning.

"Rajiv, let me show you to your room. Mani, bring Sir's bag."

Rajiv shook his head. "It's okay, I'll carry my bag."

Mani glanced nervously at Manoj and opened his mouth to say something, but Rajiv had already picked up the bag, and was smiling at Manoj.

"Which way?"

Manoj looked from the bag to Mani, then smiled. "Please follow me."

"My driver?"

"We have rooms for the drivers." Manoj nodded at the elderly watchman. "Mani."

"Yes, sir."

Manoj turned back to Rajiv and smiled. "He'll sort it out. Come."

He led Rajiv through the archway and down a stone path. On each side of the path, patches of grass fought a losing battle against the sand and salty air. Manoj gestured toward a long, low building on the left. "That's the administration building." He looked back over his shoulder. "My office is in there."

To the right was a large patch of open sandy ground dotted with more coconut palms, and behind it was what looked like a private house in a separate compound. Unlike the cream painted concrete of the administration building, the walls were built from red laterite stone blocks under a terracotta tiled roof. Polished wooden pillars supported a verandah which ran the full width of the bungalow, and the piece of lawn visible through the gate in the boundary wall was lush and green, unlike the patchy grass along the pathway. "What's that over there?"

Manoj looked back to see what Rajiv meant, then smiled. "That is Guruji's accommodation while he's here." He pointed ahead to a large double height building, "And that is the meditation hall." He stopped in his tracks and turned. "I trust you will join us for the meditation?"

Rajiv nodded as noncommittally as he could, then changed the subject, "How many residents are there in the ashram?"

Manoj beamed proudly. "We have around two hundred and fifty *shishyas,* students, staying full time on the ashram. Perhaps another twenty or so outside the ashram, and starting this evening we will have another fifty arriving for Guruji's programme."

"Staff?"

Manoj smiled proudly. "Through the grace of our Guru, and the selfless service of our students, the ashram runs like a well-oiled machine with minimal staff." He walked on and pointed to another building to the left of the meditation hall. "That is our dining hall and kitchen. The students prepare all the food." He looked back over his shoulder, "Vegetarian of course."

"Of course." Rajiv made a mental note to eat outside the ashram. "Are you also a volunteer, Manoj?"

Manoj shook his head and stopped. Turning around to face Rajiv, he said, "No, no, Guruji insists I receive a salary." He smiled, "But of course, I would be happy to work for him for free. It's such an honour."

Rajiv returned his smile. "I'm sure." Rajiv liked to think he was good at reading people. Years of questioning suspects, trying to extract the few grains of truth from whatever someone was telling him, had honed his instincts for bullshit. And right now, he could smell it. "And how long have you worked for him?"

Manoj straightened up and pulled his shoulders back, but all it did was push his belly further forward. "Five years now."

Rajiv nodded thoughtfully. "Atman must be very happy with your work."

Either the praise embarrassed Manoj, or he was a better actor than Rajiv thought, because his face coloured and his smile grew broader even as he looked away.

A young woman in white appeared from further up the pathway and as she approached, she glanced warily at Rajiv's uniform, then raised her hands in *namaste* and nodded at Manoj. Manoj did the same with his own hands, nodded with a smile, then once she was past, he gestured in the direction she had come from. "Shall we?"

"One of the students?"

"Yes."

"Are there many women students?" Rajiv asked, falling in step beside Manoj, as he led him along the path between the dining hall and the meditation hall.

"I think about eighty percent. I haven't counted."

"All Indian?"

Again, Manoj stopped in his tracks and turned to look at Rajiv, his face beaming. "No, people come from all over the world to see Atman." He reached out and placed a hand on Rajiv's arm. "You'll see tonight."

## 33

Once past the two halls, the ashram opened up and ahead between the coconut palms Rajiv could see the sea. A steady onshore breeze carried the sound of waves crashing against the beach. The path forked and Manoj took the left between the palms toward a two-storey building, its once cream facade peeling and stained from the constant onslaught of the sea air.

"This is the men's dormitory."

"And the women's?"

Manoj waved in the direction they had come. "The right-hand path goes there." He stopped at the foot of the steps that led up onto the verandah, his face serious. "We don't encourage mixing between the male and female residents. The vibrational energy is different and Guruji says it slows one's progress."

"Really?"

"Yes." Manoj smiled, "But then you don't have to worry about that. You are married."

Rajiv frowned. "How do you know that?"

Manoj grinned. "I saw your ring."

"Hmmm, maybe you should work for me, Manoj. We can always use someone with good detective skills."

"Ha!" Manoj seemed to find the idea highly amusing, because he didn't stop chuckling as he led Rajiv up the steps onto the verandah. Directly ahead was a set of stairs leading to the first floor and to the right, along the verandah, were five doors with a single window to each side of them. A western man in white stood in the third doorway watching them and when Rajiv nodded in his direction, he raised a hand in a reluctant wave, then stepped back inside the room.

"Your room is up here," Manoj announced, already halfway up the stairs.

Rajiv followed after him, while Manoj paused at the top to catch his breath. "I think you will be very happy with the view," he said after a moment.

Rajiv stepped out onto the second floor verandah and looked around. To his left was the broad expanse of the Arabian Sea, dotted with fishing boats. Directly in front, he could just make out through the coconut palms, the building that must be the women's quarters. It was a similar design, but three times as long as the block he was in and looked fully occupied. To his right were the dining and meditation halls and between them and the women's dormitory, he could see through to the immaculately manicured lawn of Atman's bungalow. He noticed a figure in white moving along the bungalow's verandah, but it was a little too far for him to see who it was.

"This way, please."

Rajiv followed Manoj to the last room on the sea end of the verandah. The door was open and Manoj was already inside, but Rajiv stopped and gazed out at the ocean. He hadn't been to the seaside since he was a kid, and even then rarely. But he still remembered how the vastness had taken his breath away, and even now, after so many years, it had the same effect. Pristine golden sands stretched to his left and right in a gentle arc and far to the right on a promontory stood the Kapu Lighthouse, built all the way back in 1901. He closed his eyes, inhaled a lungful of fresh sea air, and smiled. Coming here may not have been such a bad idea after all.

He heard Manoj clearing his throat and blinking his eyes open, he turned to see him standing in the doorway with a large iron key in his hand. Attached to it was a block of wood with the number ten hand painted on it in white. "Here is your key. There is a change of clothes for you on the bed." He smiled. "For the meditation this evening. The water should be hot. We have solar, so it's only hot in the evening."

He thrust the key toward Rajiv. "If there is anything you need, please tell me."

Rajiv took the key and nodded. "I'm sure it will be fine."

"Good. Six-thirty at the hall then."

Rajiv nodded and waited for Manoj to walk away before stepping inside the room. There was a single bed on each side of the room with a bookshelf at the head of each. Behind the bookshelves on each side was a steel railing with several empty clothes hangers. A set of white cotton clothing lay folded on the right-hand bed, so he set his bag and his uniform cap down on the left-hand bed and examined the room. At the rear was a door, which he assumed led to the bathroom, and on the right above the bed was a small shuttered window. He leaned over and unlatched the shutters, swinging them open. Immediately, the sea breeze filled the room, and he took another deep breath. It certainly beat the dusty, smoggy air of Bangalore. He fixed the shutters open with the hooks at the bottom of the frame, then walked over toward the bathroom and glanced inside. Cracked white tiles covered the floor and continued halfway up the wall. A pink plastic bucket was filling up drip by drip under a leaking tap, and to the right of the door was a squat toilet. The room smelled of disinfectant, and despite the cracks in the tiles and cobwebs in the corner near the roof, was clean.

He walked back out and unzipped his bag, removing his toilet kit and a spare uniform. The toilet kit he placed on the edge of the sink in the bathroom and then he shook out his folded uniform and placed it on the clothes hangers. He studied it for a moment. It was creased but hopefully it wouldn't look too wrinkled in the morning.

He checked his watch. He had two hours before the meditation. Time to explore.

## 34

Despite the heat and humidity, Rajiv kept his uniform on. A policeman's uniform allowed him access to places without question and as it was his first time there, he wanted to take advantage of that. He pulled the door closed behind him, not bothering to lock it. There was nothing worth stealing, and walked toward the stairs. Three of the doors had large padlocks on them, and only the one near the stairs appeared to be occupied, although the door was closed. He jogged down the stairs and walked along the verandah. Here, all five rooms looked occupied, and Rajiv did a quick mental calculation. Assuming each room had two beds, there should be up to twelve male students. He paused outside the third door and smiled at the westerner who was reclining on a bed, reading a paperback.

"Good evening."

The westerner looked up in surprise, then sat upright, placing the book on the bed beside him.

"Good evening," he replied, a frown creasing his forehead. "Is something wrong?"

Rajiv increased the width of his smile. "Not at all. I'm staying upstairs for a few days. Just thought I would familiarise myself with the surroundings."

The man relaxed and stood up. Walking toward the door, he smiled and held out his hand. "I am Thorsten, from Germany."

"Detective Inspector Rajiv Sampath, Bangalore Police."

Thorsten raised an eyebrow. "Bangalore? That's a long way from here."

Rajiv nodded, "Yes. Mr... Atman, your guru, was just there, and I accompanied him here."

"Aha." Thorsten still looked puzzled. "You are his... student?"

Rajiv thought quickly. It would be useful to have people on his side, and if he just said he was looking after security, he might not establish the same relationship. "It's a bit early to say. I only met him two days ago, but so far, I like what I see."

Thorsten smiled. "He is a great Being. Once you surrender to him, great things will happen in your life."

"Well, that's good to hear. Have you been here long?"

Thorsten stepped outside the room and leaned back against the doorframe, much more relaxed. "This trip, two months, but I try to come twice a year. "

Rajiv nodded, as Thorsten, warming to the subject, continued, "I was going through a bad time in my life, and Atman helped me a lot. He has given me a lot of peace."

"Okay." Rajiv smiled, as his phone vibrated in his pocket. He pulled it out and glanced at the screen. *Aarthi*. "I'm sorry, excuse me, I must take this call."

"Of course." Thorsten nodded, but stayed where he was.

Rajiv turned and walked back in the direction he had come, putting distance between them. He took the three steps down off the verandah, and only then answered the call. As he held the phone to his ear, he glanced back and saw Thorsten still watching. He turned his back on him and began walking down the path.

"Hello, Aarthi, where are you?"

"I've just arrived, Rajiv. I'm at the entrance. Where are you?"

Rajiv smiled at the sound of his wife's voice, the underlying tension he had felt since leaving Bangalore melting away. She had arrived safely.

"I'm also here. How was the journey?"

"Good. A little tired now, but it's okay."

Rajiv smiled again, stopping in the middle of the pathway. He heard a noise and looked up to see a crow cawing at him as it hopped between the fronds of a coconut palm. "Okay, go and freshen up. I think there's a meditation this evening."

"Yes, at six-thirty. Will you be there?"

Rajiv was reluctant to commit. "I'll be around. Don't forget, I'm working."

He heard her sigh, "I know, but... what will happen here? You can relax a bit. It's not Bangalore."

Rajiv grinned. "No, that's for sure. Let's see how it goes. But... I've been thinking..." Rajiv's grin turned into a grimace as he struggled for the right words, "I want to keep things professional, so... please don't tell anyone that I'm your husband."

"What? Why?"

Rajiv sighed. "I just..." What did he tell her? The things he had read, and that John had told him, lurked in the back of his mind, but he also didn't want to contaminate her experience. What if he was wrong? Instead, he gave her another explanation, one he'd been working on during the long car journey. "I don't want people to think I'm taking advantage of my position. I know you have booked and paid for this, but you know what people will say."

"Who will say?"

"I don't know, Aarthi, but I don't want to take a chance. You know how hard I work to protect my reputation. Everything must be above board."

She was silent for a while and he could almost picture her thinking it over. It was a discussion they'd had many times before throughout his career. Colleagues took money to look the other way, to quash a case, even to arrest the wrong person. But Rajiv always refused. His career had suffered for it, but at least he could sleep at night. He had joined the force to uphold the law, not break it.

"Okay."

He could hear her disappointment, but he felt a weight leave his shoulders. He would make it up to her later. "Message me your room number, so I know where you are. I'll still find you... come and see you... but we'll keep it professional unless we are alone."

"Okay... I'll miss you, Rajiv."

Rajiv grinned. "I'm here. What to miss? I'll see you soon. Now go and get yourself settled in."

Rajiv ended the call and looked around. The crow had flown off, and a squirrel scampered across a patch of sandy ground to his left. He took a deep breath of fresh, salty air. He had to admit; he was feeling more relaxed than he had felt in a long time... but he was here to do a job, and the job always came first. Slipping the phone back into his pocket, he set off along the path.

## 35

It took about ten minutes for Rajiv to patrol the complete boundary of the ashram. The eight-feet-high boundary wall Rajiv had seen at the front continued along the entire perimeter, except unusually, for the wall that bounded the beach. There it was lower, around five feet high and missing the barbed wire that topped the wall on the other boundaries. There was a steel mesh gate in the wall allowing access to the beach. A digital keypad operated the lock, but when Rajiv wiggled the gate, it clicked open. He punched a few numbers into the keypad, but there was no sound. Either the salt air had corrupted the electronics or the batteries were flat.

Stepping through the gate, he walked out onto the top of the low dune, his feet sinking into the soft surface and his uniform shoes filling up with sand. Looking left, the beach curved gently for about a kilometre before ending in a rocky outcrop. A single fisherman stood ankle deep in the water, staring out to sea, and several wading birds ran back and forth in front of the surf pecking at holes in the sand. To his right, the beach was a little busier. There was a couple walking just above the high-water mark, and further down toward the lighthouse, groups of people played in the surf.

A movement close by caught his eye. A stray dog yawned and stretched in the sand, then trotted toward him, stopping just out of reach. It tilted its head, sniffed the air, and then curled its lips in a low growl.

Rajiv grinned. For some reason, dogs always hated police uniforms. "Come here, boy," he called out. The dog gave a lazy wag of its tail, then, losing interest, cocked its leg over a piece of driftwood, emitting a faint splash of urine before turning its back on Rajiv and walking away.

Rajiv shrugged and stepped back inside the ashram, pushing the gate shut behind him.

After emptying the sand from his shoes, he continued on his way, noting the security cameras on each corner and making a mental note to check they were working and that the feed was monitored and recorded.

He passed the rear of the women's dormitory, the open windows and excited chatter in complete contrast to the men's block. No-one noticed him pass though, and he continued on his way, passing several other buildings that looked like storerooms until reaching Atman's separate compound. He stopped in the open gateway and looked inside. The compound ran parallel to the main ashram stretching from the road to the beach, the bungalow sitting at the halfway point. In contrast to the ashram, the lawn areas were lush and green and the landscaping along the boundary was well planted and maintained. Several stone sculptures were dotted around the compound — statues of Buddha, Ganesha, and even a Nataraj, the dancing form of Shiva.

Cane chairs and occasional tables occupied the verandah facing the beach, and several fans turned lazily in the roof above them. It was all beautifully and well maintained, looking more like the holiday home of a wealthy industrialist. At the end nearest the road was a parking area, and a man was washing the Range Rover in front of an open garage housing two white Mahindra SUVs. The high wall and gate shielded the compound from the road, preventing passers-by from knowing what lay within.

Rajiv wondered if any of the students ever commented on the contrast between the ashram and Atman's private quarters. He shook his head. Probably not. People rarely questioned anything.

He turned his back on the compound — he'd explore it in more detail later, probably during the meditation — and followed the ashram boundary toward the front. There was little more of interest, and not long later, Rajiv stepped into the parking area. A minibus stood with its doors open, the driver standing barefoot on the roof rack, passing bags down to Mani, who stacked them in a pile. A group of Indian women chattered excitedly in front of a white-clad volunteer who was checking names off on a clipboard.

There was no sign of Aarthi

Rajiv wandered over to the guardroom beside the gate and poked his head inside. A single flat screen TV attached to the wall showed the feeds from twelve cameras. Rajiv studied them for a moment, checking their coverage. The entire boundary appeared to be monitored, however one feed was blank, a camera by the beach, and Rajiv made a mental note to mention it to Georges. A key cabinet was bolted to the wall beside the screen and beneath it was a wooden table, bare apart from a phone charger and several dirty *chai* glasses. To the rear of the hut was a single cot, and a shirt hung from a hook on the wall. The windowless room was dark and musty, the only light coming from the single bare lightbulb hanging from a wire and the flickering of the television screen. Rajiv shook his head. He'd seen it all before. The money was always spent elsewhere, leaving the staff to exist with the bare minimum of facilities.

Rajiv turned, his eyes on the unloading of the mini-bus but his thoughts elsewhere. From a security point of view, the weak point was the beachfront boundary. The wall was easy to climb over, and the gate lock wasn't working. However, the cameras would pickup anyone trying to get in... when they were working. But then if Mani wasn't watching the screens...

Before he could take the thought any further, he saw Manjunath appear in a doorway to his right. He was drying his hands with a thin cotton towel, his hair slicked back with water.

"Sir."

"Is that your room?"

"Yes, sir."

"All okay?"

"Yes, sir."

"Good. I'm in room ten at the far end near the beach, but call me if you need anything."

"Yes, sir." Manjunath looked as if he wanted to say something more.

"What is it?"

Manjunath looked down at the ground and cleared his throat before looking up again. "Um, sir... can I attend the meditation?"

Rajiv studied him, keeping his expression blank, hiding his surprise. His first instinct was to say no. Manjunath was on duty, not on holiday and besides, he hadn't taken Manjunath for being the spiritual type. But after a moment, he changed his mind. It couldn't do any harm.

"Okay, but..." He looked the constable up and down, "change out of your uniform. Try to blend in and keep your eyes and ears open."

"But sir..."

"What is it now?" Rajiv growled.

"How will I meditate with my eyes open?"

Rajiv counted to ten before replying, "It's a figure of speech. We're here for a reason, so I want you to keep alert for any security risks."

"Ah, yes..." Manjunath flushed with embarrassment. "Of course, sir. Thank you, sir."

"Off you go." Rajiv watched the young constable turn eagerly back to his room. "Oh, Manjunath... your wife..." He racked his brain trying to remember her name. "Sushmita?"

"Sushila, sir."

"Yes, that's right. Isn't she from around here?"

"Yes, sir," Manjunath beamed with pride. "The next district, sir."

"So, have you learnt the local dialect from her?"

"I understand it, sir, but I don't speak it."

Rajiv nodded slowly. "Good. Don't let anyone know you understand. Let's keep it between us."

Manjunath frowned, confusion evident on his face.

Rajiv dismissed him with a jerk of his head toward the driver's room, then turned away to look at the minibus.

Although most people spoke English, Kannada was the official state language, and the one Rajiv had used to speak to Mani, the watchman. However, this region had a language of their own, Tulu, and it was one Rajiv didn't speak, let alone understand. Having someone on his team who did though might come in useful.

## 36

Flip-flops, slippers, and sports shoes littered each side of the footpath, as if mocking the dimly lit sign which said, 'please put your footwear in the shoe stand.'

Rajiv hesitated by the almost empty shoe stand, looked down at his scuffed brown shoes, then decided against removing them. He wasn't planning to stay.

He climbed the steps to the meditation hall, stopped in the doorway, and peered inside the open double doors. The hall was already full, five minutes ahead of the scheduled time. Hundreds of students, all in white, sat cross-legged on folded blankets and cushions on both sides of a central aisle. The left side was all women, while the right-hand side had a small group of men seated near the front, and more women behind them. A spotlight shone down on a high-backed armchair draped in a white cloth in the centre of the stage and to the right was an altar with various idols garlanded with flowers. To the rear of the stage was a huge framed photo of Atman seated in a similar armchair, a blissful look on his face, his eyes rolled back, only the whites of the eyes visible.

A low hum of excited conversation filled the hall, as did the sweet, fragrant smell of incense.

Rajiv scanned the seated students looking for Aarthi, but from the back, in the low light, and dressed in white, the women looked the same, the only difference being the hair colour. Based on the hair colour alone, Rajiv estimated at least half the students were westerners.

He heard footsteps behind him, and he turned to see Manoj hurrying along the path toward him. He cast a disapproving look at Rajiv's uniform, while he slipped off his flip-flops, then pushed past, saying only, "Atman is coming."

Rajiv watched him hurry down the aisle toward the stage, then turn and gesture for the students to stand up. The excitement levels rose as everyone struggled to their feet, heads turning toward the door.

Rajiv suddenly realised everyone was looking at him. A heat spread across his cheeks and he quickly stepped back out of the doorway and out of sight. At the same time, he turned to see Georges and Atman walking toward him. Both had changed into white clothing, Atman in a well fitting linen shirt and matching pants, Georges in a long Indian *kurta* and loose pants. If Atman had noticed Rajiv's uniform, he didn't show it, instead fixing Rajiv with a broad smile. He was already barefoot, and walked straight up the steps, winked at Rajiv, then stopped in the doorway as a hush came over the hall. Georges jogged up the steps after removing his footwear, nodded at Rajiv, his face serious, then stopped behind Atman. Atman placed his right hand over his chest and moved his gaze from left to right and back again. Rajiv couldn't see the reaction, but not a sound came from the hall. Atman paused a moment longer, then dropped his hand and entered the hall, with Georges following immediately behind him. Rajiv stepped forward to look inside, but Georges had turned, blocking the doorway, reaching for the door handles on each side. His eyes flicked to Rajiv's uniform, then back to his face as he pulled the doors closed, leaving Rajiv standing alone on the step outside.

He stared at the closed door for a second, then turned around and stood with his hands on his hips, looking back down the pathway. Manjunath hurried toward him, a worried look on his face. He had changed out of his uniform and was wearing a loose cotton shirt and a white *lungi* wrapped around his waist. "Am I too late, sir?" he panted, his eyes flicking from Rajiv's face to the closed door.

Rajiv shook his head. "Just in time. Go on in. I'll debrief you later."

Manjunath nodded, stepped forward, and gently eased the door open a little and peered inside. With a final nervous glance back at Rajiv, he opened the door just enough for him to slip through, then the door clicked shut behind him.

Rajiv smiled and turned to gaze up at the sky. The last rays of the departed sun highlighted a single wisp of cloud high above in the night sky, while down below, moths danced in the light of the lamps lighting the path. Apart from the ever-present sound of waves on the beach, the ashram was silent, as if Rajiv was the only person left alive. The thought somehow comforted him. For so long, his life had been filled with constant calls on his attention. Even when he was off duty, his phone would ring or buzz with messages. For the first time in a long time, longer than he could remember, he was truly alone. He felt his cheek twitch and then his mouth breaking into a wide grin. Perhaps Muniappa had done him a favour?

He stepped down onto the path and walked away from the hall, disturbing a tiny frog that hopped across the path and then disappeared into the darkness. Rajiv chuckled. When he was a young boy, he and his friend Tarun used to catch them in the field behind the village school, and hide them in the lunchboxes of the girls in his class. What was Tarun doing now?

Without realising, Rajiv found himself at the entrance to Atman's compound. Tasteful lighting highlighted the polished wooden pillars on the verandah and hidden spotlights lit up the varied statuary around the garden. Rajiv glanced at his wristwatch. He probably had an hour to an hour and a half before the meditation ended. Time to put it to good use.

## 37

Rajiv walked down the pathway toward the house. The compound was quiet, the house apparently empty. But then a flash of movement in a window caught his eye. He kept his attention on the window as he walked closer. He could see a middle-aged man moving around inside a kitchen and heard the whistle of a pressure cooker. Rajiv ignored him and turned his attention to the verandah. The highly polished red-oxide floor glowed in the soft lighting reflecting off the wooden pillars. Several planter's chairs faced the ocean and hanging baskets filled with ferns and flowers swung lazily in the sea breeze. He was still around ten metres from the house when a figure stepped out on to the verandah and faced him, watching him approach.

Max.

"How can I help you, Rajiv?"

Rajiv waited until he was at the foot of the steps leading up to the verandah, then smiled. "Good evening, Max."

Max dipped his head in acknowledgement, but the wary expression on his face didn't change.

Rajiv glanced around the compound. "I'm just familiarising myself with the layout of the ashram." He looked back at Max, keeping the smile fixed on his face.

Max frowned slightly. "You didn't want to join the meditation?"

Rajiv shrugged and shook his head at the same time. "I'm not here on holiday. I'm here to look after security."

The lines on Max's forehead eased away, and the stiffness went out of his shoulders. He half smiled, and with one hand gestured across the lawn toward the ocean. "I think we are quite safe here."

Rajiv nodded thoughtfully, his expression serious. "Perhaps. But the wall along the beach is easily climbed and the lock on the gate to the beach isn't working. The gate is unlocked."

"Yeah," Max sighed. "The salt air plays havoc with the electronics. I'll get it checked."

"Yes," Rajiv continued. "And I'm not convinced Mani can keep an eye on the security feed in the guardroom. He's busy unloading luggage, leaving the screens unattended, and..." Rajiv didn't want to get the old guy in trouble, but needed to make a point, "he's probably asleep the rest of the time."

Max nodded slowly, his eyes fixed on Rajiv's face, then seemed to come to a decision. He turned sideways and gestured for Rajiv to come onto the verandah. "Come inside. I'll show you what we have here."

Rajiv smiled and jogged up the steps, following Max across the verandah toward the central door that led into the house. Max paused in the doorway and shot a glance at Rajiv's shoes. Rajiv took the hint and stood with one hand on the door frame as he slipped off his footwear. To his left on the wall beside the door was a large framed photo of

Atman seated in meditation. A garland of orange marigolds hung from each corner of the frame, and on a small table in front of it, an oil lamp burned steadily behind a glass shield.

Rajiv nudged his shoes together at the side of the doorway and stepped into a large living room. The polished red-oxide floor continued inside, but here a large luxurious silk carpet filled the centre of the room. A long white-covered sofa wrapped around a central coffee table on three sides and on the open fourth side was a large high-backed armchair, again just like the sofa, covered in white cloth. A fan rotated slowly from the wooden rafters high above and the air was filled with the soft, sweet scent of sandalwood and flowers.

"This is where Atman meets people privately," Max said with a nod of his head toward the sofa, but continued on past a long wooden dining table on his right. The table was set for three, but could easily accommodate ten.

Max led Rajiv into a well-lit hallway. The first door on the right opened into a kitchen, and Max paused beside it. "This is Siddu, our cook."

Rajiv looked inside at the man he had glimpsed in the window. He wore a stained vest and his *lungi* was doubled up and tied around his waist, revealing a pair of thin legs from the knees down. At the sound of his name, he turned from the gas burner where he was frying something, his eyes instantly widening at the sight of Rajiv's uniform. Rajiv raised a hand in greeting, smiling to put the man at ease. Siddu dipped his head but remained silent.

On the far side of the kitchen near a door that opened to the outside, a young boy sat cross-legged on the floor, watching curiously as he peeled a stack of onions. Rajiv smiled at him, but before he could say anything, Max was already walking away down the corridor, past a closed door on the left and into an open courtyard that took up the centre of the building.

The courtyard was open to the stars, the corridor dividing and running around each side. Rajiv had seen this layout before, back in the village when he was a kid. It was common in the old days before people insisted on filling all the space on their land with concrete buildings. The central courtyard acted as a natural air-conditioner, the warm air being drawn from the outer rooms into the courtyard and then dispersed into the air above. It was simple, but highly effective.

Max gestured to three doors on the left side of the courtyard. "Those are our bedrooms and a bathroom. The office is on this side." He led Rajiv to the right and opened a door, flicking on a light switch as he entered.

Rajiv followed him in and looked around. The room was functional, with none of the niceties of the other parts of the house. A row of battered filing cabinets lined the wall to the left, and in the wall opposite the door was a window, shuttered from the outside. An office desk took up the centre of the room and on the right-hand wall a giant flat-screen TV flickered with the feeds from multiple cameras.

Rajiv studied the screen, recognising the various parts of the ashram just as he had seen in the guard hut, but in higher definition.

"We monitor the feed from here, too," Max paused, then pointed at the blank corner of the screen. "But it looks like one camera is out."

"Yes, on the beach wall. You said 'we?'"

"Yeah, Georges and I."

Rajiv chewed his lip. "Is that enough? I mean, there's only two of you."

Max shrugged. "One of us is always with Atman anyway, and if not, it's usually because we're all in the house."

"Hmmm, okay. Recording?"

"Yes." Max pointed toward a hard drive beneath the screen. "It's stored there and only written over after thirty days."

"Power backup?"

"A generator that kicks in within thirty-seconds of a power outage. But there's also an inverter for all the cameras and screens, that supplies the power during that thirty-second gap. So we're covered."

Rajiv nodded, satisfied. "So we just need to get the gate to the beach and that camera sorted."

"I'll get one of the maintenance guys to look at it right away."

"Good. How do you control access at the front entrance?"

"There's a bell beside the gate and..." Max pointed to the top left of the television screen. "Those two feeds cover the front gate. So we don't open the gate until we see who it is."

Rajiv stared at the screen for a moment, a question on the tip of his tongue. In the end he had to ask... "Can I ask you a question, Max? As a friend?"

Max frowned. "Yes, of course."

"Why does Atman need security? He's a... guru. A spiritual leader. Why would there be any risk to his safety?"

Max shrugged and looked away, seeming to find the television screen very interesting. Rajiv waited. From experience, he knew people had a natural inclination to fill the silence if you left it long enough. After a long moment, when it was clear to Max that Rajiv was still waiting for an answer, he spoke. "We've had some issues before."

"Like what?"

Max shrugged again and looked down at the floor. He cleared his throat, scuffed the floor with his toe, then finally looked up. "Sometimes this path... the spiritual path... attracts people who aren't always stable... mentally. They can go a bit crazy, make accusations," he shrugged again and thrust out his lower lip, "maybe try to harm him."

"Is that what happened in Sri Lanka?"

Max looked up in shock, his eyes widening, then glanced away. "Um... yeah... something like that."

Rajiv waited for him to say more, but Max had turned his attention to the desktop and was shuffling some papers around.

Rajiv slapped him on the shoulder and gave him a big grin. "Then we'll have to make sure it doesn't happen again, won't we?"

Max looked up, relieved, and gave a weak smile.

"Good. I think I've seen enough here. I'll see myself out."

Max relaxed even more. "It's okay, I'll walk you out."

Rajiv stepped back to allow Max to walk past him and gave the room a quick scan. He noticed a large old-fashioned safe sitting in the corner nearest the door, and above it, another sturdy looking steel locker.

"What's that?"

Max stopped in the doorway and turned to see where Rajiv was pointing. He flushed, "ahhh..."

"A gun locker?"

Max looked surprised, but nodded.

Rajiv nodded slowly, but said nothing. Instead, he pretended there was nothing unusual about a gun locker in the home of a man teaching love and forgiveness and walked toward the door.

"Let's go, shall we?" he slipped past Max into the corridor and stopped. "Oh, and which room is Atman's?"

Max pointed to his right at an ornately carved double-width wooden door in the wall at the opposite end of the courtyard. "Atman's suite is there."

Rajiv pursed his lips. "Any other access to it?"

"No. Only one entrance."

Rajiv walked over and studied the door. It was carved from solid teak and now Rajiv was close enough he could see the carvings in more detail. The main scene taking up most of the door's surface was of a young man playing the flute in a forest clearing, surrounded by groups of young women. "Lord Krishna"

"Yes. A scene from the Bhagavad Gita."

"He stole the clothes of the *gopis,* the milkmaids, while they were bathing." Rajiv turned to face Max, "Then he commanded them to come out of the water, naked." Rajiv shrugged, then continued, observing Max's reaction, "Apparently, to teach them non-attachment. Sounds sexist to me."

The young man's eyes widened and moved from Rajiv to the scene on the door and back again.

Rajiv turned away and looked back at the door. "Beautiful work though." He noted the tiny peephole in the middle of the door and, incongruously, the electronic keypad above the door handle.

"Who has the combination?"

"Only Atman and Georges."

Rajiv turned and raised an eyebrow. "Not you?"

Max shook his head.

"Hmmm." Rajiv smiled. "Well, I think Atman has nothing to worry about. This place looks secure enough to me." He grinned at Max. "In fact, I don't think there is any need for me here at all."

## 38

The smell of coffee and bacon hit John's nose as he made his way slowly down the stairs. He needed both.

He and Steve had hit the bottle pretty hard the night before. John liked to think he could handle a few drinks, but his throbbing temples were telling him otherwise.

He stepped into the dining room where Steve sat at the dining table, tapping away on an iPad and looking fresh as a daisy.

"Good morning."

John put on a brave face and smiled in return.

"Morning." He pulled out a chair, sat down, and reached for the coffeepot.

"I think it's gone cold, mate." Steve turned his head and called out, "Marisel? Can you bring us some more coffee, please?"

"Yes, sir," came the reply from the kitchen. "John Sir, good morning."

John smiled at Steve's housekeeper, who was standing in the doorway. "Good morning, Marisel."

"Bacon and eggs, sir?"

"Perfect, thank you." He turned back to look at Steve. "How do you get bacon here in Dubai? Isn't it *haram*?"

"You can get everything here, mate. What do you think we were drinking last night?"

"Huh," John grinned. "True."

Steve moved the iPad away to the side of the table. "I was just messaging Maadhavi. She says hi."

"Pity she's not here. When is she back?"

"Another week."

Before he could say any more, the doorbell rang, and Steve glanced at his phone on the table. He tapped on the screen, then held it up for John to see.

John leaned over and looked closer to see a live feed from above Steve's front door. Ramesh was looking up at the camera and frowning.

"Bloody Madrasi has come for a free breakfast." Steve grumbled, but with a grin on his face. He stood up and disappeared out of the room.

John poured himself some coffee and took a sip as he heard the front door opening. John made a face. Steve was right, the coffee was cold.

A moment later, Steve walked in. "Look what the cat dragged in."

John pushed back his chair and reached out to shake Ramesh's hand. "Good morning, Ramesh."

The young man briefly returned John's smile, the whites of his eyes reddened with fatigue, then shook his hand and thrust an envelope at him with the other.

"It's all done."

"That was quick."

Ramesh nodded, but said nothing, glancing around the room, his eyes taking in the tabletop, Steve's phone, and

Marisel walking out of the kitchen with a tray holding two serving bowls.

"I suppose you want some breakfast while you're here?" Steve growled. "Might as well. Marisel set another place, will you?"

"Of course, sir." She set the serving bowls in the centre of the table and smiled at Ramesh. "Hello, sir."

Ramesh gave her a genuine smile. "Good morning, Marisel. I'd love some of your coffee."

"On its way, sir."

John waited for Ramesh to pull out a chair and sit before taking his own seat and sliding the contents of the envelope onto the table.

A couple of unused passport photos, and a folded sheet of paper, lay beside the familiar dark blue of a British passport. John picked the passport up first and opened it. It looked well used, and the pages were full of visa stamps.

"Looks like a genuine passport."

"It is," Ramesh replied with a hint of pride.

John glanced at Ramesh with raised eyebrows.

"I have a contact at the embassy. The wear and tear and the visa stamps, I added myself. I've stuck with the name John. Makes it easier for you."

John flicked through the pages and nodded. John Harris, British citizen, date of birth not too different from his. "Very good."

"He does a good job, I have to admit," Steve added, causing Ramesh to raise his eyebrows in surprise.

"What happened to you this morning, Steve? Are you feeling okay?"

"Credit where credit is due." Steve muttered.

"And the Indian Visa?" John interrupted.

"eVisa for thirty days. I've printed out a copy for you."

John picked up the paper and took a quick look. "Thank you."

"Will thirty days be long enough?"

John pursed his lips while nodding slowly. "I hope so."

He slipped the documents back inside the envelope while Marisel set a plate and cutlery in front of Ramesh. Ramesh waited until she had left the room before clearing his throat. "I know it's unprofessional of me but..." he hesitated, looking down at the empty plate in front of him, and adjusted the position of his fork. "Given that it's my home country, I have to ask..."

John helped him out. "Why?"

Ramesh nodded, only then making eye contact. John thought for a moment. He liked to keep his plans to himself, but Ramesh had looked after him when they had gone to Syria, and he had no reason to distrust him now.

"It's a long story."

## 39

The three men sat silently while Marisel cleared away the empty plates.

"Bring us some more coffee please, Marisel," Steve asked as he pushed back his chair. "Let's sit by the pool."

John could see his story had affected Ramesh, who remained sitting, a deep frown on his forehead. It took him a moment to realise Steve and John were standing, and he shook his head as if shaking off a trance. Steve slid back the French windows, and they stepped outside onto the terrace. It was still relatively cool, and the well tended foliage bordering the swimming pool was full of the sound of birds.

Steve gestured toward the coffee table. "Grab a seat." He walked toward the edge of the pool and stared into it. "The bloody pool cleaner is broken again," he grumbled, then walked back to join Ramesh and John at the coffee table.

"I won't charge you for the passport."

"I'm sorry?" John glanced at the young man in surprise.

"It's on the house."

"I think you've got a temperature today, Ramesh, not me." Steve quipped.

Ramesh shook his head, still frowning deeply. "No. People like this need to be stopped. I've seen it so many times." His voice rose, "They prey on the devout and the faithful, promising them a glimpse of God and all they're doing is exploiting them." He punctuated the sentence by banging the heel of his fist on the table.

Steve looked over at John, his eyes wide, eyebrows raised.

John looked away, turning his full attention to Ramesh. "You don't have to do that. I'm happy to pay."

Ramesh was shaking his head before he had finished, "No, no. I won't hear of it." He took a breath. "Look, John. I know what you and Steve did in Syria. I believe you can stop this man." He paused, searching for the words, "... I'm not that type of person. I mean, look at me." He gestured toward himself. "I'm... better at a keyboard. So anything you need, I'll do it. You know my skills... and it's all on the house."

John studied him for a moment, then reached over and gave his arm a squeeze. "Thank you, Ramesh. I appreciate that."

He sat back in his chair, glanced at Steve, who, uncharacteristically, was watching quietly, then looked back at Ramesh.

"If you don't mind me asking... why? It sounds like... it's maybe personal for you too?"

Ramesh nodded, his gaze across the pool, eyes focused on some point in the distance. He was about to open his mouth when Marisel came out with a fresh pot of coffee.

"Thank you, Marisel," Steve smiled at her. "We'll serve ourselves."

She smiled and moved back inside, while Steve poured

black coffee into three cups and passed them out. He and John took a sip and waited for Ramesh to continue. He sat, turning the cup on the table with his fingertips once, twice, three times, before finally speaking.

"Years ago, when I was a teenager, there was a guru who came to our house."

## 40

John stepped forward and smiled at the immigration official behind the plexiglass screen. "Good evening." He slid his passport and the photocopy of his eVisa through the slot and waited, willing himself to relax. He had left Dubai without any problems, the Dubai Immigration official giving his passport only a cursory glance before stamping it and waving him on.

The immigration official frowned, and John's heart rate increased. The official leafed through the passport, then stabbed at the keyboard in front of him with two fingers before looking up.

"Your first time in India, Mr John?"

"Yes." John had checked the visa stamps in the passport before getting off the plane, just in case.

The immigration official, a thin middle-aged man with skin the colour of polished ebony, smiled, exposing a set of brilliant white teeth, and John breathed out. "Welcome to my country."

John mirrored his smile, relaxing a bit more. "Thank you. I'm excited to be here."

The official leafed through the passport again, found an empty page, and stamped it with a resounding thud.

John smiled genuinely this time and reached for his documents. "Enjoy your stay."

"Thank you," John replied as the official bobbed his head from side to side in that characteristically Indian way he recognised from previous visits. John did the same and the official's smile widened even more as John stepped away from the counter and moved past.

He was in.

He checked the overhead screen for the correct baggage claim area, then removed his phone from his pocket and switched off the flight mode. By the time he reached the luggage belt, the phone was already vibrating with incoming messages. The bags hadn't come out yet, so he stood with one eye on the belt and the other on his phone as he scrolled through the messages. The first couple were from the local phone provider welcoming him to India, but one from Ramesh caught his immediate attention. He tapped the screen with his thumb, opening the message and frowned.

*Atman has left Bangalore for his ashram in Udupi.*

"Shit," John cursed out loud, surprising an elderly couple standing next to him. They edged away from him, but John ignored them, his mind whirring away. *Udupi, Udupi...* he visualised a map of India, trying to remember where it was. Giving up, he opened the mapping app on his phone and searched. When the results came up, he cursed again. The elderly couple pushed their luggage cart further away as he checked the driving time. Fourteen hours from the East Coast to the West Coast. He groaned. Add in toilet, food and fuel stops, it could take him fifteen to sixteen hours. The belt started moving, and he put his phone away and stepped forward. His eyes roamed the bags on the belt, while his mind weighed the options. He'd already arranged for a rental car and was mentally prepared for the six-hour drive to Bangalore, but to add another eight plus hours on to that, particularly with most of it at night on poorly lit roads wasn't filling him with joy.

He spotted his bag, stepped closer, and removed it from the belt. Pulling out the handle, he pushed his way past the other passengers and looked for the exit. He would clear customs and then find a flight to the other side of India.

## 41

John caught a late night flight into Mangalore, the closest airport to Udupi. Despite the transit and travel time, he had saved at least ten hours, and from there it was just an hour and a half drive north up the coast to Udupi. But it was dark and three days of almost constant travel had wiped him out. He needed a shower and a good night's sleep. Atman could wait one more day.

He found a hotel in the old Port area of the city, on the edge of the backwaters. The large one-bedroom suite promised views over the river and out across the Arabian Sea, but right now, just after midnight, all John could see was a broad expanse of black space. Anyway, he wasn't there for the view.

He didn't bother unpacking. Although the hotel was plush and comfortable, he wanted to be nearer Atman. While waiting for the flight, he had researched the ashram and its surroundings. There were a couple of guesthouses nearby and that's where he preferred to be.

He still did not know what he was going to do, but

trusted that an opportunity would present itself. Grabbing an ice-cold bottle of Kingfisher from the mini-bar, he popped the top, sat down on the bed, and picked up his phone. With one hand, he dialled Adriana, and while the phone connected, took a long draw from the bottle. He wasn't a beer drinker, but the ice cold liquid sliding down his throat was just what he needed.

"John?"

He grinned at the sound of her voice and wiped his lips with the back of his hand. "Hey."

"Where are you? Have you reached Bangalore?"

"Plans have changed a little. I'm in Mangalore."

"Mangalore?" He could almost hear her frowning. "Where's that?"

John chuckled. "It's on the opposite side of India. On the West Coast."

"Why? I thought you were going to Bangalore?"

John took another quick sip of beer before replying, already feeling a slight warmth spreading through his body. "Yeah, but he left Bangalore and has come to his ashram on the West Coast." He could hear the clicking of a keyboard.

"Udupi?"

"Yes." He glanced at the digital alarm clock beside the bed. "Are you still at work? It's late."

"What else is there for me to do if you aren't here?"

John chuckled.

"So, what's your plan now?"

"Sleep first. I'm shattered." He picked at the label on the beer bottle with his thumbnail, "And tomorrow I'll drive up the coast and take a look at the ashram. I'll find a guest-house and base myself there."

"Okay. But..." Adriana paused, "then what? You can't go

into the ashram. They might recognise you. I still don't understand what you can do."

John made a face. Neither did he. "I..." he sighed. "Yeah. I don't know. But something will come up."

There was silence from Adriana for a while, and John could hear the background noises of her office. Other voices, phones ringing, and her breath. Eventually, she replied, "Please be careful."

John grinned. "I will, don't worry. The sooner this is done, the sooner I can come back and see you."

"Yes."

John took a deep breath. "I'd better go. It's after midnight here. I'll shower and go to bed."

"Okay."

"I love you, don't forget that."

"I love you too, John. Be careful."

"I will, good night." He ended the call, dropped the phone onto the bed and stared at the torn label on the beer bottle.

He suddenly felt very sad.

## 42

Aarthi was happy. Very happy. The people in the ashram were so nice. Friendly. Glowing. Everyone walked around with a smile on their face as if floating on clouds of bliss. The previous evening's meditation had made her feel so relaxed, and she'd had the best night's sleep for a long time. She was so happy she had come.

The only thing that could make it better was if Rajiv would spend more time with her. She was used to his work taking over his life, but had hoped that here on the coast, hundreds of miles away from Bangalore, he would allow himself to take things a little easier. She had glimpsed him briefly the previous night, but he had been busy and, despite promising to come and see her, she still hadn't met him. Fortunately, she was enjoying herself so much it made up for it.

Now, as she sat in the dining hall eating breakfast, she kept one eye on the door, hoping he would come in. The food was simple, vegetarian and light, just enough to stop them from being hungry, but not too much that they would fall asleep during the next meditation. She took another mouthful and tuned back into the surrounding conversation.

The lady opposite her, what was her name...? Rashmi, that's right, Rashmi from Delhi, was busy recounting the miracles she had experienced since she had started following Atman and his teachings. She was a large boisterous woman who, Aarthi learned quickly, liked to dominate every conversation. In contrast, her daughter, Priyanka, a slim young woman, perhaps in her late teens, sat quietly beside her. She had thick glossy black hair that tumbled onto her shoulders, a soft gentle face, and clear caramel skin. She lifted her eyes, catching Aarthi looking at her, and smiled shyly. Brilliant white teeth, and large dark eyes like deep pools of liquid ebony. Aarthi smiled back, and Priyanka blushed and looked back down at her plate. Aarthi continued studying her. How could someone so beautiful be so shy? And apparently so different to her mother? It was so refreshing. She reached out and placed a hand on Priyanka's arm. "How long have you been following Guruji's teachings?"

Priyanka looked up, glanced sideways at her mother, who was still in full flow, and shrugged. "I don't know, maybe a couple of months?"

"And what do you feel?"

Again she glanced at her mother, who was unaware that anyone else was talking. "Good, I think." She looked down at her plate, then up again. "It's helping me with my studies." Her confidence seemed to grow as she spoke. "I'm more relaxed. Not stressed anymore."

Aarthi nodded and smiled encouragingly. "What are you studying?"

"Medicine."

Aarthi raised her eyebrows. "You want to be a doctor?"

Priyanka's eyes darted to her mother, then down at her food, but said nothing.

Aarthi watched for a moment. It was as if the light had gone from her face. She changed the subject. "Is this your first time here?"

Priyanka took a mouthful of food and nodded, still not looking up.

"Me too. In fact, it's the first time I've done anything like this. Perhaps you can help me? Show me what to do? I'd really like that."

Priyanka looked up, stared at Aarthi for a moment, then smiled. "I'd like that too."

## 43

Rajiv stepped into the dining hall and looked around, hoping to spot Aarthi. But in a sea of white-clothed people seated at long communal tables, it was hard to spot an individual.

He felt like an idiot in his uniform, even more so as he'd had to leave his shoes outside, and was standing there in his socks. The suspicious glances thrown his way by some students didn't make him feel any more comfortable. He brushed off the feeling and scanned the hall. The genders were separated; the women sitting on the left side of the hall and the men on the right. Whether that was a rule or the preference of the students, Rajiv didn't know, and he was about to turn his attention to the students on the female side of the hall when a figure stood and hurried toward him.

"Good morning, sir."

"Good morning, Manjunath." Rajiv looked him up and down. Unlike Rajiv, the constable was dressed in a long white shirt and a white cotton *lungi*. "I see you have made yourself at home."

"Yes, sir." Manjunath grinned. "It's very nice here. But..." He frowned. "You didn't come to the early meditation?"

Rajiv shook his head. "No."

"Sir, it was very nice, sir. You should come." Manjunath lowered his voice and leaned in. "He is very powerful, sir."

Rajiv nodded. "I'm sure he is. Maybe next time. What's for breakfast?"

"*Poha,* sir. Can I get you some?"

Rajiv shook his head, "No, thank you." He'd noticed his uniform belt getting tighter recently and was attempting to cut back on carbohydrates. But his stomach growled in protest. "I'll have a coffee later." He nodded toward the table Manjunath had left. "Finish up and get changed. I want you in uniform."

The smile faded from Manjunath's face. "Sir?"

"We have work to do. I want to visit the local station."

Manjunath's shoulders slumped. "Yes, sir."

"Half an hour. No more."

"Yes, sir."

Rajiv watched the young constable walk back to his table and shook his head. Did he think he was on holiday?

Turning, he walked back toward the entrance, stopping only to scan the tables where the female students were sitting. There she is. Aarthi spotted him at the same time and half stood, raising a hand. He shook his head and made a gesture. *Later.* He didn't want to embarrass her in front of her fellow students. He was in full uniform, after all. Turning away, he moved toward the door, but not before noticing the look of disappointment on his wife's face.

## 44

Approximately sixty kilometres south of Rajiv, John mopped up the last of the egg yolk with a rasher of bacon and popped it into his mouth. He caught the eye of the waiter and signalled for the bill. Despite only six hours sleep, he felt refreshed and ready to go. The two plates of bacon and eggs, and a French Press full of coffee had helped too.

Signing the bill, he instructed the waiter to send it immediately to the front desk as he was checking out, and caught the elevator back to his room. His bag was already packed, and taking one last look around the room, spotted his phone charging on the bedside table.

"Shit. That was lucky," he muttered to no-one in particular, unplugged it, rolled the cable up, and stowed it in the side pocket of his bag. He tapped the phone screen awake and checked for messages. One from Adriana, sent late in the night. *Check your email.*

He smiled, switched to the email app, scrolled past the email from a Nigerian prince offering him several million dollars and opened Adriana's.

*Hey, take a look at the attached news articles I found after we spoke. I miss you. XXXX.*

John tapped on the first attachment and waited for it to open.

*Australian woman killed by rogue truck driver'*

His jaw clenched as he speed-read the article, then cursed out loud, "Bastards."

He tapped on the next attachment. Another news article.

*Brother of Australian woman insists she was murdered.*

"Yup," John sighed. "It wouldn't surprise me."

As he scrolled through the article, a photo appeared about halfway down. Atman smiling, his eyes looking directly at the camera. John's heart did a little jump, feeling the intensity of his gaze as if he was there with him in the room. Several emotions fought for dominance. There was no denying John had felt something in his presence, something otherworldly. But the knowledge of the things he did, the way he used his position, filled him with disgust and... anger.

His grip tightened on the phone, and his jaw clenched. Closing the article, he tapped reply on the email and typed, *See if you can get hold of the brother. He might have some information that will help us catch this bastard.* John closed his eyes and took a deep breath, calming himself, then added, *I miss you, too. Speak soon.*

Slipping the phone into his pocket, he stood and stared blindly out the window, paying no attention to the broad expanse of the Arabian Sea spreading out before him. He was in the right place; he was sure of it, and he would do whatever it took to make sure Atman was brought to justice. This time, he wouldn't get away.

It took almost half an hour before John finished clearing his bill. Stepping outside, he waited for the bellhop to load his bag into the trunk of the rental car. Standing on the top step, he took a deep breath and inhaled the warm, humid, slightly salty air. The smells brought back a flood of memories. Wonderful memories intertwined with the absolute worst. India had changed his life beyond all recognition. It had changed him, too. The John Hayes standing here now was nothing like the version of him that had come to India for the first time with Charlotte. That time he had felt something had ripped his heart from his chest and it had set him on a journey of revenge, but also, now he looked back on it, a journey of growth. The things that had transpired in his life since then, had made him harder, tougher, but also confident, self-reliant. What was that saying? Rough seas make good sailors? Yes. There was nothing he felt he couldn't handle, as long as he set his mind to it.

But why did India keep pulling him back? There was something about the country and its people that seemed to have got under his skin. It felt a part of him, familiar, comfortable, even though the events that brought him here were filled with violence, stress and loss.

An image flashed in his mind's eye, bringing with it a pang of sorrow. "Charlotte," he whispered.

"Sir?"

John snapped out of it, focusing on the smiling young man standing at the bottom of the steps.

"Your keys, sir."

John returned his smile and stepped down, taking the car keys from the bellhop and slipping him a hundred rupees.

The bellhop grinned and dipped his head in thanks.

"Happy journey, sir. Please come back again."

"Thank you," John looked at the name tag on the young man's uniform. "Sushant. Have a good day."

He walked around to the driver's side and opened the door of the small Korean hatchback. It was white, underpowered, and boring, but it blended in with most of the other traffic on the road, and that was the main thing.

He climbed in, turned up the air conditioning, and entered his destination into the GPS. One hour and fifteen minutes to the *Anandsagar* Ashram. Staring at the route on the phone screen, he felt an uneasy sensation in his chest. He frowned and took a deep breath. Was it too much coffee or nerves? Exhaling slowly, he put the car in drive, nodded at the hotel security, and pulled out of the hotel forecourt. Whatever it was, the only thing that would get rid of it was taking action.

## 45

"Wait here."

"Yes, sir."

Rajiv climbed out of the police Bolero, donned his uniform cap and straightened his uniform. The station looked like so many others he had visited in his career. Dusty, in dire need of maintenance, and busy... always busy. It didn't matter how small the town was, there was always something happening at the police station.

A group of young men argued with a constable as he wheeled a motorcycle toward the back of the compound, adding it to a row of other seized two wheelers. Near the compound wall a woman squatted in the dirt, staring straight ahead, while her two small children played a game with pebbles beside her. Tears streaked the dust on her face, and she paid no attention to Rajiv as he walked past.

A corrugated fibreglass roof provided shade for the outdoor waiting area in front of the entrance, where several members of the public waited patiently in the plastic chairs lined up in front of a battered steel desk.

Rajiv stood in front of the desk and cleared his throat.

The constable seated behind the desk grunted with irritation, looked up from the well-worn ledger he was writing in and then jumped up, standing to attention.

"Sir."

"I'm here to see Inspector Prakash Rao."

"Yes, sir. He's..." The constable turned his head to look inside the station entrance.

Rajiv followed his gaze and saw a tall officer standing just inside the entrance. Next to him was a westerner and judging by the body language, the conversation wasn't going well.

"He's busy, sir, but shouldn't be long."

Rajiv nodded at the constable. "I'll wait," he replied, then switched his attention back to the corridor. The westerner looked angry and the police officer appeared to be trying to placate him. Rajiv stepped closer, trying to hear what was being said, but the conversation had ended and the man was walking out. He brushed past Rajiv and marched across the compound toward the main road. Rajiv watched him go, then turned back to see the tall officer standing in the doorway pinching the bridge of his nose with his thumb and forefinger.

"Inspector Rao?"

The Inspector took a deep breath, dropped his hand and seemed to notice Rajiv for the first time. He frowned.

"Detective Inspector Rajiv Sampath, Bangalore Police." Rajiv stepped forward and extended his hand.

Rao stared at him blankly for a moment, then nodded. "Ah yes," he sighed. "I was told you were coming." He shook Rajiv's hand, his grip firm, his gaze direct. "Why don't you come inside?"

Rao turned and walked back into the station, down the corridor, stopping beside an open door at the end. He gestured for Rajiv to enter. "Take a seat. I'll organise some coffee."

Rajiv walked in and looked around. The office was sparsely furnished but immaculate. Two plastic chairs stood in front of a basic wooden desk, the surface clear apart from a neat stack of files on one end, a telephone, and two mobile phones lined up side by side.

Three filing cabinets sat against one wall and above them were several framed certificates and a photo of a young Prakash Rao on parade at the Police Academy. Rajiv stepped closer to get a better look.

"Batch of 2002."

Rajiv turned in surprise. He hadn't heard Prakash come back in.

"Sometimes I think those were the best days of my career."

Rajiv raised an eyebrow.

"Things were a lot simpler then." Prakash gave a sad smile, then walked around the desk and sat down. Rajiv joined him at the desk, removed his cap, sat down, and placed it in his lap.

"So what brings you here to our district, Inspector Sampath? I was told you were coming and to extend any assistance but I'm not sure why?"

"Please call me Rajiv."

Prakash gave a nod of acknowledgement. "Prakash."

"The *Anandsagar* Ashram."

Prakash narrowed his eyes but said nothing.

"I was instructed to come down and oversee security for the ashram and the ah… guru, Atman."

Prakash nodded slowly. After a moment, he spoke. "Okay. If there's anything I can do to help, please let me know."

Rajiv shrugged. "Well, to be honest, Prakash, I don't know why I'm here. I mean... it's an ashram. He's a guru. What security does he need?"

Prakash shrugged and stuck out his bottom lip at the same time, but said nothing.

"Have you had any reason to be concerned about the security of the ashram? I mean, have there been any threats?"

Prakash looked down at the desk and moved the two mobile phones slightly, as if wanting to make sure they were perfectly aligned. "Not, not that I'm aware of."

Rajiv studied him for a moment. There was something Prakash wasn't telling him. He would try another tack. "Between you and me, Prakash, it's a complete waste of my time being here. I have so many pending cases in Bangalore..." he raised both hands, "but they have sent me here to baby-sit a holy man."

Still no response.

"Part of me thinks my boss prefers me out of the way." Rajiv decided to go with his gut feeling. "You know how it is in our job, Prakash. Politics and influence preventing us from doing our job properly."

At this, Prakash looked up. He stared at Rajiv and opened his mouth, about to speak, when his eyes flicked to the door.

"Sir?"

Prakash nodded and gestured at the table.

A constable entered with a stained melamine tray. He placed it on the table and removed two steel tumblers and placed one each in front of Rajiv and Prakash. He gestured at a bowl of sugar on the tray. "Sugar separate, sir."

"Thank you, Rakesh. Please close the door on your way out."

Prakash watched him leave, waited for the door to close, then gestured at the steel tumbler in front of Rajiv. "Sugar?"

Rajiv shook his head, grinned, and ran a hand down his stomach. "Thank you, but no. I'm trying to lose weight. My uniform doesn't fit like it used to. Too much time behind a desk."

Prakash smiled as he scooped a heaped spoonful of sugar into his coffee and gave it a stir. "Life's too short, Rajiv." He picked up the tumbler between thumb and forefinger and blew the steam off the top before taking a sip. Nodding his approval, he sat back in his chair and watched Rajiv drink his.

"Very good, thank you."

"We might not get all the resources we need, but at least we can have a good coffee."

Rajiv smiled in support. The coffee was good.

They sat in silence for a minute while Prakash sipped his coffee then placing the tumbler down on the desk, he made a face and swivelled his chair so he was side on to Rajiv. Fixing his gaze on something outside the window, he said, "The ashram."

Rajiv waited for him to say something else, but he didn't. Rajiv frowned and took another sip from his tumbler.

Eventually Prakash spoke. "The westerner I was talking to when you arrived. His sister was at the ashram."

## 46

Prakash turned back to face Rajiv and removed a file from the top of the pile and opened it in front of him.

He started reading from a sheet of paper. "Trevor Hughes, twenty-five, Australian citizen. Brother of Sally Hughes, killed in a hit-and-run accident just over three months ago." He looked up, gave Rajiv a meaningful look, then reached for the files on his left. He slid the whole pile into the middle of the table and started sorting through them. After a moment, he pulled out a file and opened it up. "Mathilde Solberg, twenty-four, Norwegian citizen. Drowned while a resident of the ashram." Again, he looked at Rajiv.

Rajiv watched him, wondering what point he was trying to make.

Prakash went back to the files, pulled out another. Opening it up, he read, "Kaaveri Narayanan, twenty-two years old. Indian citizen. From Chennai. Reported missing eight months ago. Has not been seen since she left the ashram one evening."

He closed the file, sat back in the chair, and stared at Rajiv as if waiting for him to comment.

Rajiv took the hint. He placed his coffee down and sat forward. Nodding at the files, he said, "Two accidents and a missing person."

Prakash shrugged.

"What are you trying to say, Prakash?"

"What do they all have in common?"

"They were all residents of the ashram."

"And?"

Rajiv frowned. "All young women."

Prakash snapped his fingers and pointed at Rajiv.

Rajiv raised his eyebrows. "So... are you saying there is foul play involved?"

"I'm not saying anything. But there seems to be a connection."

Rajiv frowned and sat back. "And when you investigated? You did investigate?"

"I did."

This time it was Rajiv's turn to ask, "And?"

Prakash chewed his lip before answering, "Let's just say I was discouraged from spending too much time in digging further. I was... guided toward the conclusion that had to be made and encouraged to close the case in each instance."

"By whom?"

Prakash smiled and shook his head. "You've been in this game longer than I have, I'm sure. You know how it goes."

Rajiv stared back at Prakash, a million thoughts running through his head. After a while he said, "So what's going on there?"

Prakash made a face. "I don't know. I've never been able to get close enough to find out." He exhaled loudly, "And to be honest Rajiv, there are enough calls on my time where I can do something, that I've not paid it anymore attention." He gestured toward the pile of files. "There are more in there. I've spared you the details, but if I'm to keep my job here, then I have to direct my attention elsewhere. Do you have children, Rajiv?"

Rajiv shook his head.

"I have two daughters. They love it here. Their school, their friends, all here. My wife too. Very happy. We've made a home here. How do you think they will like me being transferred to some village in the middle of nowhere to serve out the rest of my career?"

Rajiv nodded. He knew what it was like. A constant tightrope walk between doing what was right and keeping the job.

"I understand." He shook his head. "It's a daily battle for me, too. I often wonder who the real criminals are."

"Yes," Prakash chuckled. "Well, let me know if there is anything you need. If I can help, I will."

"Thank you. Hopefully, I won't need anything." He took a deep breath and forced a smile. "All going well, I will be back in Bangalore within a couple of days."

## 47

John pulled the brim of the baseball cap lower and glanced at his reflection in the rear-view mirror. With the dark Ray-Ban copies he'd bought at the petrol pump on the way, and the three days' growth of stubble, he was confident he wouldn't be recognised immediately. He turned his attention back to the phone screen on the holder mounted on the dashboard. According to the GPS, he would pass the ashram in two hundred metres.

He slowed further. The road was narrow, just under two lanes wide, even narrower in places, potholed and broken in others. A mongoose scampered across the road in front of the car and John grinned. Wasn't that supposed to be good luck?

A high wall appeared on the left side, security cameras mounted on the corner. John angled his face away slightly but doubted they could see into the car. Keeping his speed slow but steady, he followed the wall and passed a gate with the name *Anandsagar* painted across it. He was in the right place. The gate was closed, and the wall was too high for him to see inside, so he kept driving as the wall continued along the roadside.

He passed another large closed gate, in the same colours as the ashram but with the word "Private" painted across it. Reaching the end of the wall, he continued for another five hundred metres, then did a three-point turn and headed back the way he had come. He didn't want to go past too often in case he was noticed, but figured one more time wouldn't hurt.

Just before the ashram came into view, he reached forward and angled the phone toward the side window of the car and turned on the video camera. As he neared the ashram, he observed how the wall ran from the road down to the beach and how, even on this side, there were cameras at regular intervals. He drove past the main entrance again, making sure he didn't look directly at the gate, in case the cameras were on him, then continued until he was out of sight, then pulled over onto a dirt clearing to the side of the road. Removing the phone from the phone holder, he turned off the video recording and played it back, studying the images, looking for anything he had missed with his own eyes.

The wall and the gate were too high for him to see inside from the road, and the boundary walls on each side were also too high. He switched the phone off and stared out the windscreen. What did he do now? How did he look inside without getting caught?

He looked to his right across the road and through the rows of coconut palms toward the sea. Perhaps the beach boundary would be less secure? Probably not, but it was worth a try. He glanced at his watch. Almost midday, a time when most people were indoors, avoiding the peak heat. If he walked along the beach now, he would stick out like a sore thumb. He would leave it until evening. In the meantime, he would check into a guesthouse, hope they had good internet, and try to find some satellite images online or even photos, anything that could help him get an idea of the layout.

He slipped the gear stick into drive and turned the wheel, about to pull out, when he saw a police vehicle approaching. His heart jumped, and he stiffened, watching it approach. His eyes took in the details as he tightened his grip on the steering wheel, ready to flee. It was a white Bolero, with two people inside, the driver and one other. His eyes flicked to the number plate, and he frowned. *Strange.* KA01. A Bangalore registration.

He narrowed his eyes, peering through the windscreen as the vehicle got closer. It showed no sign of slowing, in fact, neither of the occupants spared him a look as it passed. But there was something about the passenger that made John look closer. Something familiar. Then a shaft of light filtering through the coconut palms lit up the passenger's face and John gasped.

No fricken way!

## 48

John found a guesthouse at the southern end of the beach almost a kilometre south of the ashram.

The accommodation was basic but clean and the Wi-Fi was slow but useable. There was a small living room on the ground floor that opened out onto a paved sitting area, and on the first floor a bedroom and bathroom, the bedroom with a view through the coconut palms toward the sea.

The owners, a fisherman and his wife, lived in a separate building on the side, with a dog and several chickens. They were a shy couple, seemingly nervous about having a foreigner stay with them, but relaxed considerably when John handed over a month's rent in cash.

The husband said little, perhaps unable to speak English, but the wife was fluent. She explained that their son was away in the US, working for a software company and it was his money that had enabled them to build the guesthouse.

The heat outside was now almost unbearable, even with the constant sea breeze, so there was little more John could do until the temperature dropped. He fired off a couple of messages to Ramesh in Dubai, stripped down to a pair of shorts, and lay on the bed with the ceiling fan at full speed, but the fan did little to cool the room down. John had underestimated the temperatures and needed to take that into account when planning anything.

He still had no idea what he was going to do, but once the sun was lower in the sky, he would take a walk along the beach and see if he could see into the ashram. Perhaps then an idea would come to him.

In the meantime, he thought back to the person he had seen in the police vehicle. Detective Rajiv Sampath, of the Bangalore Police. What the hell was he doing here?

## 49

The sun was now at a forty-five degree angle, turning the sky orange and the sea golden. The wind had picked up slightly and while it was still warm, it was manageable.

John had taken another drive past the front of the ashram, this time checking the properties on the opposite side of the road, looking for anywhere he could use as an observation point. But there was only another small village house and several vacant plots of land. Nowhere for him to hide and nowhere high enough for him to see over the wall. Everything now depended on the beach.

John adjusted the peak on his baseball cap and kept walking in the hard sand just along the edge of the water. Tiny almost translucent crabs scuttled away in front of him, seeking safety in their holes above the waterline, and white-headed Brahminy kites circled in the updrafts high above him. John paused and looked up, once again marvelling at the large birds. They appeared to be flying just for the joy of flying, no agenda, nowhere to go, nothing to do, not a worry in the world, and for a moment, he envied them.

A dog barked from the edge of the beach where the sand gave way to grass and tangled creepers, but when he glanced in that direction, the dog gave a wag of its tail, still unsure whether John was friend or foe.

Ahead, John could see the beginning of the ashram wall standing out in a row of unfenced properties. He kept on walking closer, his eyes continuously scanning the ashram from behind his dark Ray-Bans. He committed everything to memory, looking for anything that might give him an advantage.

Unlike the other boundaries, the wall bordering the beach looked considerably lower, perhaps to enable the residents to have a view of the ocean. It seemed to be around five feet high, and behind it, as John got closer, he could see several two-storey buildings. Judging by the number of doors and the layout, he assumed they were the accommodation blocks.

He kept on walking, taking sidelong glances as the wall passed to his right. There were two gates in the wall, from which steps led down a rudimentary sea wall into the sand. Nearer the end of the ashram boundary, a gap in the coconut palms appeared and when he glanced inwards, he could see what appeared to be an open area, but he needed to climb higher up the beach to see more.

Past the ashram, several multi-coloured single-hulled boats were lined up above the high-water mark and around them fishermen busied themselves repairing their nets. They glanced at John as he passed, but paid him little attention, returning their focus to the work at hand.

John continued on toward the northern end of the beach, then turned around and began his walk back, his calves burning with the unfamiliar effort of walking in the sand.

As the sun went down and the heat reduced, the beach was slowly becoming more occupied. Two small boys attempted to launch a homemade kite, only to get it snagged in one of the coconut palms, and a young couple sat watching the sunset while their child played in the sand. John smiled at them as he walked past and they stared back, unsure what to make of the westerner walking along the beach.

Surprisingly, though, John had seen no one from the ashram. Perhaps they had a full program of activities that kept them busy? John thought back to his stay in Atman's Sri Lankan ashram. The ashram ran on free labour, that of the students, and there hadn't been much spare time available. When you weren't in class, you were cleaning the rooms or preparing food. John shook his head as he remembered. It was a convenient way of keeping costs down, all dressed up in the guise of serving one's guru. Meanwhile, the ashram was raking in cash from donations and course fees.

As John got closer to the ashram boundary again, he casually angled his path upwards until he was above the high-water line. The sand here was deeper and softer and his calves protested at the effort. He walked slowly, one eye on the ashram and the other keeping a careful eye on his footing, avoiding the flotsam and jetsam deposited by the sea.

John reached the wall and angled his head down and away from the security cameras on the corner. Once past them, he could easily see over the wall and across a broad expanse of lawn to the bungalow beyond.

John kept walking, taking sidelong glances, memorising the layout but trying not to look too interested in case anyone was watching. He guessed the bungalow was where

Atman stayed. It looked far too luxurious and well kept to accommodate the ashram students.

John passed the gate and gave it a casual push as he walked past, but it didn't budge. He kept walking.

Half way along another wall bisected the property running from the beach boundary toward the road, separating the lawn area from the rest of the ashram and once past John could see the accommodation blocks and beyond them a larger building, which must be the main hall. Here the grounds were sandy and filled with coconut palms. A stone path ran from the gate in the wall back into the ashram. John gave the gate a push with his hand as he passed, and it swung open.

He stopped.

Should he go inside? He looked left and right, and over the wall into the compound. There was no-one around, either nearby on the beach or inside the compound. John hesitated. He glanced toward the camera on the end of the wall, then started walking again. The sun was now just above the horizon; the sea rippling with a golden fire. He would come back once the sun had set completely.

## 50

Rajiv leaned on the door frame and looked left toward the setting sun. He had finally submitted to wearing something more suited to the climate than his police uniform and had changed into the ubiquitous white *kurta* and loose cotton pants that all the male ashramites were wearing. He felt much cooler, less conspicuous, and even relaxed. The security checks were done, and it looked like there was nothing for him or anyone in the ashram to worry about.

The sun was an orange ball in the sky and the sea beneath it looked as if it was liquid gold. He took a deep breath of the ocean air and allowed his eyes to lazily roam the seascape. The silhouettes of several fishing trawlers were just visible near the horizon. Nearer the shore, a local fisherman seated on an inner tube bobbed on the waves as he fed out his net.

Rajiv turned his attention to the beach. A pack of stray dogs wrestled down by the surf, startling a small flock of Sandpipers and sending them into the air. A group of fishermen tended to their boats above the high tide line and a couple sat in the sand while their child played nearby.

Perhaps if Aarthi got some free time, he would take her for a walk along the beach. They had done nothing like that for years. He checked his watch. What was she doing now? He'd tried without success to find her during the afternoon chores, but hadn't been able to track her down, and he hadn't wanted to embarrass her by barging in while wearing his uniform. That was another reason he had changed. He missed her.

Even though he worked dreadful hours when he was on duty in Bangalore, not a day went by without seeing her. Apart from the quick phone call when he arrived, and a glimpse in the dining hall, he hadn't spoken to her since.

He watched a lone figure walking along the edge of the surf. His police mind subconsciously noted the details. A male. Colourful, fashionable clothing. Not someone from the ashram and likely not local. Probably someone from the city. Maybe a local tourist spending the evening by the seaside. Udupi town wasn't far away.

He switched his attention back to the sunset and smiled. It really was a beautiful sight, and it was rare that he was getting the time to see it. He watched the sun sink lower, once again thinking of Aarthi, wishing she was standing here now sharing the experience. But then... she seemed to be loving the program. She had been smiling and laughing in the brief glimpses he had of her. He was happy for her. He checked his watch again. Maybe he would join the evening meditation? He'd see her there.

Rajiv pushed himself away from the doorframe and took one more look at the beach. The lone male was closer now and had made his way up onto the soft sand above the high-water line. His body language and skin colour suggested he was a foreigner. Maybe Rajiv had been wrong? Perhaps he was from the ashram? A resident who had popped out for an evening walk before the meditation? Rajiv didn't blame him. There was only so much sitting around one could do.

He watched the man approach, his cap and sunglasses now visible. Yes, definitely a foreigner. In fact, something about him looked familiar. Rajiv must have seen him somewhere in the ashram.

The man reached the ashram wall and walked along it, passing Atman's section of the ashram and approached the gate into the public section. The gate swung open. Rajiv shook his head—Max had obviously not got around to fixing it yet. The man stopped but didn't come in. He looked around, then continued walking.

Rajiv frowned.

That was strange.

## 51

The sun had set by the time John made his return to the ashram gate. Moonlight reflected off the white sand of the beach and he easily made his way along the shore. He was no longer barefoot, deciding instead to wear his running shoes. The sand slowly seeping inside the shoes was a small price to pay for the ability to run across rough ground if necessary. He still wore the baseball cap and now pulled it low over his face as he neared the end of the wall and the cameras mounted on the corners.

Ducking down, he pressed himself close to the wall and moved sideways along it until he reached the gate. Hopefully, it was still unlocked. Taking a breath, he pushed it with his fingertips. It creaked open. Opening it just wide enough, he slipped through and stood motionless just inside the gate, listening, waiting.

There was no-one in sight and not a sound apart from the crash of waves on the beach behind him. Ahead, the path leading into the ashram was lit at regular intervals by soft yellow lamps at about waist height, but off the path there were deep shadows. John waited a moment longer, ready to flee if someone had spotted him, then slipped off the path into the shadows and moved deeper into the ashram.

If he was spotted, he would bluff his way through it, assuming most ashram residents wouldn't know everyone, and if it was security that caught him, he would say he had taken a wrong turn off the beach and was trying to find his way back to the road.

Once his eyes adjusted to the lower light levels, he found the going underfoot quite easy, unlike when he had been exploring the ashram in Sri Lanka. Here there was little that could grow in the sandy soil, and apart from the regularly spaced coconut palms, there were a few scattered creepers and the occasional patches of grass trying to establish themselves against the constant onslaught of sand and salt.

He moved steadily toward the large building on the left that he had spotted from the beach and then stood on the edge of the shadows. It was, as he suspected, an accommodation block. He waited and watched for any movement, but there was no one around, so he moved closer, then stepped up onto the verandah that ran along the front. All the doors were locked, but he could see in through open windows and judging by the clothing in some rooms, this was the block for the female residents.

He stepped back down into the sand and made his way through the trees toward the other block on the right-hand side. Similar in layout, but smaller, it appeared by the contents of the rooms to be the male block. Again there was no-one around, the room doors locked and the rooms empty. John glanced at his watch. He guessed everyone was in the evening meditation. That made his job much easier.

Continuing on, he entered deeper, keeping to the shadows, memorising the layout. He neared a large building, which he assumed was the meditation hall. He couldn't see in, the windows set well above eye level, but when he stopped and concentrated, he could hear soft chanting over the sound of the wind and the waves.

Cautiously, he made his way along the side of the building toward the entrance and paused at the corner. He scanned the surroundings for security cameras, but so far, they only seemed to be on the boundary walls.

There was no sign of anyone, almost as if the ashram was deserted. He peered around the corner at the entrance to the hall and what he saw confirmed his previous assumption. Footwear filled a row of low shelves beside the steps, and more were scattered on the ground below it. John estimated a few hundred people must be inside the hall.

He checked his watch again. If they ran to the same program he had experienced in Sri Lanka, he still had almost an hour before everyone came out, which gave him a free run of the place, assuming everyone was inside. Feeling more confident, he stepped away from the meditation hall and began exploring the other buildings.

He walked through the large dining hall into the kitchen where large covered pots were lined up on the gas burners. The pots were still warm, and he lifted the lid off a pot and inhaled the steam. His stomach growled, and he realised he hadn't eaten since that morning. He took another look inside the pot at what appeared to be a thick *dal*, but eating would have to wait. He had more important things to do.

Another building housed the administration offices, and he tried the doors of each room as he passed, but all were locked and here, unlike the accommodation blocks, the windows were closed and the lights off so he couldn't see inside.

John followed the path toward the front gate and

stopped on the edge of the parking area, his heart rate increasing at the sight of the white police Bolero parked to one side. John didn't move, his eyes scanning the parking area, but there was no sign of the police. His eyes dropped to the number plate. A Bangalore registration. It was the same one that had passed him when he was outside in his car. Rajiv's vehicle. What was he doing here in the ashram?

John waited a moment longer, then skirted the parking area, keeping to the shadows. He noted the cameras over the gate, fortunately pointing outwards, the gate secured with a large heavy duty bolt. There was a row of motorcycles parked under an open-sided lean-to, and a stone-walled well.

In a building next to the front gate, he spied through an open door, an elderly security guard dozing in his chair in front of a flickering television screen. John carefully made his way closer until he could see inside the guardroom. The guard was fast asleep, his snores audible over the tinny sound of music coming from the cellphone on the desk. John shook his head. All the security in the world was only as good as the people monitoring it. He moved closer until he was standing right at the edge of the door and peered inside. The screen showed the multiple feeds of the security cameras. John studied the screen, memorising the locations, estimating the coverage of the cameras, but they all appeared to be focused on the boundary. There was a blank feed on the top right-hand corner which, judging by the other cameras, covered one corner of the wall along the beach. The night vision capability of the cameras was average, too.

There was a cabinet on the side wall above the guard's head, the door half open, and John could see keys hanging on hooks inside. On a desk in front of the guard was a telephone, the mobile phone playing music, and a couple of stained cups.

The guard stirred in his chair and John jerked back out of sight and waited, his body tensed, ready to flee, but a moment later the guard's snores resumed.

Having seen enough, John eased past the door and checked the other rooms attached to the guardroom. There was a locked room housing the generator, and then a room with a cot in each corner, presumably accommodation for the drivers. The light filtering through from the window was just enough for John to see a police uniform hanging on a hook on the wall above one cot. He looked for others, but there was only the one. Probably the driver. Where was Rajiv staying?

John checked his watch again, then moved on. The guard was still snoozing, so John moved quickly away from the carpark back into the ashram. He wanted to check out the bungalow.

## 52

Rajiv couldn't settle.

He opened his eyes and stretched one leg carefully in front of him, then gasped as the blood flow resumed, sending a sensation of pins and needles through his left foot. He had a pain just below his left shoulder blade and he was hungry.

He looked around. The hall was now completely silent, the chanting and breathing exercises long finished, and everyone sat still, eyes closed, in complete silence. Turning his head sideways, he glanced at the man seated to his right. His head was slumped, chin resting on his chest, and a long string of saliva ran from the corner of his mouth, ending in a wet patch on his shirt. Rajiv half smiled. He was definitely asleep.

In contrast, the man to his left sat ramrod straight, his legs crossed in half-lotus position, a beatific smile across his face. Rajiv stared for a moment, then shrugged. He wished he could feel whatever that man was feeling.

Turning his attention to the front, he could see Atman seated on the white armchair in the centre of the stage. His eyes were rolled back into his head, only the whites of his eyes visible, and both his hands were raised in the air, palms facing outwards as if blessing the audience.

Beside him, seated on a cushion to the left of the stage, was Georges. His eyes were also closed, but a deep frown creased his forehead.

Rajiv closed his eyes again and took several deep breaths. Everyone else in the hall seemed to be enjoying themselves. Everyone except him. Was there something wrong with him? He wasn't feeling calm or blessed. In fact, he couldn't get the morning's conversation with Inspector Rao out of his head.

Being here was a waste of Rajiv's time. He had so many outstanding cases in Bangalore he could deal with. Instead, he was providing security for a guru who, if all the evidence was correct, was a serial sexual predator, laundering money for powerful interests, and may or may not have had people killed.

But then how could all these people in this hall be feeling what they were feeling? How could he be scamming them all? Even Aarthi? She was an intelligent, discerning woman. Surely she must see through him?

He clenched and unclenched his jaw. It was so confusing and wasn't giving him any mental peace. The more he thought about it, the less he could relax, a feeling of frustration filling his body. This wasn't why he joined the police. This wasn't what he stood for.

Taking a deep breath, he exhaled slowly. No. That didn't work. He clenched his jaw again and opened his eyes. Checking his watch, he frowned and stifled a groan. Still another painful hour to go.

Forget this. He needed to move around. Get his thoughts in order.

## 53

Rajiv eased the door closed behind him and winced at the sound of the latch clicking home. He paused for a moment, then stepped away from the door, rolled his shoulders around and shook out his legs. How these people sat still for hours on end was beyond him.

Outside the hall, the ashram was silent apart from the rustle of the breeze in the coconut palms overhead and the distant sound of the waves breaking on the beach. He inhaled a deep breath of fresh, warm, salty air and exhaled slowly. He'd much rather be outside doing something than sitting around indoors with his eyes closed. It was the same when he was at work. Properly at work. He never enjoyed sitting behind his desk with the endless paperwork that increased with his rank. He preferred to be out on patrol, on the streets, talking to people, solving problems directly.

He stepped down from the entrance and looked for his flip-flops in the dim amber light thrown by the lamp over the entrance door. He found one pair that looked just like his, but it was a size too small, and he continued sorting through the pile of footwear until he found his own. Next time, he would keep them somewhere else.

Slipping them on, he set off with no destination in mind. He just needed to get moving again and followed the path away from the hall, deep in thought. He really didn't want to spend much more time at the ashram. Aarthi wanted him to relax, but he couldn't, not while he was working. There was so much to do back in Bangalore, and the longer he stayed away, the tougher it would be to catch up when he got back.

He would put in a call to Muniappa in the morning, but would have to be careful how he worded his request. If Muniappa realised Rajiv wanted to come back, then he would insist on him staying at the ashram. Rajiv had to make Muniappa think it was his idea to return.

Rajiv passed the fork in the path where it led off toward Atman's bungalow, and a movement caught his eye. He stopped and looked closer.

There it was again. A man stood in the shadows with his back to him, staring out at the bungalow. Rajiv frowned, then carefully stepped sideways into the shadows.

Who was it? Everyone was supposed to be at the meditation. What was the man doing?

The light wasn't enough to make him out and if he hadn't moved, Rajiv would never have spotted him. Rajiv narrowed his eyes, striving to get a better look, then crept forward, keeping to the shadows off the side of the path. His foot caught on a fallen palm frond, and he stumbled, just catching his balance in time, and he froze, holding his breath. The man turned, the sound alerting him, and Rajiv kept as still as he could, hoping he wouldn't be seen in the darkness. After a moment, the man turned back to face the bungalow, and Rajiv exhaled, allowing himself to straighten up. He still couldn't see the man clearly, but there was something about him, his shape, his posture… he wasn't a local.

## 54

John stood close to the gap in the wall, keeping to the shadows, and observed the bungalow ahead of him. There was a security camera just above his head, but he was confident he was standing in its blind spot. He couldn't guarantee it hadn't recorded his approach though, despite his precaution, but hoped the guard was still sleeping.

The bungalow was well lit, as was the compound, and John couldn't see many options to approach unobserved. He visualised the position of the cameras based on what he had seen in the guardroom and thought for a moment.

Along the boundary wall that divided what he assumed to be Atman's compound from the rest of the ashram, was a strip of planting about a metre wide. It was mainly shrubs, heliconias, alocasias, and small palms between knee and waist height. At regular intervals were floodlit statues of Hindu gods and figures from Indian mythology, but in between, if he kept himself low enough, the foliage would provide him with cover. He could circumnavigate the bungalow, but still wouldn't be able to cross the lawn and approach the building itself. *Fuck it*, John muttered under his breath.

There had to be something incriminating inside the bungalow, and now, while all the occupants of the ashram were busy in the evening meditation, it was the best time to look for it. Turning his wrist, he glanced at the luminous dial of his G Shock. He still had time. Shit, what should he do?

He allowed his gaze to fall back on the bungalow itself. There was light in most of the windows he could see from his position, but he had yet to see any movement from inside. There must be staff, perhaps a cook, and a housekeeper. He could bluff his way past them if he acted with authority, but who else was there? John assumed that wherever Atman was, Georges would be with him, and perhaps the other guy... John frowned as he tried to remember his name... Max... yes Max, the other Israeli.

There was a sound behind him and he flinched, pressing himself closer to the wall, deeper into the shadow, his body tense, his breath caught in his throat, but then he heard it again. The creaking of a branch in the wind. He breathed out, forcing himself to relax, and turned his attention back to the house. There was still no movement inside.

He had two choices. He could hang around indefinitely, waiting for something to happen that he could use against Atman... but that could take forever.

Or he could force the issue. Make something happen. It was risky... but John hated sitting around.

Decision made, John took a deep breath, then stepped out of the shadows.

## 55

Rajiv kicked off his flip-flops and sprinted forward across the lawn, his bare feet on the grass not making a sound and he slammed his shoulder into the back of the intruder, forcing him flat against the wall of the bungalow. There was an audible whoosh as the impact forced the air from the intruder's lungs, followed by a grunt of pain.

Rajiv didn't hesitate, grabbing the man's right hand by the thumb and twisting his arm up behind his back. He forced the man's head against the wall with his left hand and growled, "Don't move."

The man remained silent. He was of a similar height to Rajiv and well built, but that was all he could make out in the darkness. He struggled to get away, and Rajiv twisted his right hand higher up his back, causing an involuntary groan to escape the man's lips.

"Max!" Rajiv shouted. "Max! Outside now. We have an intruder."

The man struggled again, and Rajiv kicked his legs apart, putting him off balance. He hoped Max had heard him, because he wasn't sure he could continue to deal with the man alone.

"Who are you?" he growled.

There was no response. On a hunch, he switched to English. "Who are you?"

"Fuck off."

Rajiv had been right. He was a foreigner.

He heard a noise to his left and turned his head to see Max on the verandah, peering into the darkness, a flashlight in one hand and what looked like a handgun in the other.

"Over here."

Max stepped off the verandah onto the lawn and advanced slowly, his weapon held at the ready, the barrel resting on the wrist of the hand holding the flashlight.

"Here."

The beam of the flashlight played across Rajiv's face, and he looked away quickly to preserve his night vision.

"I see you."

"Good." Rajiv increased the pressure on the man's right arm slightly to get his attention and then said, "I am a police officer. My friend here is armed. So I suggest you think carefully about what you do next. Do you understand?"

"Yes."

"Good. I'm going to release your arm now. I want you to turn around slowly and keep your back to the wall. Understood?"

The man grunted.

"Is that a yes?"

"Yes."

Rajiv released the man's arm and stepped back.

The beam of Max's flashlight lit up the man's face, and Rajiv raised his eyebrows in surprise.

"What are you doing here?"

Max looked sideways at Rajiv, his weapon and the flashlight still pointing at the man's head. "You know this man?"

Rajiv sighed. "You could say that."

## 56

John blinked in surprise.

What the...?

He could understand Max being there, but Rajiv?

Detective Inspector Rajiv Sampath, a man he trusted and respected. Helping Atman even after being shown evidence of the crimes he had committed, evidence that exposed him as a fake, a sexual predator, a murderer. John ground his teeth together. He couldn't believe it. He'd thought Rajiv was better than that.

And did the Bangalore police even have jurisdiction here?

John took a deep breath and exhaled slowly.

And who was the third guy? The guy they'd caught sneaking around the bungalow? A westerner, but not from the ashram, surely? He wasn't dressed like one of Atman's acolytes. In fact, he was all in black like a ninja and if John hadn't spotted Rajiv sprinting across the lawn, he would never have noticed him.

John sat back on his haunches in the undergrowth and

watched the scene play out in front of him. He'd been lucky. A minute earlier and that would have been him pressed up against the wall with a gun pointed at his head. He would need to be extra careful from now on.

Rajiv and Max pushed the intruder toward the verandah, then forced him to kneel with his hands behind his head.

Max maintained a safe distance standing to one side, but kept his weapon trained on the prisoner, while Rajiv crouched down and questioned him.

John couldn't make out what they were saying, the background noise from the surf making their conversation inaudible. He saw the prisoner shaking his head, then Rajiv stood and spoke to Max. They seemed to disagree about something, Max raising his voice and gesturing toward the prisoner with his handgun. Rajiv stepped closer, raising his own voice, and then reached up with his hand and moved the weapon away.

Max glared at him, then stepped back and lifted his shirt, slipping the weapon into the waistband of his pants.

Rajiv turned back to the prisoner and said something. The man released his hands from the back of his head, his arms falling to his sides, his chin dropping to his chest, all fight gone out of him.

John shifted his position, easing his legs out slowly, trying not to make a sound or disturb the surrounding foliage. It looked like he wouldn't be able to move for a while, so he might as well make himself comfortable. He leaned back against the wall, moved slightly so his view was undisturbed, and settled in for a lengthy wait.

## 57

John rubbed his face and sat up in bed, giving up on trying to sleep longer. The soft light of dawn was already filtering into the room through a gap in the curtains made by the gentle sea breeze. John stood and walked over to the window, drawing back the curtains and leaning on the windowsill. The sea and sky were grey, the division between the two almost indistinguishable, the ripples in the otherwise flat surface of the ocean the only difference to the sky above.

The previous evening, John had remained hidden in the garden for four hours until he judged it safe enough to move.

He had watched Rajiv make a call, and a short while later, several uniformed police arrived and took the intruder away. It was only then that Atman, accompanied by Georges and Manoj, made their appearance, and went inside the bungalow. Around thirty minutes later, Rajiv exited the bungalow and stood on the verandah alone, his hands on his hips, gazing out to sea. He then walked slowly back toward the ashram, his head down, seemingly deep in thought.

When the lights finally went out in the bungalow, John decided to move, making his way slowly back through the shadows of the ashram onto the beach and back to his guesthouse.

He'd stayed awake for a long time, unable to sleep, his mind racing away, trying to come to terms with what he had seen. He just couldn't understand what Rajiv was doing there. It made no sense. After all, he had shared with him, why would he be here protecting Atman? And the western intruder? What was his story?

Eventually, tiredness got the better of him and he drifted off into a restless sleep that only lasted until the sun's rays appeared in the morning sky. He pulled on a shirt and walked outside, across the sandy ground and out onto the beach. He spotted the fisherman owner of the guesthouse sitting on the trunk of a fallen coconut palm and he could smell the distinctive scent of a hand-rolled *beedi*.

He stood beside him and the old man nodded a greeting and offered a puff on his cigarette. John smiled, shook his head and stood beside him, gazing out to sea.

"Dolphin."

John looked at where the old man was pointing. He couldn't see anything for a while and then something black and shiny appeared on the surface and then disappeared again. It was just visible to John's naked eye, and he marvelled at the elderly fisherman's eyesight. He kept watching and a moment later, a little further on, it reappeared. John grinned. For some reason, the sight filled him with joy. He turned and smiled at the old man, then sat down beside him.

He wasn't sure how much English the man spoke, having only dealt with his wife the day before, but he thought he'd try, anyway.

"John." He held out his hand.

"Pankaj," he replied, switched the *beedi* to his left hand, then shook John's with a broad, strong, calloused hand.

"Do you see a lot of them here?"

"Some days."

"Whales?"

"No."

John nodded and kept his eyes on the ocean, hoping for another glimpse.

"Do you still fish?"

Pankaj tossed the finished *beedi* into the sand, cleared his throat and spat to the side. "Only what we eat. I'm old now."

"Hmmm."

"Not much fish now, either."

John turned and studied his face, burnt black and lined with the relentless sun exposure. The man glanced sideways at John, then returned his attention to the ocean.

John made a gesture with his head as if encompassing all the other fisherfolk living along the beach. "What will everyone do? If the fish run out."

Pankaj shrugged. "All the young people have left. Gone to the city, some overseas. They send money back."

John looked past him at the neighbouring properties, run down, unmaintained, slowly decaying into the earth, but with one of the greatest views on earth.

As if reading his mind, Pankaj said, "Some sell their land." He sniffed and nodded up the beach toward the ashram. "They buy it."

John frowned. "The ashram?"

Pankaj nodded.

"What for?"

Pankaj shrugged. "I don't know, but they own most of the land along here now."

"Are they good people?"

Pankaj turned and stared at John for a moment. "You are not one of them, are you? Ashram people?"

John shook his head. "No."

Pankaj stared a moment longer, then he shook his head. "No. I didn't think so. No, they aren't good people."

"What do you mean?"

Prakash turned away and stared out to sea again, but said nothing for a while.

John waited for an answer and when one wasn't forthcoming, he, too, returned his gaze to the ocean. There was something calming about the vast open space in front of them.

"Sometimes you can't fish because of the weather. Sometimes the weather is okay, but there are no fish. Money runs short. Then your children need money for school fees, your daughter is getting married, a family member gets sick."

John nodded slowly as if he understood, but wasn't sure what point Pankaj was trying to make.

"There's no money from the government. We have a fishermen's union, but they have no funds." He jerked his head in the ashram's direction again. "They offer loans." He sniffed and spat in the sand again. "Social programs." He turned and looked at John again, and this time, his eyes flashed with anger. "But if you don't pay them back, they take your land."

"Can they do that? Legally?"

Pankaj shrugged. "Who are we? We are fishermen. Poor.

No education. They are rich. Actors, actresses, politicians, they all go there. What can we do?"

John sighed loudly and shook his head. The same story the world over. Maybe he could get Adriana to do a story about it, but he doubted things would change.

"I saw him once."

"Who?"

Pankaj nodded up the beach again. "Guruji."

"Atman?"

He nodded.

"And? What do you think? Is he..." John searched for the words, "a real guru?"

Prakash made a face, his eyes on the sea again, and he said nothing for a while. "He has something... maybe... but when money and fame come... it's hard to let go."

John dug his fingers into the sand, then watched it slide through the gaps in his fingers. "Yeah. I went to his ashram once. In Sri Lanka."

Prakash half turned and regarded him from the corner of his eye. "And?"

John pursed his lips. "The teachings are... good, but the man is flawed. He's not God."

"Do you believe in God?"

John took a breath, giving himself time to think. How did he explain himself? His beliefs were complicated, but somehow he felt this simple man sitting beside him held more wisdom than more worldly, educated men of his age.

"Not anymore. I mean, not in the usual way. I've seen too much hatred... cruelty... horror... to believe God is up there watching over us."

"I understand." He reached over and gave John's thigh a squeeze, just above the knee, the gesture giving John comfort and they both lapsed into silence, watching the sea change colour as the sun rose higher behind them.

A dolphin, much closer this time, leapt out of the water, twisted in the air and splashed back down again in a spray of water.

Pankaj chuckled. "That is God, John."

## 58

Rajiv, now back in uniform, drummed his fingers on the dusty desktop of what doubled for an interview room and waited for the prisoner to be brought in. The room was dusty, the floor in dire need of a sweep, and decaying boxes of files lined two of the walls, but it was the only room in the station that was free.

Rajiv had read the file on the table in front of him, but it told him little of the man's motivations, although deep down Rajiv had a suspicion.

There was a hesitant tap on the door, and it cracked open. "Sir?"

"Come in."

The door opened wide to reveal a constable escorting a young western male in black clothing. His sun bleached hair was ruffled and his deep tan failed to disguise the dark circles under his eyes. He obviously hadn't found the cell conducive to a good night's sleep.

Rajiv gestured to the plastic chair pulled up in front of the desk. "Take a seat." He glanced at the constable behind the prisoner. "Remove his cuffs."

"Sir?"

Rajiv simply raised an eyebrow, and the constable hurried to remove the handcuffs from the young man's wrists.

"You can leave us, constable."

This time the constable didn't question Rajiv, and he stepped outside and closed the door behind him.

Rajiv studied the man in front of him. He had broad shoulders, a lean face, and the lines around the corners of his eyes suggested significant time spent in the sun.

He glared back at Rajiv. "I'm an Australian citizen. You can't keep me here."

Rajiv nodded slowly. "I know you are an Australian citizen. But if you commit a crime in India, you are still subject to India's laws."

"And what crime have I committed?"

Rajiv ignored the question and reached forward for the file and flipped it open.

"Trevor Hughes, twenty-five years old. Currently resident of Anjuna Beach, Goa. Long-term tourist visa. You've been in India for quite some time." He looked up. "What are you doing in Goa, Mr Hughes?"

"None of your business."

Rajiv sighed, closed the file, and sat back in his chair. He brushed an imaginary speck from the table in front of him. "This aggressive attitude of yours will not help you."

"What do you care? As if the police help anyone. If you did your job properly, I wouldn't be here now."

Rajiv could feel the seed of irritation germinating in his gut, but kept his face calm, expressionless. "My job? And what, in your opinion, is my job?"

Trevor sneered and shook his head.

Rajiv regarded him for a moment, then asked, "What were you doing at the *Anandsagar* Ashram last night?"

Trevor shrugged and fixed his attention on the window behind Rajiv.

"You are not a resident of the ashram, I know that. In fact, you are staying in a guesthouse on Kapu Beach." Rajiv leaned forward and opened the file again and ran his finger down the top sheet of paper. "According to this rather extensive file we have built on you, you have been there for the past three weeks."

Trevor's eyes blazed, and he leaned forward and jabbed a finger at Rajiv. "Then the file should tell you that my sister was also a resident of Kapu beach until they murdered her in cold blood. And you bastards have done nothing about it. Corrupt motherfuckers."

And there it was.

Rajiv sat back in his chair and waited for Trevor to calm down a little.

"Sally Hughes, killed in a hit-and-run accident approximately three months ago. An unfortunate accident."

"She was murdered," he snarled. "By those bastards at the ashram."

Rajiv's phone vibrated on the table with an incoming call. He glanced with irritation at the screen. It wasn't a number he recognised. He cut the call and asked, "And what makes you think that? I've read the file. You've made this allegation before, but there is no evidence to back up your accusations."

The phone vibrated again, and Rajiv reached over and cut the call without looking at it, his attention fully on the man in front of him.

Trevor was shaking his head, ill-disguised contempt plastered all over his face. "You are the same as the rest of them. Lazy, corrupt, only wanting to please your powerful masters."

Rajiv had had enough. He leaned forward, placed both hands on the desk, his arms outstretched, and in a low voice, he growled, "You know nothing about me or how I do my job. I suggest you tone down the accusations or you will find yourself back in that cell and I will forget where I put the key."

Trevor matched his glare, the two men in a battle of wills, then he looked away.

"Now. Tell me what proof you have that she was murdered."

Trevor swallowed and looked down at his lap. "I don't have any proof."

"What was that? I can't hear you."

He looked up. "I said, I don't have any proof."

"No, I didn't think so. Now listen to me. Whatever opinion you think you have about me, you are wrong. If a crime has been committed, and there is evidence, then I will prosecute the crime. But..." Rajiv pointed at the file. "I've read the reports. There is nothing to suggest murder. The only crime we have right now is one of trespass, which is why you are here now."

The phone vibrated again. Rajiv glanced at the phone screen, suppressed a curse, then quickly picked up the phone. "Sir."

"Let him go."

"Sir?"

"I said let him go. Don't waste your time, Rajiv."

Rajiv blinked. "But..."

Muniappa interrupted him, "I'm happy you've done your job. I knew I'd made the right decision sending you there to look after security. Well done on catching the intruder, but your orders are to release him immediately."

Rajiv frowned and rubbed his face with his spare hand.

"The ashram will not be pressing any charges."

Rajiv glanced at Trevor, but he was not paying him or the call any attention.

Muniappa continued. "I would like to add that the Chief Minister is very impressed. He asked me to commend your efforts in keeping our esteemed guest safe. Keep up the good work, Rajiv. The CM is watching your career with interest."

A million thoughts raced through Rajiv's head, but not a single one he could voice. All he could manage was, "Yes, sir."

The line went dead, and Rajiv placed the phone slowly back on the table.

"You are free to go."

"What?" Trevor looked up, his eyebrows raised in surprise.

"Yes."

Trevor frowned. "Who called you?"

"That's none of your concern. But I would suggest you stay away from the ashram. You might not be so lucky next time."

Trevor pushed back his chair, but hesitated and looked at Rajiv again, as if expecting him to change his mind.

Rajiv nodded. "The constable will give you your things on the way out."

Trevor, still puzzled, stood up and turned toward the door.

There was a question on the tip of Rajiv's tongue, and he had to ask it.

"Why do you feel your sister was murdered, Trevor?"

Trevor turned back to face Rajiv, the anger returning to his face. "Because she called me the day before she died. That fake fucking god-man raped her and she, my beautiful, loving sister, who never hurt a fly, had the guts to complain about it."

## 59

"Who is this?"

"Someone who trusted you and now wonders why." John braked to avoid a stray dog that had decided at that moment to cross the road.

There was no answer on the other end, and John glanced at the phone screen on the dashboard holder to see if the call had been cut.

"John?"

"I can see why you are a detective," John quipped, making no effort to keep the sarcasm from his voice.

There was the sound of muffled voices on the other end, then Rajiv's voice came back on the line again. "Wait one sec."

Three cars ahead of John, a white police vehicle pulled off the road and stopped. John braked suddenly and pulled to the side of the road next to a village shop. He saw the passenger door of the police SUV open and the familiar figure of Rajiv Sampath step out, a mobile phone pressed to his ear. He walked to the rear of the vehicle and looked around.

John sank lower in his seat, but there were enough people standing outside the shop blocking Rajiv's view that he was confident he wouldn't be seen easily.

"I guess by the number you're using, you are now in India."

"Again, great detective skills."

"Why the hostility, John?"

John exhaled loudly. "Well, why don't we start with, why are you protecting Atman? After what I shared with you?"

"Wh…" John heard Rajiv sigh. "It's complicated, John. But…." Rajiv sighed again and John could see him rubbing his face with his free hand. "I would have thought you would have allowed me the benefit of doubt."

John screwed up his face and thought for a moment. "That's why I called you."

"Hmmm."

John watched Rajiv pace slowly in a circle, and then stop, phone pressed to his left ear and his right hand on his hip. He stood staring into the field beside him, still silent.

A goods vehicle honked as it passed John's car and then again when it passed the police vehicle. Rajiv turned slowly, not saying anything, and looked directly at John's car.

"Shit," John cursed under his breath.

"Stay where you are. I'm coming to you."

The phone went dead and John cursed again, "Bugger." His heart raced. He'd done nothing wrong, but might have some explaining to do, and it was a situation John hadn't planned for.

Ahead, Rajiv had returned to his vehicle and opened the door. He said something to the driver, then closed the door and stood watching the vehicle pull out onto the road and drive away. Only when it had disappeared around the next bend did he turn and walk back toward John's car. John allowed himself to relax a little. Rajiv obviously didn't want to be observed by his men.

John continued watching as he approached. He looked pretty much as he remembered him, perhaps a little thicker around the middle, a bit weary around the eyes, but still in an immaculate uniform, his carriage straight and confident.

Rajiv opened the passenger door, removed his cap, and climbed in. Placing the cap on his lap, he turned sideways and looked John up and down. He said nothing for what seemed like an eon, then reached out his hand and smiled a genuine smile. "You are looking well, John."

John grasped his hand in his and, despite his misgivings, returned his smile with as much warmth and respect as it had been given.

"You too, Rajiv. Life seems to agree with you."

"I can't complain." He patted his waist, "A bit too much time behind a desk, but all said and done life is good."

John nodded slowly, still smiling. "That's all we can ask for."

"Hmmm." Rajiv looked forward through the windshield at the villagers gathered outside the shop. None of them were shopping, instead treating the shop as a meeting point. "Let's go somewhere less conspicuous. We have a lot to catch up on."

## 60

"Filter coffee?"

John nodded. "Black, though."

Rajiv spoke in Kannada to the waiter and waited for him to leave before turning back to face John. They were seated in the rear corner of a small restaurant open to the road. Rajiv sat with his back to the wall, his eyes moving constantly, observing the road outside and the constant ebb and flow of customers. John sat sideways, leaning his back against the side wall where he could see Rajiv, but also be aware of what was going on around him.

The coffee appeared almost immediately, steaming hot and served in stainless steel tumblers set in deep saucers. Rajiv picked up his tumbler and poured it into the saucer and back again, cooling the liquid until it was suitable to drink. John watched him, then took a sip of his own and set it back down again. It was too hot, and extremely strong, the staff unused to making coffee without milk.

"So..." Rajiv said after a moment. "I always suspected you would turn up, but perhaps not so soon and definitely not here."

John smiled with the right side of his face. "And I too did not expect to see you here. A bit out of your jurisdiction, aren't you?"

Rajiv took a deep breath, his shoulders rising, and then he exhaled loudly. "Yes... well," he shrugged. "It wasn't my decision."

John narrowed his eyes, waiting for Rajiv to explain.

Rajiv turned the tumbler around with his fingertips, then looked up. "You remember my boss?"

John nodded.

"We don't always see eye to eye, as I'm sure you can imagine."

John nodded again. He had never liked SP Muniappa, an overweight slug intent only on pleasing his masters.

"He put me in charge of Atman's security while in Bangalore and for some reason Atman wanted to keep me around when he came here. My boss jumped at the chance to get me out of the office for a while."

"So..." John took a sip of the coffee. Still too hot. "It wasn't your choice to be here?"

"No."

John studied his face, searching for any sign of untruth. Satisfied, he replied, "Good. But I have another question."

"I'm sure."

"What was going on last night?"

Rajiv raised an eyebrow and leaned back in his chair. "You were there?"

John grinned but said nothing.

Rajiv shook his head and gave a wry smile. "John Hayes. You haven't changed."

"I don't think you have either, Rajiv, which is why I was surprised to see you in the ashram."

Rajiv shrugged. "Yeah. I read what Adr..."

"Adriana."

"What Adriana sent me. But as I said when we first spoke... on the phone... there's nothing I can do, John, unless I catch him in the act."

"I know."

"And what you've described, the evidence Adriana provided, while useful as background, doesn't help me here."

John nodded and had another attempt at drinking his coffee. It was finally cool enough, and he took a larger sip.

"Is it that bad?"

John looked up. "Was it that obvious?"

Rajiv chuckled. "Written all over your face. Have some milk and sugar in it."

"Eww. No, thank you."

Rajiv grinned. "One day, you should come home. My wife Aarthi, she makes wonderful coffee."

"I'd like that."

Rajiv's expression suddenly became serious. "She's in the ashram too."

## 61

"Who? Your wife?"

Rajiv nodded.

John winced. "Why?"

Rajiv shrugged. "She's always been spiritual, and she believes he's a great teacher."

"Tell her to be careful, but... no disrespect... is she a similar age to you?"

"Yes."

"She should be okay, then. His tastes seem to run to young girls or foreign women."

"Bastard."

"He is, Rajiv. Don't let that smooth, charming exterior fool you. He's rotten inside. You've met Georges too, haven't you?"

"Yup."

"Another charmer."

"Huh. It's crazy, but... I've always thought myself to be an excellent judge of character, John. I have to be in this job. My instincts are good. I'm rarely wrong. But I've been completely wrong with Atman."

"Yeah, I know." John sighed and turned to look out toward the road. "Look, I don't understand it either." He looked back at Rajiv. "I fell under his spell in Sri Lanka. He… definitely has something… and maybe… when he started he had good intentions, but… someone wiser than me said, 'the lure of money and fame is hard to let go of.'"

"He's not the first."

"No." John shook his head. "That guy in Punjab. The one who made the movies about himself?"

Rajiv groaned, "I know."

The two lapsed into silence, sipping their coffee and watching the activity in the restaurant.

"You still didn't tell me what happened last night. The westerner. You let him go this morning, too."

"You were at the station?"

John grinned. "I followed you."

Rajiv shook his head again. "Maybe you should have my job." He sighed. "Trevor Hughes, Australian. His sister was at the Ashram, but she died about three months ago."

"Run over by a truck."

"See, you should do my job."

"And what was he doing last night?"

Rajiv stuck out his bottom lip and frowned. "I don't know. But I do know he believes she was murdered. She told him Atman raped her, and the next day she was dead."

"Coincidence?"

"What do you think, John?"

"There are no coincidences. Not with something like this."

"Yup."

"I'm glad you let him go."

"I had no choice."

John raised an eyebrow.

"I was told to."

"By whom?"

"Indirectly by the Chief Minister of Karnataka."

"Fuck."

"Yes, fuck."

"You know they'll kill him too, don't you?"

"I don't know that," Rajiv scoffed.

"Come on Rajiv, don't be so naïve. Why else would they let him go? It's not forgiveness or love for your fellow man, or any other such bullshit. Mark my words, this young man will meet with an unfortunate accident sometime soon."

Rajiv stared back at John, but didn't say anything.

"Which is why we have to stop them."

"John, John, no, no..." Rajiv began shaking his head vigorously. "You can't go taking the law into your own hands again."

John smiled with his mouth, but not his eyes. "What do you mean again?"

"No, there will be a legal way. I'll find something. Something incriminating. We'll get him deported, get the ashram closed down."

"Okay." John turned his hands over, palms facing upwards, and gestured toward Rajiv. "Well, good luck with that." He leaned forward, placed his forearms on the table, and lowered his voice. "But if you've got the Chief Minister influencing your investigations, then I don't see you having much success."

John waited for a response, but Rajiv remained silent and wouldn't meet his eyes.

"This guy has more wealth than we can imagine, is highly connected, and no-one will believe any of the things we know about him. He's a man of god for... god's sake. He's untouchable."

"So then, what do we do?"

"I don't know, Rajiv, I don't know. But there are two things of which I am sure. He needs to be put out of business and it will be a damn sight easier for me to do something about it than you."

Rajiv narrowed his eyes and stared back at John. John held his gaze, not knowing what was going through Rajiv's head, but sensing a fierce mental debate.

"And what makes you think that?"

John winked. "Sometimes you've gotta have faith."

"Who told you that? Atman?"

John grinned. "George Michael."

"Who?"

"Doesn't matter. But you need to trust me, Rajiv."

Rajiv looked away, exhaled loudly, and fiddled with the empty coffee tumbler on the table in front of him.

"Okay, okay..."

John waited.

"Okay..." Rajiv nodded, then looked up at John. "There's someone I think you should meet."

## 62

Aarthi suppressed the feeling of irritation and forced a smile on her face as her eyes roamed the dining hall. There was no sign of Rajiv anywhere, and she hadn't seen him at all that morning, neither in the meditations nor at breakfast.

She returned a wave from one of her fellow students, a young lady from Germany, but continued her scan of the students seated at the tables. No, he definitely wasn't there.

Was it her fault? Was she expecting too much, wanting him to take time off and learn meditation? She knew he had a job to do, but taking time out to go within, to still the mind, and to imbibe some of Atman's teachings would only help him. He needed to de-stress. His world was a dirty one and while he never brought it home, there were signs it was affecting him. She knew when he'd had a bad day, or when something was troubling him, even though he never talked about it. Sometimes she caught him staring into space and had to ask him a question again because he hadn't heard her the first time, or she could feel him tossing and turning in the bed, unable to sleep. It was as if there was a third person in their relationship. She loved him with all her heart, but having to share him with his job was wearing thin. When Meenu had suggested joining Atman's retreat and when she heard that Rajiv would be here too, it was as if the Divine was watching over them and sending an opportunity for them to strengthen their relationship and to give Rajiv much needed peace of mind.

But he had only attended one meditation, and she had barely seen him the rest of the time. He seemed to be avoiding her, and during the brief interactions they had together, he appeared tense and on edge. What was going on?

She spotted Meenu at their regular table and made her way between the other diners to sit down.

Maybe if she spoke to Atman himself? The thought sent a thrill shivering up her spine. To actually speak to him! Her heart began to race. Would she have the courage to see him face to face as an individual, not an anonymous member of the crowd? But it would be worth it if he could help them. He could encourage Rajiv to slow down, to take time for himself. Atman was always talking about how the inner world was more important than the outer world. Maybe if he spoke to Rajiv, Rajiv would actually do something about it?

Aarthi pulled out her chair, slid her food tray onto the table and sat down. She smiled at Meenu on her left, nodded a greeting to the others sitting opposite her, and then felt a hand on her arm. Turning, she saw the large liquid eyes of Priyanka brimming with excitement. Her face was flushed and her mouth stretched wide in a broad smile.

"Aarthi, guess what?"

Aarthi returned her smile and reached over to squeeze

her hand. "What's happened, Priyanka? You look very happy. Did you have an experience during the meditation?"

"Yes, well... no." She looked down shyly, then looked up again. "It's better than that."

Aarthi raised her eyebrows, and grinned. "Better than that?"

"Yes!" Priyanka glanced at the others sitting around them and then leaned closer, continuing in a low voice, "Atman has asked me to come and see him. Tonight, after the evening meditation."

"Really?" Aarthi felt a brief pang of jealousy.

"Yes." The young girl was almost hopping in her seat. She took hold of Aarthi's arm. "He's impressed with my progress, but said something is holding me back on a psychic level. He said once that is cleared, there will be no stopping me."

Aarthi was listening, but struggling to understand her emotions. What was wrong with her? Was she not doing the meditations properly? Perhaps she was paying for sins in her past? Was that why she wasn't making progress? She forced herself to focus on the young lady beside her. "Wow. He told you this himself?"

Priyanka shook her head. "No, that manager... um, Mr Manoj."

Aarthi nodded.

"He came and saw me after the meditation. He said Atman had asked him to tell me."

Aarthi took a deep breath and smiled. She would try harder herself. She would make progress, she knew it. It was only a matter of time. But in the meantime, this beautiful, innocent, young lady should make the most of the opportunity God was giving her. She placed a hand over Priyanka's. "I'm thrilled for you. You deserve it."

Priyanka blushed even more and looked away.

"What does your mum say? She must be excited."

Priyanka glanced toward her mother, who was sitting on the other side of the table, three seats along. "I haven't told her."

Aarthi frowned. "Why?"

Priyanka looked back at Aarthi with those deep, dark eyes. A look of sadness flashed briefly across them. "I... it's... she might..."

Aarthi's frown deepened. "It's okay, you can tell me."

Priyanka looked down at her plate and Aarthi saw her throat move as she swallowed. "She... I don't..." Looking up, she studied Aarthi, her eyes moving as they roamed Aarthi's face. "I don't tell her everything."

"Okay."

"She's..." her voice became more forceful, "she's very... controlling. I want this to be for me, not her."

Aarthi glanced at Rashmi, who was carrying on a loud conversation with those around her. "I understand. It's okay" She looked back at Priyanka and gave her a reassuring smile. "You are a beautiful, intelligent, and confident young woman. You can make your own decisions."

Priyanka smiled shyly and looked away. "Thank you," she murmured.

The two sat silently for a moment, Aarthi staring at the untouched food on her plate. She felt Priyanka's hand on her arm again.

"Hey, will you come with me? He can bless you, too."

Aarthi frowned and shook her head. "No, no, he's asked for you, not me."

"But he won't mind, I know. He's not like normal people, he's a great being. He loves everyone. Please come with me."

Aarthi thought fast. Maybe it would be a good time for

her to ask for his help with Rajiv? She wasn't going selfishly. She obviously had more inner work to do on herself before she could see him, otherwise he would have sent for her. But if she went to seek help for another, surely that would be alright?

Aarthi turned and smiled at Priyanka. "I would love to come with you."

## 63

"That's him."

John didn't need to see who Rajiv was pointing at, the young Australian man quite obvious amongst the Indian customers standing around the tea stall.

"Let's go."

But Rajiv was already climbing out of the car. John got out and followed him across the road. Several villagers eyed Rajiv in his police uniform and sidled away, but Trevor had his back to them. It was only when Rajiv was almost beside him that Trevor, perhaps noticing the look on the tea stall owner's face, turned around and cursed.

"For fuck's sake. I thought I was free to go."

Rajiv raised both hands, palms facing out. "It's okay. I'm not here to arrest you."

Trevor's eyes flicked past him, noticing John for the first time, and he frowned.

Rajiv continued, "I want you to meet someone."

John stepped forward and held out his hand. "John Hayes. I think I can help you."

## 64

They had moved to a wooden bench under a stand of trees, off the road and to the side of the tea stall. After the initial suspicion and curiosity from the locals, they were now ignored and John sat with his back against the trunk of a coconut palm, watching a pair of crows peck through the contents of an overturned trash can.

Rajiv stood nearby, sipping on his third coffee of the morning, while they both waited for Trevor to finish reading through the news article on his phone.

"So that was you?" He looked up while slipping his phone back into his pocket.

John nodded. Rajiv had forwarded Adriana's article about the events leading to Atman fleeing Sri Lanka to Trevor's phone, and he'd spent the last five minutes going through it.

"He's an evil bastard."

John nodded again.

"I wish you had stopped him there… in Sri Lanka. My sister would still be alive."

John took a deep breath and sighed. "Yeah. I'm sorry," he shrugged. "I tried."

Trevor didn't answer, just stared down at the sandy ground in front of him. John remained silent, fighting the guilt he had suppressed for so long. He thought he had come to terms with it, but when he learned of the death of Trevor's sister, it had brought things to the surface. Now, with the young man beside him, still seeking answers, he felt even worse.

"Nah... it's not your fault, mate," Trevor turned to look at John. "You did more than anyone else."

John frowned and kicked at a pebble lying between his feet.

"She was so full of life... and happy here. It's because of her that I came over. She told me about this great teacher who had changed her life... brought her so much peace." Trevor exhaled loudly. "She'd had a tough breakup back home, didn't handle it well. Then, after she came here, she was... how do I say it... I want to say reborn, but that sounds a bit 'born again'... She was like I remember when we were growing up. Full of hope, joyful..." he trailed off.

John glanced up at Rajiv, who was staring into the paper coffee cup in his hand.

"I was in Bali, surfing," Trevor continued, "and she convinced me to come over." He shrugged. "But sitting still, contemplating my navel for hours isn't my thing. I stayed a few days, then moved up to Goa. If I had known..."

John reached over and gave the young man's shoulder a squeeze. "Don't blame yourself. It doesn't help. What's happened has happened," he paused. "Sorry, that sounds callous, but trust me, I know... you have to move on."

Trevor turned his head and stared at John, his expression at first angry, but then, as John held his gaze, his face softened and a look of deep sadness came over him, and he looked away.

"But..." John added, "despite what they say, I've also found revenge to be a useful part of the healing process." He glanced at Rajiv again, but the detective was looking in the other direction, finding the crows beside the trash can very interesting.

John turned and looked back at Trevor, who was regarding him with renewed interest.

"What do you mean?"

"It's a long story, one for another time, but just know that I too have suffered a significant loss in the past, and..." he glanced over at Rajiv again, "sometimes one has to take matters into their own hands."

Rajiv cleared his throat. "I ah... I'll leave you guys to it. I have ah... things to do."

John nodded.

"Just... whatever you do, be careful. There's a limit to how much I can... um... look the other way."

"I know." John half smiled. "Thank you, Rajiv."

Rajiv nodded at Trevor, then walked away toward the road. John stayed silent, his eyes on his friend as he stood on the edge of the road and waved down a passing villager on a motorcycle. He had a brief discussion, then climbed on the back, at the same time pulling out his phone and holding it to his ear.

As he disappeared up the road, Trevor asked, "How much do you trust him?"

John pursed his lips, his eyes on the disappearing motorcycle. Only when it was out of sight did he reply, "With my life, Trevor. With my life."

## 65

"I can't hear you. Say that again." Rajiv raised his left hand and covered his ear, while pressing the phone harder to his right ear.

"I said I'm meeting Atman this evening."

Rajiv tightened his grip on the phone and waited while the motorcycle swerved around a pothole. "What do you mean, Aarthi? Meeting?"

"Yes, it's so exciting. One of the other students, Priyanka, I can't remember if I mentioned her, a young girl from Delhi..."

Rajiv frowned as he concentrated on Aarthi's voice, trying to hear her above the wind noise.

"... She's been making great progress and Atmanji has noticed. He asked to see her this evening, and she asked me to come with her."

Rajiv clenched his jaw and closed his eyes, forcing himself to stay calm. "Where?"

"At his bungalow. Is everything okay Rajiv, you sound tense... where are you?"

"I'm just heading back to the ashram..." This wasn't a

conversation to be had over the phone. "Where are you now?"

"I'm near the dining hall. Why?"

"Meet me at the front gate. I'm almost there."

"Why, Rajiv? What's going on?"

"Just meet me there," Rajiv struggled to keep the irritation out of his voice. "Just do this for me, please." He ended the call and tapped on the motorcyclist's shoulder. "*Bega, bega*. Faster, faster."

A minute later, the bike pulled up outside the ashram gate and Rajiv climbed off. "Thank you," he said to the motorcyclist and then strode toward the gate and pounded on it with the heel of his hand, at the same time looking up at the camera.

He was about to bang the gate again when he heard the bolts being slid open and the gate swung inwards. Rajiv marched in, nodding a thank you to Mani, and looked for Aarthi. She was standing in the archway that led from the carpark into the ashram and when she saw him she smiled and waved. She looked excited to see him, but a hint of concern tinged her smile as she noticed his uniform.

"Rajiv, where have you been? I've not seen you since yesterday."

"Just work." Despite his concern, Rajiv couldn't help smiling. "You look beautiful."

Aarthi blushed with pleasure.

She really did. Her thick glossy hair tumbled loosely onto her shoulders, and her face glowed with happiness. The retreat was doing her the world of good. Rajiv sighed. Which only made what he had to say even more difficult. He glanced around to make sure no-one was in earshot, then, taking her arm, led her to one side. "Don't go and see him."

Aarthi blinked in surprise, the smile leaving her face. "Why?"

"Just..." Rajiv took a deep breath. What did he say? "He's not what he seems."

"Oh Rajiv, don't start this again. Why do you have to be so suspicious all the time? For once, just once, can you leave your policeman's brain to one side?"

"You don't understand, Aarthi..."

"No, I don't understand, Rajiv. Why can't you just relax? This job of yours is taking over our life."

Rajiv bit his lip.

"You're not even trying. You've not been to any of the meditations and you've been negative right from the beginning."

"Aarthi, I have a job to do."

"Yes, but you are taking it too seriously. What is there to worry about here?" She made a gesture with her hand to encompass the surrounding ashram. "Look at this place. It's beautiful. People are happy, kind, full of unconditional love."

"I..."

"No, Rajiv, it's not fair. You can see how much good this is doing me, yet you want to ruin it with your suspicion and cynicism. Do you know why I'm going to see him? Not for me. For us. To help us Rajiv... don't you understand that? I love you and this obsession with your job... it's..." she trailed off. "It's coming between us, Rajiv."

Rajiv felt as if a stake had been driven through his chest. He knew he spent most of his waking hours at work but hadn't realised it was affecting Aarthi so much. Taking a deep breath, he reached out and held her shoulders with his hands. He looked down at her and waited until she looked up and her eyes met his. "I'm sorry. I didn't realise... I'm really sorry."

Aarthi gazed back at him, her eyes moist, but then she smiled. "It's okay... I... I'm being selfish."

Rajiv shook his head. "No, no, you are not. It's me who has been selfish. I promise when we are back that I will try harder. I'll take some time off."

Aarthi smiled wider.

"But you have to trust me now, please."

Aarthi's smile slipped, her eyebrows knitting together, "What do you mean?"

Rajiv released his grip on her shoulders and looked around. There were a couple of students talking at the other end of the pathway, and the security guard was back in his room. Looking back at Aarthi again, he said, "You must not meet him alone. He is not a good man. I know you don't believe it, but I have evidence of..."

"Of what, Rajiv?"

Rajiv exhaled and made a face. He had to tell her. "Sexual assault, kidnapping, probable murder."

"Don't be ridiculous!"

"It's true."

"No, no... it's not possible. Guruji? No, no way."

Rajiv didn't say anything. She had to come to terms with it on her own.

She was shaking her head and not looking Rajiv in the eye. Again she said, "no, no..."

Movement by the gate caught his eye, and he turned to see it swing open and Atman's Range Rover pull inside and stop. There was no sign of movement from inside and with the light reflecting on the windscreen, Rajiv couldn't see who was inside.

Rajiv looked back at Aarthi. She hadn't noticed the car

arrive, still lost in the denial of what Rajiv had told her. "Aarthi, listen to me. Whatever happens next, just act normally."

"What?"

But Rajiv had already turned back to watch the Range Rover.

The rear passenger door opened and Atman stepped out. He closed the door, straightened his shirt and then stood looking directly at them.

Rajiv's heart began to race, even though there was no way Atman could know what they were talking about.

The lights flashed on the Range Rover as Georges locked it, and walked around to join Atman, then they both walked toward the archway.

Rajiv swallowed, took a step away from Aarthi and forced a smile.

"Rajiv," Atman stopped in front of him and flashed a broad smile. His eyes twinkled, and Rajiv suddenly felt that he had been wrong about everything. "You are looking very official in your uniform."

"Yes, I ah..." Rajiv looked over Atman's shoulder at Georges, who looked back without an expression on his face. "I was dealing with our uninvited guest."

"Oh yes," Atman made a dismissive gesture with his hand, still smiling. "Not important. Sometimes people lose their way. But thank you. I know I can rely on you." His eyes moved to Aarthi, who was standing beside him, her hands held in *namaste*, a nervous smile on her face.

"I'm sorry, we haven't met yet. You are?"

"Aarthi, Guruji."

"Aarthi," he repeated quietly, still smiling. Then he reached out, placed his hand on her head and Aarthi visibly shivered. Rajiv felt a hot spark of anger ignite in his gut.

"Close your eyes, my child."

*Child.* Rajiv repeated the word in his head, his anger growing, but doing his best to keep the smile on his face. He watched his wife's face flush and her eyeballs move behind her closed lids and realised he had never hated any man more in his life.

Atman removed his hand from Aarthi's head and she opened her eyes. They sparkled and her shoulders rose and fell as she took rapid, short breaths.

"Something was troubling you, my child, but don't worry. Everything will be fine now."

"Th-th-thank you, Guruji." Aarthi bent down as if to touch his feet in the traditional sign of respect shown to a guru, but he placed his hands on her shoulders and stopped her. "There's no need for any of that. Just keep up your practice. The Universe will guide you."

"Y-y-yes," Aarthi stammered a reply and he let go of her shoulders, winked at Rajiv and said, "you need to spend more time with your wife, Rajiv."

Rajiv blinked in surprise and opened his mouth to protest, but Atman was already walking away, Georges following close behind.

Rajiv frowned. How the hell did he know?

Aarthi moved beside him and he fought back the feeling of jealousy as he looked down at her. She was still breathing quickly, her mouth slightly open, colour in her cheeks.

"What did he do to you?"

Aarthi finally dragged her gaze away from the retreating form of Atman and looked up into Rajiv's eyes. "I... I don't know." Her eyes searched his face while she struggled to find the words to describe her experience. "There was this tremendous heat from his hand and then I felt a rush of energy up my spine." She smiled up at him. "And then I had a feeling that everything was going to be okay, just as he said."

"Hmmm." Rajiv realised he was clenching his jaw, and he forced himself to relax. Getting angry wouldn't help him or Aarthi.

"Rajiv, surely you are wrong about him."

"I wish I was, Aarthi, I wish I was."

"But... he has so much power... he's not like us... he's..."

"He's not God, Aarthi. I'm sorry, but he has all the urges of a normal man."

"But..."

Rajiv sighed. "Aarthi, he raped a woman in his ashram in Sri Lanka, and is suspected to have raped and murdered another young Sri Lankan girl. And by young, I mean young. Early teens."

Aarthi was covering her mouth with her hand, her eyes wide and her head shaking.

Rajiv continued, "And he has raped an Australian woman here, Sally Hughes, and after she reported it, she was killed in a hit-and-run accident."

Aarthi gripped Rajiv's arm, and a tear rolled down her right cheek.

"I didn't want to tell you. I know how much this means to you, being here, this retreat, but..." He took a deep breath and shook his head. "I couldn't let you see him on your own, knowing what I know."

"Why don't you arrest him?"

"Huh." Rajiv shook his head. "If I catch him, I will. But I can't do anything about what he's done in Sri Lanka, and I don't have proof of the rape and murder here."

"So... it's possible he didn't do it?"

"Come on, Aarthi. The woman's brother told me this

morning that she called and told him he had raped her. Then the next day she was hit by a truck."

"It could have been an accident."

"You really think so?"

Aarthi said nothing for a while and then when she replied, it was barely over a whisper, "No."

"Promise me you won't be alone with him."

Aarthi stepped closer and threw her arms around Rajiv and buried her head in his chest. "I promise."

Rajiv glanced around to see if they were being watched, then relaxed and put his own arms around her, hugging her tight. "I would never forgive myself if something happened to you."

Aarthi lifted her head and looked up at him. "But what about Priyanka?"

## 66

"So, what were you planning to do?"

Trevor leaned forward, his elbows on his knees, and rubbed his face with his hands. He exhaled loudly, the sound like a balloon deflating. "I don't know. I hadn't thought it through." He paused. "I was just so angry that the police weren't doing anything and that..." he sat up and gestured down the road in the direction of the ashram, "bastard... is getting away with it."

John nodded. He understood. He'd been in the same position himself.

Trevor continued, "I thought I would get inside his house and... I don't know... teach him a lesson." He sighed again. "Stupid, I know."

"Hmmm. You were lucky Rajiv caught you."

Trevor turned to look at John, his forehead creased. "What do you mean? You say you trust him, but there he is, protecting the bastard."

The right side of John's face formed a smile, but there was no amusement in his eyes. "It's complicated. Even for him."

Trevor raised his eyebrows, still watching John, waiting for a further explanation.

"Look. Detective Rajiv Sampath is a good man. One of the most honest, honourable men I know. He believes in justice, in upholding the law, in doing his job to the best of his ability. You were trespassing... he caught you."

"Okay. Then why are we talking to him?"

"Because he is also in the difficult position of not being allowed to do his job properly. Sometimes he can't bring people to justice because of their connections, political influence, money... The legal system here is ponderous. It can take ten years before a case comes to court, if it even gets that far. If you have money, or know someone powerful, nothing will ever happen. Witnesses, victims, they get paid off, threatened, even... killed."

A flash of anger passed across Trevor's face. "So my sister will never get justice."

John shook his head. "Sadly, not by conventional means, no."

"Fucking..."

"Yes."

The two sat in silence, the only sound the cawing of the crows who had moved to a tree above them, and the background conversations from the tea stall.

"I still don't understand why you have taken such an interest in this," Trevor eventually broke the silence.

John didn't reply immediately. He wasn't sure how much he could trust the young man sitting beside him. He understood his loss, but until he had proven himself in action, John reserved his judgement. But he had to tell him something.

"A lifetime ago," he began, "my wife was raped and murdered in Bangalore."

"No…" Trevor shifted on the bench so he was facing John. "I'm… I'm so sorry."

John acknowledged him with a nod, the memory, despite the passing of time, still raw, and continued, "The men that did it… they were connected politically, wealthy, and influential." John realised he was gripping the wooden bench with his fingers and he let go and flexed his hands. "The police investigation ground to a halt. Nothing happened."

"Rajiv was involved?"

"Yup. But it wasn't his fault." John stared blindly across the patch of sand in front of them, images flashing across his mind's eye. Faces of the men who no longer walked the earth.

"And?"

John shrugged. "Let's just say, those men… the men who did it… they are no longer around."

"Prison?"

John shook his head.

"Shit… fuck… really?"

John said nothing, instead concentrating on his breathing, relaxing his body, stilling his mind.

"Wow," Trevor said eventually. "But… how… I mean… how did it feel… afterwards?"

John turned and regarded the young man sitting beside him. Young, idealistic, his whole life ahead of him. He didn't deserve to experience such sorrow at such a young age. But then no-one did. "It didn't bring her back." John looked away again. He could see across the road and through the trees a patch of the Arabian sea. A deep blue behind the mottled greens of the coconut palms. A patch of calmness amongst the constantly moving leaves. The memories still disturbed him, but at the same time, it all seemed so long ago, almost as if it had happened to someone else. If he had to experience it all over again, would he do it differently? The answer came immediately.

He turned back to look at Trevor. "It didn't bring her back, Trevor. Nothing ever will. But as much as you feel that your heart has been ripped from your chest, eventually it fades away. Life carries on. People forget. They carry on with their own lives as if she never existed. Just a figment of my imagination. It sucks, big time. To be honest, I have trouble remembering her face now. Just fragments. And I feel guilty about that. But I'll tell you one thing, if I had sat around and done nothing, if I had not taken action, and those motherf… those men had got away with it, I could never live with myself."

Trevor nodded slowly, then looked away, staring off into the trees.

Eventually he said, "Yeah."

John reached over and placed a hand on his shoulder. "I'm not saying it's easy. I'm haunted every day by what I've done. Nightmares, guilt… but it was worth it," he sighed and dropped his hand to his side. "In fact, that's how I got involved with Atman. Trying to find something that would give me peace. His teachings have helped. Meditation, breathing exercises…" he shrugged, "but you can learn that from a book, or on YouTube. There's a million teachers out there."

"That's why I surf. It stills the mind. Just me and the waves. But even that I don't feel like doing anymore."

"You should. It's important."

Trevor chewed his lip but didn't say anything.

"Anyway, to answer your original question, I'm involved because I decided back then to never stand by and do nothing if I see something wrong."

"All it needs for evil to flourish is for good men to stand by and do nothing."

"Something like that."

Trevor sat up straight and slapped his thigh with the palm of his hand. "So what do we do then?"

John grinned. "Honestly? I have no idea. But between the two, maybe three of us, I'm sure we can come up with a plan."

## 67

"Where are you?"

John frowned, "Ah, why?"

"Because it's a conversation I don't want to have on the phone."

John thought fast. Should he tell Rajiv where he was staying? He'd told Trevor he trusted the policeman with his life, and anyway, it probably wouldn't take long for him to find out.

"Okay, I'll text you the address."

"I'm coming now."

The line went dead and John sat up in bed. He had stripped off and was lying shirtless under the ceiling fan. Not to sleep, but to think during the hottest part of the day. He crossed to the bathroom and splashed cold water over his face and slicked back his hair before pulling his shirt back on. What was so urgent that Rajiv was coming to see him?

He walked downstairs and out onto the verandah. There was no sign of Pankaj and his wife, and the dog that seemed to have made the property its part-time home, didn't even look up from where it was sleeping in the shade, near their house.

John didn't have to wait long, Rajiv's Bolero pulling up outside the gate in a little over five minutes from the call. John watched him step out of the car, raised a hand in greeting, and beckoned him inside.

Rajiv had changed out of his uniform and looked like a member of the ashram in a white *kurta* and a pair of leather sandals. He glanced at the owner's house as he passed, then stopped in his tracks as the stray dog raised its head and growled at him.

"Ignore him," John called out. "He's more noise than anything else."

Rajiv nodded and walked forward. Sure enough, the dog growled once more, then decided he wasn't worth the effort and went back to sleep.

John led Rajiv along the verandah and gestured toward one of the planter's chairs that was set up facing the ocean. "Take a seat. I'm sorry I can't offer you anything to drink. I don't have anything, and I think the owners are having a siesta."

Rajiv made a dismissive gesture with his hand and stood in front of the chair, his hands on his hips, and looked out toward the beach and the ocean beyond. "Nice spot."

"Yeah." John stood beside him and shaded his eyes with his hand. "It's a pity about the reasons for being here. I might enjoy it more."

Rajiv narrowed his eyes and continued staring out to sea. After a while, he sighed, turned around and sat down in the chair.

John looked down at him. "What's up? Why the secrecy?"

Rajiv pursed his lips while the fingers of his right hand tapped nervously on the arm of the chair.

John moved to sit in the other chair and waited for an answer.

"Whatever you decide to do, it needs to be done quickly."

John raised an eyebrow. "Why? What has changed?"

"Arrgh." Rajiv covered his face with his palms and pressed his eyeballs with his fingertips. Dropping his hands, he turned to face John.

"My wife Aarthi is in the ashram."

"I know. You told me."

Rajiv exhaled loudly. "She was planning to visit Atman this evening. In his bungalow."

"You've not told her about him?"

"I hadn't. I have now."

"And?"

"She didn't believe me at first. At least, she didn't want to believe me."

"He's very convincing. It's not her fault."

Rajiv nodded and looked down at the floor.

"And now? You've talked her out of it?"

Rajiv nodded again, then thumped the arm of the chair with the heel of his hand and stood up. He paced to the end of the verandah and back again.

"What if I hadn't been here, John? What if I hadn't been able to warn her?"

John said nothing, allowing Rajiv to voice his thoughts.

Rajiv kept moving around, his body seeking an outlet for his agitation. "He has to be stopped. He has to."

"That's the plan."

Rajiv stopped in front of John. "I know, but..." he moved back to his chair and sat down. "I know he's done bad things, but to be honest, until now he was just another villain. I come across so many in my job, John. I've seen people do things you wouldn't believe. I've hardened myself to it. Built a shell around me. I... I... don't allow it to get personal. But this time it is. If anything happened to Aarthi... I..." he trailed off, shaking his head. Taking a breath, he continued, "I've saved Aarthi this time, but next time it will be someone else's Aarthi. Someone's wife, daughter... sister."

"I'll stop him."

Rajiv nodded slowly and sat back in the chair, his eyes on the sea again. "I know, John. I believe you." He turned to look at John. "And I'll help you. As much as I can, given..." he gestured toward himself.

"Yup." John didn't need him to finish the sentence. He and Rajiv had been in similar situations before. Rajiv had a duty as an officer of the law, but sometimes lines had to be crossed.

"Tell me about the security. There are cameras on all the boundaries, but one on the beach doesn't work."

"It does now. It's been fixed."

"Damn. The gate?"

"Also fixed."

John made a face. "Okay. Where else are the cameras?"

"On all corners of the bungalow. Covering the verandah and the lawns. They are monitored both in the guardroom beside the gate and also in a room in the bungalow."

"You've been in the bungalow, right?"

"Yes."

"Tell me what you saw."

Rajiv described the layout, including the office with the security system.

John nodded. "He had a similar room in Sri Lanka. Did you see a safe?"

"Yes. A big one."

"That will be full of cash, I'm sure."

"Huh," Rajiv scowled. "There's a gun safe too."

"Really? Did you see inside?"

"No. But both Georges and Max are armed. Handguns. I've not seen them clearly, but they look like Glocks."

John shook his head. "So much for spirituality."

"I know. And they won't be licensed. It's hard enough to get a license for Indians, but foreigners?" Rajiv shook his head. "My guess is they brought them when they arrived into India."

"There's a chance there are more weapons in the gun safe, too."

"Yes, and I can't do anything about it," Rajiv growled. "I have to turn a blind eye. Pretend I haven't seen them."

"Do you have a weapon?"

"I was told not to bring one. Mustn't defile the ashram with an instrument of death."

John chuckled.

"But I brought my Browning. It's locked in the glove box of my vehicle."

John grinned. "Good. It might come in useful later."

"I hope not."

"There's no point in sugarcoating things, Rajiv. Georges and Max are ex-Israeli army. Battle hardened, and extremely loyal to their boss. It's likely to get messy."

Rajiv made a face, but said nothing.

"Tell me about Atman's room."

Rajiv sighed. "I didn't get to see inside."

"So, it's at the end of the internal courtyard, right?"

"Yes. The building is oriented toward the beach, with the

entrance off the lawn, so I guess you would call it the back of the bungalow."

"One sec." John stood up and went inside, picked up a dog-eared paperback from the bookshelf, and tore out the flyleaf. He found a pen, then walked back outside. "Draw the layout on here."

Rajiv sketched the layout and handed it back to John.

"So, this whole end is his room?"

"Yes. There's a large wooden door here." Rajiv pointed at the sketch. "Heavy. It looks really thick, and there is a digital keypad to unlock it. According to Max, only Georges and Atman have the code."

John leaned back in his chair, rested his elbows on the armrests, and steepled his fingers in front of him.

"Staff?"

"I've only seen a cook and a houseboy."

"Will they be a problem?"

"I doubt it. It's just a job for them."

"Hmmm, so we've got Atman guarded by two heavily armed, battle hardened men, a compound filled with security cameras, and a secure..." John made quotation marks with his fingers, "'strong room' with no way of gaining access."

Rajiv didn't say anything.

"Piece of cake then."

Rajiv sat forward. "There's one more complication."

# 68

Aarthi's eyes were closed, and she held her hands in *chin mudra* on her lap, palms up, the tips of her index fingers forming a circle with the thumbs. But she wasn't meditating.

Her mind raced at a hundred miles an hour, millions of disturbing thoughts fighting for prominence inside her head. She still couldn't believe that the man sitting on the stage in the front of the hall was a fraud.

But was he? The things she had felt during meditation, she had never felt before. The deep sense of inner peace, the passing of time in what felt like seconds, the energy vibrating through her body, at times causing her spine to stiffen or her body to shake. Had she imagined that?

She heard a noise and opened one eye. Ahead of her and slightly to the right, one of the students was shaking their head violently up and down while rapidly inhaling and exhaling through their nostrils. It wasn't the first time she had witnessed something like this. She had read about it too before coming on the retreat. The activation of the sacred *kundalini* energy near the base of the physical spine was something only a few gurus could do, and once it became active and spread through the body, it caused the meditator to shake, perform spontaneous *yoga mudras*, and even *pranayama*, the yogic breathing currently being performed by the student in front of her. She had experienced something like that when Atman had placed his hand on her head. Surely that meant he was genuine?

But what about the things Rajiv had told her? She trusted her husband and knew he wasn't one to make accusations lightly. She now understood why he had been so reluctant for her to come. It made sense to her now.

She opened both eyes and gazed at the man sitting on the stage. Unusually, he was alone, the powerfully built man who normally accompanied him everywhere, not present at this afternoon's meditation. Good. There was something about him that unnerved her. He had never spoken to her, or even looked at her, nor given her any reason to dislike him, but there was something about him that didn't sit right with her.

She turned her head to look at Priyanka sitting beside her. The girl sat poker straight in full-lotus position, and Aarthi envied her flexibility. Her eyes were closed, her lips slightly apart, and a look of bliss filled her face. She had never looked so beautiful as she did now, like an angel in physical form.

Aarthi turned back to face the front and closed her eyes again, but unlike Priyanka, her forehead was crinkled, her eyebrows knit together. She had to prevent Priyanka from visiting Atman. If Rajiv was right and Atman assaulted this innocent creature, Aarthi could never live with herself.

She took a deep inhalation through her nostrils and slowly exhaled, consciously releasing the tension she was holding in her body, and said a silent prayer to the universe. *Please, please help me protect this girl.*

She kept repeating her request over and over in her mind like a *mantra*, her body relaxing more and more, until what seemed like a moment later, she heard a voice from the stage.

"Slowly come back... move your fingers and toes... rub your palms together, create heat between your palms... and then place your hands over your face... when you are ready, open your eyes."

Aarthi blinked her eyes open and dropped her hands to her lap.

She looked up toward the stage, where Atman was now standing, his left hand held to his chest, and his right hand held up, palm facing out toward the hall, and a broad smile across his face.

"Bless you all." He bowed his head, then turned and walked off the stage.

Murmured conversation rippled through the hall, and in that moment, Aarthi got an idea.

## 69

John and Rajiv agreed they must prevent Aarthi and Priyanka from spending time alone with Atman, but after an hour of brainstorming, they had failed to come up with a workable solution. Rajiv was confident he had convinced Aarthi, but Priyanka was another matter.

In the end, Rajiv returned to the ashram in time for the end of the afternoon meditation session, leaving John alone in his chair, staring out at the ocean.

Experience had taught John that sometimes he had to give his mind space to work things out. Usually he went for a run, the physical activity helping still his mind, but even though the sun had begun its descent, it was still way too hot to be performing physical activity outside.

Instead, he slowed his breathing, and narrowed his vision to a single point on the ocean, until without realising it, his breathing matched the rhythm of the waves crashing on the beach. His inhalations coincided with the incoming waves, and as he exhaled, the water receded. He began to feel that he and the ocean were one. Thoughts continued to appear in his mind but he paid them no heed, letting them fade away with each exhalation until they too slowed and there was just him and the vast expanse of grey-blue space in front of him.

Time slowed down and the outside world receded. He could no longer hear the wind, the surf, the birds in the trees. He could no longer feel the wind on his skin, nor his body touching the surface of the chair. It was as if the physical part of him had ceased to exist, leaving behind just an awareness that had no physical form.

After some time, something moved in the ocean, pulling him back, and he blinked. There was movement again, and the corners of his mouth twitched. A feeling of intense joy surged through his body and he began to smile. The smile broadened, and a sound escaped his lips, the beginning of a laugh which bubbled and grew inside him, until he was laughing out loud. His eyes moistened, and he wriggled his fingers as he became aware of his body again and then rubbed his eyes, clearing his vision.

He stood up from his seat, at first unsteady as the sensation returned to his limbs and then he stepped forward and placed a hand on one of the verandah pillars and watched the dolphin that had caught his eye, leap forth from the ocean once more, twist in the air and then hit the water side on sending a spray of water into the air. There was another splash as another dolphin followed it, then another, a whole pod, dancing and cavorting in the ocean, for no other reason than the joy of being alive.

John's laughter subsided, but the feeling of bliss remained, his face beaming, his body filled with a warm glow of tingling energy.

Any doubts he had before had disappeared, replaced instead by a certainty that everything was going to work out.

He still didn't know how, but had faith the solution would come to him. It always had in the past, and there was no reason it wouldn't in the future.

The pod of dolphins gradually moved out of his line of sight, and he moved back to the chair and picked up his phone. He needed to make a couple of calls.

## 70

"So you think it will work?"

"As long as someone clicks the link. That's all I need. The worm will do everything else."

John ran his fingers through his hair. "Okay. How quickly can you do it?"

"I'll put something together now. Maybe an offer of a donation. Greed usually works best." The enthusiasm in Ramesh's voice was noticeable, even over the phone line. "Then we just need someone to open the email and click the link."

"Hmmm." John turned his wrist and looked at the time on his watch. "The next meditation won't start for around an hour, so there will still be staff in the office. If you can send it within that time, there is still a chance."

"I'll do it, John, don't worry."

"Okay. Call me as soon as you get something. If you can get control of the cameras, it will make everything so much easier."

"John, as soon as someone clicks on that link, I'll have

access to everything in their system. All their files, emails, everything. And if the security system is connected, I'll have that too."

"Good. Time is of the essence, Ramesh."

"Understood."

"Thank you." John ended the call. The faint wisp of a plan was forming in his subconscious. He could feel it even if he couldn't make out the details. All he could do was take one step at a time and let the outcome look after itself.

He had another call to make.

"*Bom dia!*"

"John! Is everything okay?"

John smiled at the sound of Adriana's voice. "Yeah. All good. How are you?"

"Missing you, of course." John could hear the sounds of a busy office in the background.

"I miss you too. Hopefully not long now."

"Good, good. Tell me what's happening."

John filled her in on the events of the past two days, leaving nothing out. Adriana listened quietly, not interrupting once until he had finished. "So um... the policeman... Rajiv is going to help you?"

"As much as he can. His hands are tied to some extent, but he knows what Atman is really like now. He believes me." John sighed, "But the reality is it's going to be down to me."

"How about this guy, Trevor?"

"He's determined. I can see it in his eyes... I... recognise it."

"Hmmm." Adriana was quiet for a moment. "Do you think he will agree to be interviewed?"

"I'll ask him. I don't see why not."

"Because if we can make his sister's allegations public, then maybe that will pressure the authorities into doing something."

"Yeah," John exhaled and paced to the end of the verandah, pausing at the end with one hand on his hip, the other holding the phone to his ear, and he stared down at the ground. "It's worth a try, but it will take time."

"I know. I just feel helpless here and need to do something."

"Yeah. I'll check with him, and then you can interview him over the phone. At least get the ball rolling. I've got Ramesh working on gaining access to their computers, so hopefully he'll come up with something for you, too."

"Ramesh? The guy in Dubai who helped us with the Syria trip?"

"Yes, that's him."

"Good. Then wait, John. Between us, we'll work something out, raise awareness, get the local media involved. Why put yourself at risk if you don't have to?"

"Let's see. I don't think I have time to wait."

"John, be careful."

John chuckled. "I'm always careful, don't worry."

"That's all I'll do until this is over."

"It'll be over soon. I know it. He has to be stopped, Adriana."

"I know."

John glanced at his watch. "Hey, I have to go. I'll send you Trevor's number if he agrees."

"I love you, John. Be careful."

"I love you too. I'll call again soon."

John ended the call, closed his eyes and took a deep breath, picturing Adriana standing in front of him. When they were apart, it felt like a piece of him was missing. But he had to do this, before someone else's Adriana was assaulted, abused, or murdered.

## 71

"Sir."

"Manjunath, what is it?" Rajiv closed the door of the Bolero and turned to look at his constable. He frowned, the young man visibly agitated. "Has something happened?"

Manjunath looked around nervously, his eyes roaming the ashram carpark, then the pathway leading into the ashram, before finally settling back on Rajiv. Despite them being alone, he stepped forward and lowered his voice.

"Sir, you told me to keep my eyes and ears open."

"Yes," Rajiv replied, keeping his impatience in check.

"Well, I overheard that manager man... um... Manoj?"

"Yes, Manoj."

"I was sweeping the verandah of the offices and he was walking past and got a phone call. On his mobile."

"And?" Rajiv gritted his teeth. He wished Manjunath would hurry up and get to the point.

"He was speaking Kannada, but then when he saw me, he switched to Tulu. No-one here knows I understand."

"Yes, Manjunath, get to the point."

Manjunath gulped and looked around again. "Yes, sir. Um, I heard him ask, 'are you sure he's dead?'"

"What?" An acidic bile rose in the back of Rajiv's throat.

"Yes, sir."

"What else did he say?"

"Umm…" Manjunath frowned as he tried to remember what he'd heard. "Nothing else. Just 'well done.' Yes, that's all."

Rajiv pulled out his phone and dialled John's number

"What time was this?" he barked.

Manjunath flinched. "About ten minutes ago, sir."

Rajiv's frown deepened. He had been with John ten minutes ago. He stared at the phone screen. "Come on, pick up, pick up."

"Rajiv?"

"Oh, thank God." Rajiv felt a huge weight fall away. "You're alive."

"Last time I checked. What's going on?"

Rajiv gestured with his hand for Manjunath to wait and stepped away until he was out of earshot. "My driver overheard the manager here asking on the phone if someone was dead. I thought it was you."

There was silence from John's end, then a curse.

"Rajiv, how far is Trevor's guesthouse from you? I just called him and he wasn't picking up."

"I'm going there now." Rajiv didn't wait for an answer. He spun around, tossed the car keys to Manjunath and bellowed at the security guard, "Open the gate!"

## 72

The guesthouse was only a five-minute drive from the ashram. Manjunath, at Rajiv's urging, managed it in four and half.

But Rajiv knew in his gut it wouldn't be fast enough.

His door was open before the Bolero had pulled to a complete stop and he leaped out and ran into the property. A modest single-story house occupied the road end of the property and sitting on the front step was a startled looking elderly woman. She had been cleaning rice until Rajiv burst in through the gate, but now was frozen on the spot, her mouth hanging open, eyes wide in surprise.

"Police. Where is the foreigner staying?" Rajiv demanded.

The old woman gulped and then jerked her head over her shoulder. "Last room. By the beach."

Rajiv rushed past her down a path that ran along the side of the house toward the end of the property. Past the house, the land opened up into unkempt sandy ground dotted with coconut palms and a few straggly casuarina trees. At the end near the beach was a low set concrete building under a clay-tiled roof, a wide verandah running along the front. Three doors and three windows suggested three guest rooms. All this Rajiv took in a split second as he sprinted toward the last room. The door was closed but unlocked, and without knocking, he pushed it open and stopped dead in his tracks.

Trevor was in the room, but Rajiv was too late. His body was hanging from the ceiling fan.

"Fuck!" Rajiv roared, then stepped forward, grabbed Trevor around the legs with one arm and supported his weight while reaching up and checking for a pulse on the side of his neck. Nothing.

"Shit, shit, mother-fucking bastards!" Rajiv didn't normally swear. In fact, he prided himself on maintaining control of his language, but now seemed as good a time as any to make an exception.

"Sir?"

Rajiv heard Manjunath's footsteps as he, too, approached at a run. "Stay outside," he shouted and slowly released his hold on Trevor's legs and stepped backward toward the door. Realising his heart was hammering in his chest, he took a deep breath, exhaled slowly, then did it again. He backed out of the doorway and shook his head. Such a waste of life.

"Sir?" Manjunath spoke again and Rajiv turned to look at his constable standing behind him, peering over his shoulder at the body in the room.

"How did you know where to come?"

Rajiv couldn't speak, rage coursing through his body. He clenched and unclenched his fists, the deep breathing having had no effect on calming him down. After a moment, he forced the words out. "Speak to the lady at the front. Ask her if anyone has been here within the last hour. Get as much detail as you can."

"But sir..." Manjunath's eyes flicked over his shoulder again as he looked back into the room. "It's not suicide?"

"No."

Manjunath gulped, nodded, and headed back toward the front of the property.

Rajiv turned back to look into the room. He knew it wasn't suicide. The young Australian had been angry, but not suicidal. There was no way his mood could have changed in the couple of hours since Rajiv had last seen him. And then, of course, there was the phone call Manjunath had overheard. Still shaking his head, he muttered, "Bastards."

He took another deep breath, then pulled out his phone, moved into the doorway and took a photo of the body. He then examined the door and its frame. No signs of forced entry. Entering the room, he ran his experienced eye over the scene in front of him. A thin cotton towel was knotted around Trevor's neck, the other end tied to the support shaft of the ceiling fan. An overturned stool lay near Trevor's feet, which hung just inches above the floor. Unfortunately, Rajiv had seen this before... many times.

At first glance, it looked like a textbook suicide. There was no sign of a struggle in the room. The bedcover was slightly ruffled, but that just looked like Trevor had been resting in the heat of the day. A backpack and a battered guitar stood leaning against the wall in the corner, and a pair of rubber flip-flops outside the door were the only personal possessions he could see. The young man certainly traveled light. Rajiv moved around the body and with his elbow, pushed the bathroom door open. A bar of soap, toothbrush and a half-used tube of toothpaste were the only things inside. He walked back out just as Manjunath appeared in the doorway.

"Sir, she said no-one had been in or out of the property, apart from the foreigner."

"His name is Trevor," Rajiv growled.

"Ahh... yes, sir," Manjunath hesitated. "Mr... ah Trevor came back just after midday and had been in his room all afternoon. She said she cooked lunch for him, fish curry and rice, which he ate here on the verandah, then heard him playing the guitar for a while and then assumed he had gone to sleep. He often took a nap in the afternoon."

Rajiv nodded and took another look around the room.

"So, sir, it must be suicide if no-one else has been here."

Rajiv exhaled forcefully, then walked out of the room, pushing his way past Manjunath. He walked to the end of the verandah, then looked to his right toward the front of the property, then to the left toward the beach. "They must have come from there."

"They?" Manjunath asked, clearly confused.

"You've been wanting a promotion for a while, haven't you, Manjunath?"

The young constable straightened up. "Yes, sir."

"Well then, start thinking." Rajiv glared at him. "We have a young man eating his lunch, then playing the guitar. Does that sound like a suicidal man to you?"

"No, sir."

"You've overheard a phone call where someone asks 'are you sure he's dead,' and we have a dead body."

"Yes, sir."

"So think."

Manjunath said nothing for a while. He looked into the room, his brow furrowed, then eventually turned back to look at Rajiv. "But how, sir?"

"I don't know, I don't know." Rajiv's phone buzzed in his hand and he answered it without looking at the screen, instinctively knowing who was calling. "I'm too late. He's dead."

"Fuck!"

"Yes." Rajiv glanced at Manjunath, then moved out of earshot. "They've made it look like suicide. He's hanging from the fan."

"Bastards!" John cursed again.

"I'm looking for clues, but the room is clean. No signs of struggle. No-one seen entering the property."

"It was them, you know that," John said.

"I know, John. I know."

"Such a waste. The fuckers."

Rajiv sighed and looked back toward the room. "I'm going to be tied up here for a while. Promise me, John, that you won't do anything stupid while I'm away."

He waited for a reply, but John was silent.

"John? Did you hear me?"

"I heard you," John sighed loudly. "But I'm going to do something soon, Rajiv. They have to be stopped."

"I agree, John. But wait for me."

The line went dead. Rajiv rubbed his forehead, then turned and looked back toward the room. Manjunath stood just outside the doorway, staring at the body of the young Australian still hanging from the ceiling fan. Rajiv gritted his teeth and moved back toward the room. He couldn't worry about John right now. He had a job to do.

## 73

Aarthi thrust two fingers down the back of her throat and instantly felt her body heave as she triggered the gag reflex and emptied the contents of her stomach into the toilet bowl.

She coughed and spat, then heard a concerned voice in the background.

"Are you okay? Should I come in?"

Aarthi shook her head even though Priyanka was on the other side of the locked bathroom door and couldn't see her. "No," she gasped, "it's okay." She repeated the exercise, this time dry retching as her body struggled to empty itself. Stomach acid burnt her throat and beads of sweat coated her forehead. Satisfied she had done enough, she pushed herself to her feet, flushed the toilet and then moved to the washbasin, where she washed her hand and rinsed out her mouth. She peered at her reflection in the cracked and stained mirror. The whites of her eyes had reddened, and her face was pale with the effort of vomiting. Good.

She unlocked the door and pulled it open. Priyanka

hovered just outside, her eyes wide, worry written across her otherwise pretty features. "Should I call for the nurse?"

Aarthi shook her head, then slowly shuffled out of the room toward the bed. Priyanka held her by the arm and helped her, then eased her down onto the bed.

Aarthi laid back on the pillow, her eyes closed, her forehead creased, mouth slightly opened as her chest moved up and down with uneven breaths. "It must be something I ate at lunchtime."

"Oh, no." Priyanka sat down on the edge of the bed and held Aarthi's hand.

"I'm really sorry, Priyanka, I wanted to come with you to see Atman, but..." She winced and grabbed her stomach as if something were moving inside. She was laying it on thick, but hoped the innocent young woman would believe her.

"No, no, don't you worry about that. Just rest." Priyanka squeezed her hand. "Your health is more important."

Aarthi opened her eyes and gazed up at Priyanka. For an instant Aarthi felt a pang of regret at her deception, but then she reminded herself that she could, at the very least, be saving the girl's innocence, if not her life. "You're so kind to me, Priyanka, thank you."

"It's nothing, Aarthi. I... I wish there was more that I can do. Are you sure I shouldn't fetch the nurse?"

"No, no..." Aarthi panted, "I'm sure it's just food poisoning. I just need to give it time."

Suddenly, the girl's face lit up. "I know what. I will go to Atman and ask him to heal you."

Aarthi's stomach actually churned this time. She thought fast. "There's no need to trouble him. He's a very busy man."

"He will do it. I know he will."

"No..." Aarthi said a little too forcefully and Priyanka

flinched. Aarthi forced a smile. "I mean, remember… yesterday how he said he is only the guide and the true power lies within each of us?" She gripped Priyanka's hand. "This is the perfect opportunity to prove his teachings right."

Priyanka frowned, then her face relaxed, and she nodded slowly, "Yes, I think so."

Aarthi continued. She had to make sure Priyanka stayed with her. "Will you please stay with me? We can pray together and with your help, I will get better."

Priyanka gazed back at Aarthi with big dark solemn eyes, then she nodded and smiled. "Of course I will."

## 74

John's knuckles turned white as his grip tightened on the phone, the anger burning inside him looking for an outlet. He looked around for something to hit, something to kick, and just stopped himself from hurling his phone off the verandah into the sand. "Arrrgggh, fuck, fuck, fuck!" he roared to no-one in particular. His eyes roamed the ocean, seeking a glimpse of the dolphins again. "Where are you now, when I fucking need you?" he shouted.

But there was nothing.

A crow hopped across the sand, stopping in front of him, and cocked its head to look at him before pecking at something unseen, then flying away.

"God, huh." John scoffed. "If you exist, then why the hell do you allow things like this to happen?" He shook his head, closed his eyes, and took a deep breath. Exhaling slowly, he consciously scanned his body, relaxing his jaw, his neck, his grip on the phone. He tilted his head from side to side, stretching his neck, rolled his shoulders back, and then bounced up and down on the balls of his feet. Blinking his eyes open, he declared out loud. "Right then. It's down to me."

At that moment, his phone vibrated with an incoming message. *I'm in.*

Surprised, he tapped on the screen and called the sender back.

"John."

"That was quick, Ramesh."

Ramesh chuckled. "Yeah, I appealed to two of man's strongest vices. Greed and lust."

"What do you mean?"

"I wasn't sure who would open the email, so I sent an email offering money and a different one promising nude pics of a famous Indian actress. Someone in the ashram office prefers naked women over wealth."

"Well done."

"They won't think so. The link went nowhere, but now I have access to everything in their system."

"They won't find out?"

"They have no idea, John. In fact..." John heard the sound of computer keys, "whoever it is, is currently browsing Pornhub. Obviously disappointed with the link I sent them."

"Get as much as you can, Ramesh. Things are moving fast here. They've just killed someone else."

"Shit."

"Yeah, so I'm speeding things up. Find out whatever you can, anything incriminating. Files, accounts, call records. I'll text you Adriana's email. Send it on to her. We need to get as much publicity as we can."

"Will do."

"See what you can dig up on the manager, Manoj Shetty, too. He's as dirty as Atman, apparently."

"Guess who is browsing Pornhub?"

"Huh. Doesn't surprise me. Now, can you access the cameras?"

John heard typing again before Ramesh replied. "No."

"Damn it." John rubbed his face. He'd have to find another way to disable the security system. "Okay. Do what you can and keep me posted."

He ended the call and dialled Adriana.

"Hey."

"Hey... umm."

"Is everything okay?"

John grimaced. "No. They killed Trevor."

"What?"

"Yeah. I don't know how, but Rajiv is there now. They've made it look like suicide, but... they killed him."

*"Meu Deus."*

"Hmmm."

"That's... awful, John. Are... are you sure?"

"I'm sure. Listen, Ramesh is in their system. If he finds anything, he'll send it to you. You know what to do."

"Yes, but... John, what will you do now?"

John shrugged, then realising she couldn't see him, added, "I don't know, but..." he took a deep breath, "I'm going to end it tonight."

## 75

The landlady had seen nothing. That had to mean they had come from the beach. He instructed Manju to keep the room secure and wait for the ambulance, then he stepped off the verandah into the sand. There were footprints everywhere, going, coming, crisscrossing the sand. There was no way of knowing which ones were fresh, or which ones belonged to the killer or killers.

Rajiv assumed it was two. Trevor was a well-built surfer. It would take two men to hold him up and hang him from the fan. But how had they subdued him in the first place? There were no signs of struggle, no evidence of a fight. Rajiv frowned and walked further away from the room, out onto the dune that separated the guesthouse land from the beach. He stood on the top of the dune and shaded his eyes with his hand. The sun was low, directly into his eyes, and he turned his head to look up and down the beach. Apart from a pack of stray dogs and several wading birds standing just above the high-water mark, the beach was deserted. Rajiv dropped his hand, balled it into a fist, and thumped his thigh with frustration.

He turned back to face the guesthouse, and something caught his eye. Something in the sand glinting in the sun. He stepped closer and knelt down to take a closer look, then nodded to himself. That's how they did it.

He stuck the end of his long cotton shirt in his mouth and worked at it with his teeth until he made a hole, then tore a strip off the shirt with his hands. Covering his fingertips with the strip of cloth, he picked up the item between his thumb and forefinger and walked back to the guesthouse.

Inspector Prakash Rao was standing outside the room, hands on his hips, looking inside. Behind him was another constable and two men in dirty white coats holding a folded stretcher. Prakash turned as Rajiv stepped up onto the verandah, "He didn't seem suicidal to me."

"He wasn't. Do you have an evidence bag?"

Prakash stared at Rajiv for a moment, then turned to his constable and with a jerk of his head instructed him to provide Rajiv with a bag.

Rajiv stepped closer and held out his hand. "Check this for prints and the contents."

Prakash looked down at the syringe in Rajiv's hand and frowned. "Where was this?"

Rajiv nodded toward the beach, "Back there."

"Drug addicts. Shooting up on the beach."

Rajiv gave him a look, then pushed past and stepped into the room. He approached the hanging body and took one of Trevor's hands in his. "Does anyone have a flashlight?"

"My phone, sir." Manju stepped forward, turned on the phone flashlight and shone it at the hand. Rajiv checked the webbing between the fingers, then took the other hand.

Nothing. Squatting down, he peered at Trevor's feet. "Bring the light closer, Manju."

"Sir."

Rajiv held Trevor's right foot in both hands and separated the toes. In the webbing, between the big toe and the next one, he found a puncture wound. "See that." Rajiv took out his own phone and took a photo, then released Trevor's foot, and stood up. Turning to face Prakash standing in the doorway, he said, "I suggest you do a toxicology report on the body." He pointed at the evidence bag in the constable's hand. "I bet the contents of that syringe match what's in his body."

Prakash stared at Rajiv, his mouth slightly open, then swallowed. "How did you know what to look for?"

Rajiv shrugged. "There's no sign of struggle. He had to be drugged. It's what I would have done."

"But what made you think it wasn't suicide?"

"He wasn't suicidal, Prakash. You know that. He wasn't feeling sorry for himself. He was angry. He wanted revenge."

"But then… who would want him dead?"

"Who do you think, Prakash? Who was he angry with?"

"No, come on… that's a stretch."

"Is it? Why do you think we were pressured to release him? It's much easier to have him killed here than if he was in the station."

Prakash was shaking his head. Eventually, he sighed. "Yeah. I'll order the tests, but… you and I know it won't go anywhere."

Rajiv walked toward the door and then turned back to look at the young man, his body turning slowly in the breeze from the open window. "No," he agreed. "I'm sure it won't."

## 76

"Sir, can I ask you a question?" Manjunath asked as he started up the vehicle.

Rajiv nodded, deep in thought. He had left the crime scene in Prakash's capable hands. It was his jurisdiction and Rajiv had made his point about it being a suspicious death.

"Why didn't you mention the phone call I overheard?"

Rajiv turned his attention back to his driver. "Because we can't prove it. It will be your word against Manoj, and I don't want to alert him. I'd rather find some other way."

"Yes, sir." Manjunath pulled out onto the road, did a three-point turn and they headed back toward the ashram.

"We can prove that Trevor had been injected with something, though."

"So what do we do now, sir?"

"We go back to the ashram and carry on as normal. We have no proof. No suspects. So there is little we can do right now."

Manjunath remained silent, a deep frown on his forehead, his eyes focused on the road ahead. They had pulled up outside the ashram gate before he spoke again, "But, sir, why would they kill him? This..." he gestured at the gate, "this is an ashram. These are good people. People of God."

"Hmmmm. Not everything is what it seems, Manjunath. Just keep your eyes and ears open. Anything suspicious... come and tell me."

Manjunath nodded, still worried.

"Now give that horn a blast. The watchman obviously hasn't seen us arrive."

Manjunath tooted the horn and a short while later, the gate swung open. The guard, Mani, was rubbing his eyes, as if he had just woken up, but Rajiv ignored it. It didn't matter anymore. The threat to the ashram was from inside, not outside.

Manjunath pulled up alongside the entrance arch and stopped.

"Don't say a word to anyone, Manju. Act normal, but be alert."

"Do you think something else will happen, sir?"

"I hope not, Manju, I hope not." Rajiv climbed out of the Bolero and closed the door. His phone vibrated in his hand and he glanced at the screen. *Aarthi*. His heart jumped.

"Is everything okay?"

"Yes, yes," Aarthi replied in a low voice. "I've pretended to be sick and asked Priyanka to look after me, so she doesn't go to see Atman."

"Good idea. But why are you whispering? Is she nearby?"

"No," Aarthi's voice became normal, and she chuckled. "I guess I was getting too involved in the secrecy. She's gone to tell the manager that she can't see Atman because I am ill."

"Manoj?"

"Yes, why? Is something wrong?"

"Shit. Sorry. Um... I..."

"What's the matter?"

"Don't worry, I'll sort it out. Just stay where you are. Keep up the act."

"Rajiv?"

Rajiv ended the call and hurried down the path into the ashram. He reached the administration building, leapt up onto the verandah and rattled the door to Manoj's office. It was locked. He jogged along the verandah, jumped back onto the path and hurried toward the women's block.

Aarthi's room was the second from the end on the ground floor and as he approached, he saw the chubby frame of Manoj walking in the door. Rajiv hesitated at the foot of the verandah. He had told no one that Aarthi was his wife, preferring to keep that information secret. But Manoj had spotted his wedding ring, so he knew he was married, and perhaps Atman had also told him. Rajiv clenched his fists. No, her safety and that of Priyanka were more important than anonymity.

He jumped up the two steps onto the verandah and hurried toward her room. Stopping in the doorway, he looked inside to see Aarthi lying in her bed, a young woman, presumably Priyanka, sitting beside her, holding her hand. Manoj was standing beside the bed and looked up as Rajiv filled the door frame.

"Rajiv?" He looked puzzled. "Can I help you?"

"Is everything okay here?"

"Yes." Manoj smiled down at Aarthi. "Just a bout of food poisoning, I think. Nothing our nurse can't handle. I'll send her over right away."

"Thank you," Aarthi whispered.

Rajiv avoided making eye contact, instead keeping his

focus on Manoj. Aarthi was convincing, but he didn't trust his own expressions.

"Mr Manoj, sir, I... I... won't come to the meditation." Priyanka spoke up. "I will stay here and look after Aarthi."

Manoj smiled and rested a hand on her shoulder. "Thats okay, *beta,*" he replied, using the Hindi word for daughter.

Rajiv ground his teeth together.

"But you must go and see Atmanji later. He is expecting you."

Aarthi shot Rajiv a worried look, and he cleared his throat. "I ah... I think it's a good idea if she stays here. Maybe... Madam," Rajiv decided to preserve anonymity for as long as he could, "maybe she will need something."

"There's nothing to worry about, Rajiv. The nurse will be here, and besides, it's very important for this child's," Manoj smiled down at Priyanka again, "spiritual development, that she sees Atmanji. She will see significant benefits in her spiritual growth."

Rajiv balled his fist and bit down on the inside of his cheek. He counted to ten before responding. "She can do that tomorrow, can't she? Better she is here while," he glanced at Aarthi, "Madam is unwell."

Manoj frowned and studied Rajiv's face for a moment. "Atmanji knows best, Rajiv. If he says tonight, then there is a reason." He held up his hands and shrugged and smiled at the same time. "Who are we to question great beings like him?"

Rajiv looked at Priyanka. She was a beautiful young lady, and her eyes brimmed with excitement. He glanced at Aarthi, who looked back with a deep frown, waiting for him to say something. Turning to Manoj, he nodded. He would have to find another way.

## 77

John had been busy since Rajiv called. He still didn't have a plan, but knew that if he kept taking steps, the path would unfold before him.

Standing now in the darkness by the gate to his guesthouse, he checked he had everything he might need. He was dressed in a white cotton *kurta* and pants; the uniform worn by the ashram residents, and readily available in the local shops. Over his shoulder he carried a sling bag made from recycled rice sacks. He had been growing out his beard since he left Lisbon, and his tan had deepened since arriving in India. Dressed as he was, and with the smattering of Indian words he could throw into a conversation, he would easily pass as a long-term resident. He lifted the flap of the sling bag and checked the contents. Hidden under a cotton scarf were a flashlight, a pair of pliers with a wire cutter, and some zip ties. Rounding off his 'tool kit' was a heavy wrench. It was the only 'weapon' he could lay his hands on.

Rajiv pulled up outside the gate in the police Bolero and beckoned him over. "Get in the back and cover yourself."

John opened the rear passenger door and climbed in, wedging himself down between the seats. He reached up and pulled a cotton sheet from the seat and covered himself.

"Everyone is in the meditation, but it's better to be safe right now."

"Yeah. It finishes at eight, right?"

"Yes."

John felt the vehicle move away and then a jolt in his spine as a wheel hit a pothole. "Hey, mind the bumps, Rajiv. You'll kill me before I get inside."

"Sorry."

"So what time is the girl going to the bungalow?"

"Eight-thirty."

John wriggled his arm free and checked his watch. "So it's now seven thirty. Doesn't give me much time."

Rajiv didn't reply and John could hear him changing gear and the vehicle lurch as he avoided the worst of the potholes.

Eventually, he asked, "What you are going to do?"

John winced, not from the rough road, but because he really didn't know what to do. "Ah... I don't know. I'll think of something."

"Have faith?"

"Huh, yeah. Tell me, Rajiv, what's your role in this going to be?"

John felt the vehicle slow and then pull off the road. Rajiv kept the engine running, but said nothing for a moment. Then John felt him moving in his seat, then saw his head as Rajiv adjusted his position to look back and down at John. "I also don't know John."

There wasn't enough light for John to see Rajiv's expression, but he could hear the tension in his voice as he continued, "I have to be careful. I want the same thing you do, but

I can't afford for it to come back on me. So..." he hesitated, then exhaled loudly, "I'll play it by ear. Depending on what happens, I'll help you however I can without compromising my role as..."

"A cop."

Rajiv sighed again. "A cop. Yes."

"Well, my friend, I suppose I can't ask for more than that, can I?"

John could see Rajiv still looking at him, then his head moved, and the vehicle began moving again.

"Once inside, I'll distract the watchman while you get out of the car."

"Ok. And the cameras?"

John heard a noise as if Rajiv was drumming his fingers on the steering wheel. After a moment, he said, "I'll unplug the system in the guard hut. But I can't do anything about the screens in the bungalow."

"Okay. It will have to do, I suppose. Maybe it will give me a head start."

The vehicle slowed. "I'm at the gate now. Wait for my signal."

## 78

John pulled the sheet over his head and made himself as small as possible, not an easy task in the cramped confines between the seats. He heard Rajiv's voice and strained to hear the conversation, but couldn't follow it. John recognised the language, Kannada, but his knowledge of the language only extended to a few words. Another voice replied, then he heard the scuff of a foot on gravel and he tensed.

He heard footsteps again, this time closer to the vehicle. It sounded like flip-flops, but then he heard the person passing by and then the sound of their flip-flops on the concrete path leading into the ashram.

There was another crunch on gravel and then Rajiv's low voice.

"Okay, John."

The rear passenger door on the side away from the cameras above the gate, opened, and John felt a waft of warm air. He pulled the sheet off his face and looked up. Rajiv was holding the door open, his eyes darting nervously around. "Hurry."

With difficulty, John pulled himself upright and then hauled himself out of the car. He grabbed the sling bag from the rear seat and looked around.

"Coast is clear?"

Rajiv nodded and eased the car door closed with a click. "I sent the guard off on a false errand, and my driver will be in the meditation hall with the rest of them."

John nodded and pursed his lips.

As if reading his mind, Rajiv asked, "What do we do now?"

"You keep a low profile. It's better that when anything happens, it's a surprise for you."

Rajiv grimaced, but nodded.

John reached out his hand. "Thank you Rajiv. This will be over soon."

Rajiv looked down at John's outstretched hand, then grabbed it and instead of shaking his hand, he pulled John closer and embraced him. "Good luck, John. Be careful."

John slapped him on the back. "I'm always careful."

Rajiv released his grip and held John at arm's length. John held his gaze, then Rajiv nodded, gave John's shoulders a reassuring squeeze, then turned and walked away up the path into the ashram.

John took a breath, adjusted the sling bag onto his shoulder, and then checked his watch. He had thirty minutes.

"Right, John Hayes," he muttered. "It's all up to you."

## 79

Manoj Shetty frowned. The computer was unusually slow this evening. The screen kept hanging, and the mouse was unresponsive.

He sighed and drummed his fingertips on the desktop as he waited for the file to load. It had been a productive day. The loose end that had been the woman's brother had been dealt with, and nothing linked back to him or the ashram. He allowed himself a smile. Guruji would be proud of him... if he knew. There were some things he didn't share with Atman. Why trouble him with the murky details of running a successful ashram? He was above all that. He had to deal with things on higher levels, different dimensions, and not trouble himself with the irritations and distractions of mere mortals. That's why he had Manoj and Georges. They were there to protect him, to keep him free from the distractions of the earthly realm, so he could do the greater work he had been put on earth for.

Manoj was proud of his role. He could think of nothing greater than being in the service of a divine being like

Atman, no matter what it entailed. Everything he did was for the greater good of mankind.

The screen flickered, and the file finally loaded. Sitting forward, he ran his eyes over the screen. The final loose end. He moved the mouse and right clicked. *Move to Bin.*

There was a nervous tap on the door and he looked up, momentarily distracted. "What is it, Mani?"

Mani cleared his throat. "You asked for me, sir?"

Manoj frowned. "What are you talking about?"

Mani dipped his head and stared down at the floor.

"Come on, speak up."

"The policeman, Rajiv Sir..." he mumbled.

"Yes?"

"He said you asked for me."

"No. I didn't. You're confused. Have you been drinking again?"

Mani looked up, shaking his head violently. "No, sir, no, sir." He pinched the flesh of his throat between his thumb and forefinger. "God promise, sir."

Manoj glared at him, then made a flicking movement with his hand as if shooing away a fly. "Go back to your post. If I need you, I'll tell you myself," he growled.

Mani dipped his head, his eyes still on the floor. "Yes, sir."

Manoj continued glaring at him as he backed out of the door and disappeared from sight, then shook his head. Irritating old man. He's getting senile, he thought as he looked back at his computer. Probably time to replace him.

His hand moved to the mouse again, and he clicked *Empty Bin.*

Satisfied, he sat back in his chair. Good. All records of the Australian woman had now been deleted. Good riddance. She should have kept quiet like the others. Not everyone got chosen by Atman, but most of those who did realised how lucky they were to be selected. They appreciated it for the blessing it was.

Hopefully, the girl this evening would do the same. She was a pretty young thing, and Manoj could understand why Atman had chosen her. He would have done the same if he'd been in Atman's position.

The screen on his monitor flickered again, and he frowned. He'd have to get the IT guy in tomorrow.

## 80

Ramesh grinned. The guy was an amateur. He entered a command on his keyboard and looked back at the bank of screens in front of him. On one screen was a mirror of Manoj's computer.

Ramesh shook his head and spoke out loud, "Too late, you fat fuck." Ramesh had already copied everything in the ashram system onto one of the hard drives in his office. Every file, every document, every email. His eyes moved to the other screen, where the feed from Manoj's web cam played. He could see him frowning and then heard a curse, and the feed shook as he thumped the monitor.

"That won't help." Ramesh chuckled. The system in the ashram was old and clunky, and Ramesh guessed that his activity was slowing it down. It couldn't be helped, but at least he had copied everything.

He watched Manoj push back his chair and stand up, then walk toward the door and turn off the light in the office.

Ramesh's grin widened, and his fingers hovered over the

keyboard. Time to add something of his own. He entered a couple of commands and then sat back in his chair to watch the files upload. "Let's see how you deal with this."

## 81

John walked over to the guardroom and stepped inside the open door. He stared at the TV screen that had been showing the feed from the security cameras. It was blank; the cables unplugged. John traced the cables to where they ran down the wall and beneath the security guard's desk. There he found the hard drive that had been recording the feed. He pulled it out and dumped it on the desktop with the cables.

Spotting the key cabinet, he opened the door and ran his eyes over the hooks inside. Ignoring the motorcycle keys, he removed a large bunch which looked like it might be useful, and slipped it into his bag. There was a cigarette lighter lying next to a packet of cigarettes on the desk and he pocketed that too. It might come in handy later. Then, with one last look around, he tucked the hard drive and cables under his arm and stepped outside. He walked over to the well in the corner of the car park and tossed them in. They hit the water below with a satisfying splash and sank out of sight.

What next?

He looked toward the generator room. In Sri Lanka he

had disabled the automatic generator back-up and turned off the power supply to the ashram. Could he do that again? If he did, would that make them suspicious? John dithered for a moment and then decided to do nothing for now. His primary aim was to get into the bungalow while everyone was at the meditation, and time was running out.

Someone stepped out into the carpark and John slipped back into the shadow thrown by the trees near the well. The security guard crossed the carpark and walked into the guardroom.

*Damn.* John cursed under his breath. He had hoped for more time. He pushed his way through the undergrowth and followed the wall separating the ashram from Atman's private compound until he reached the path that led to the bungalow. Slipping through the gap, he stepped sideways into the planting that ran along the boundary and squatted down out of sight. He checked his watch. Still fifteen minutes before the meditation finished.

There was movement inside the bungalow, and he watched for a moment, hoping for another glimpse. He guessed it was the staff, but wanted to make sure it wasn't Georges or Max. He saw movement again. One of the staff. Good. He wasn't too worried about them. Dressed as he was, he planned to bluff his way in as an ashram member. If he was confident and forceful enough, he was pretty sure the staff wouldn't have the guts to turn him away. He took a breath to calm his nerves, then stood up, straightened his *kurta*, and stepped out onto the path.

## 82

Rajiv had stepped off the path and behind a clump of coconut trees as soon as he saw the security guard leave Manoj's office. He doubted the elderly man would ask him why he had been sent on a false mission, the fear of police authority being enough to deter questions, but it was easier for Rajiv to avoid the situation altogether.

He waited until he was out of sight and was about to rejoin the path when he saw Manoj leave his office and lock the door. Staying where he was, he watched the ashram manager make his way down the steps and then follow the path toward the meditation hall. Rajiv gave him a sufficient gap, then followed slowly after him. He wanted to make sure he knew where he was if John was about to start something.

Sure enough, Manoj reached the hall, slipped off his sandals outside and walked inside. Rajiv checked his wristwatch. Still fifteen minutes to go.

The sound of hurried footsteps disturbed the peace of the deserted ashram, and he turned to see the security guard hurrying toward him.

The old man stopped in front of him, his eyes darting from Rajiv to the meditation hall and back again.

"Is something wrong?"

The guard gulped. "Yes, sir."

"Well?"

The guard shot another look at the meditation hall.

"Where is Manoj Sir?"

"He's inside." Rajiv gestured toward the hall.

Mani hesitated, then looked at Rajiv. "Someone has damaged the TV."

Rajiv kept his expression neutral and played for time. "What TV?"

"The security TV, sir." Mani wrung his hands and hopped from one foot to the other. "In the guardroom."

"Really?" He placed a comforting hand on the guard's shoulder and said, "I'm sure it's nothing. Why don't you show me?"

The guard shot one last look at the entrance to the hall, then nodded and hurried back the way he had come. Rajiv slowly followed after him. He didn't know what John was up to, but the longer he could delay any reaction, the better.

The guard was already hovering outside the guardroom by the time he reached it. He was still wringing his hands together, and Rajiv gave him a smile. "Don't worry, Mani. I'm sure it's nothing."

Mani nodded and gulped at the same time, then stepped away from the door to allow Rajiv to enter.

Rajiv stepped inside and stared at the blank TV screen. Playing dumb, he asked, "Is the power on?"

"Sir, the power cable is missing."

"Hmmm. Strange."

"And the box."

"What box?"

"There was a box under the desk. Manoj Sir said it records the cameras. It's gone."

Rajiv knelt down and pretended to inspect the space under the desk. "Oh yes, I see what you mean."

"Sir, it wasn't me. I swear. Manoj Sir will kill me."

Rajiv's knees cracked as he stood up. "I'll tell him, don't worry. Now, are you sure it was here earlier?"

"Yes, sir."

"When did you last notice it?"

"Sir, just before you came back, it was here. I was watching the screen."

"Strange." Rajiv turned to look around the room. "Is there anything else missing?"

"No, sir. I mean, I don't think so."

"You don't think so?"

"I haven't checked, sir. I saw the screen and then I came to tell Manoj… I mean you, sir."

"Okay. Not to worry. Why don't you look around now and see if there is anything else missing while I look for clues?"

"Clues, sir?"

"Yes." Rajiv smiled. "You know. Signs that someone was here. You can help me."

Mani visibly relaxed, and he bobbed his head from side to side. "Okay, sir, thank you sir."

## 83

John was halfway to the bungalow when a figure stepped out the front door onto the verandah facing the ocean. He didn't know what made him do it, but as soon as he saw movement, John stepped right, off the floodlit path and into the darkness of the lawn. He continued moving slowly to his right, deeper into the shadow, and then crouched down. For a moment he wondered if he had done the right thing as his original plan was to bluff his way in, and to be caught squatting on the lawn in the darkness would be a hard thing to explain.

However, when the figure stepped further forward, he realised his instincts had saved him once again. It was Max. John crouched lower, hoping the young Israeli bodyguard wouldn't turn around, and then slowly, keeping as low to the ground as possible edged further sideways until he was hidden by the corner of the house, then turned and sprinted back toward the boundary wall and dived into the undergrowth.

He stayed as still as possible, catching his breath, hoping the noise and movement had not alerted Max, but when he dared raise his head, he saw Max was still standing on the verandah, one hand on a pillar, gazing out to sea.

John had hoped the bodyguards were at the meditation. There was no way he could bluff his way past Max. He looked down at his outfit. It was almost glowing in the darkness. "Dammit," he whispered. He couldn't get into the house and he was dressed in the worst colour possible for sneaking around in the darkness. He looked up again. Max hadn't moved. "Bugger," he cursed again. Now he was stuck.

## 84

Priyanka shivered with excitement.

She had been reluctant to leave Aarthi when she was unwell, but Mr Manoj, the manager, had insisted Aarthi would be okay. Besides, the nurse was with her now, so if anything happened, she would be looked after.

Manoj led her up the steps onto the bungalow verandah, and Priyanka took a deep breath to calm her nerves. She couldn't believe it. She was actually getting a private audience with her guru, something she never thought would have been possible. But she had worked hard since she had come to the ashram. She had done all the breathing exercises Atman had taught them, had worked on the visualisations and *mantras*, and had felt her meditations getting deeper. In fact, she was sure she had a vision of a goddess the previous day, but as soon as she tried to grasp it in her mind, her meditation had faded away and, despite trying everything, she could not calm her mind again. She had even volunteered for extra chores around the ashram in her free time, Atman explaining that '*Seva*', service to the guru, was extremely important to speed up spiritual progress. And now here she was. About to enter the great guru's private quarters. She tried hard to keep her face neutral, but the excitement was overwhelming and she felt her face breaking into a smile, her cheeks flushing with anticipation.

Manoj paused near the front door as the large foreign man, who always accompanied Atman, appeared in the doorway. He looked Priyanka up and down, then nodded at Manoj.

Manoj opened his mouth as if to say something, but then stepped back and gestured for Priyanka to step forward. "Georges will take you to see Atman now."

Priyanka gulped, then nodded shyly and stepped forward.

"Follow me," was all the large man said to her, then he turned around and walked inside the house.

Priyanka followed quickly after him. She stole a glance to left and right, but didn't register the surroundings, as she hurried to keep up with Georges. She stepped out into an open internal courtyard and followed the covered corridor around the right-hand side. A figure appeared in another doorway and she recognised the other young foreigner. His eyes met hers, then he looked down at the floor and backed into the room. As she passed, she saw he had turned his back and was looking at a black and white television screen on the wall.

At the end of the corridor was a large carved wooden door. Georges stopped and half turned to make sure she was still behind him, then he turned back to the door and entered a code into a keypad.

Priyanka took a moment to admire the carving on the door. It was Lord Krishna, and a thrill ran up her spine. She'd always had a fondness for the Hindu god and had loved the stories about him as a mischievous child stealing butter and getting up to mischief.

Her hands trembled, and she ran them down over her white *kameez*, smoothing out the wrinkles, then took another deep breath as the door beeped and swung open.

Georges turned and gestured for her to walk inside.

"Atman will see you now."

## 85

In a crouching run, John headed for the gap in the wall that led back into the ashram. He paused at the end of the wall and peered around it. Manoj was already down the path, heading back toward the office block. John straightened up, shook out the lactic acid in his quads, then stepped back through into the ashram grounds. He had to move fast.

He had been about to move earlier, once Max had gone back inside the bungalow, but Georges and Atman had appeared on the path, returning from the meditation. He had given them time to enter the house, but then the manager appeared with the young girl. The sight made John's blood boil, and it had been all he could do to restrain himself from leaping out of the garden and assaulting the man and taking the girl away. But that would only have saved her. There would be others. Atman's operation had to be shut down.

While he waited for Manoj to return along the path, the germ of an idea had sprouted in the back of his mind. It wasn't much, but it was all he had right now.

He followed the wall toward the front of the property until he reached the generator room. Where there was a generator, there should be diesel.

He looked at the padlock on the door and checked the manufacturer brand, then pulled the bunch of keys out of his sling bag and searched through them. There were a couple that matched, but it was the third one that worked and the padlock clicked open. He unfastened it from the door, dropped it on the ground, then pulled open the hasp and was about to open the door when he spotted a movement in the corner of his eye. Rajiv had just stepped out of the guardroom and their eyes met.

John hesitated, then motioned for Rajiv to move away. He understood, and held up one finger, signalling for John to wait. John pressed himself against the door, making his profile as small as possible, and held his breath as Rajiv stepped to one side, then guided the security guard out of the room, using his body to prevent the guard from looking in John's direction. He then led him away across the carpark toward the administration building, all the while keeping him engaged in conversation. John waited until they disappeared through the archway, then pushed the door open and stepped inside, the smell of diesel instantly assaulting his nostrils.

There was a light switch to the left of the door and he flicked it on, the light from the single naked bulb filling the room. The generator took up two-thirds of the room, but in the space to the right of the door was a row of jerry cans.

He grabbed the first two, but they were empty. The next two were full, and he picked them up and carried them out the door. He didn't stop to close the door or turn the light off. The quicker he moved, the quicker he could prevent the girl from being assaulted. His shoulders burned with the weight, but he gritted his teeth and continued forward at a shuffling run. By the time he reached the path to Atman's bungalow, though, he had to put the jerry cans down and bent forward, his hands on his knees as he sucked in air. A moment later he forced himself upright, hefted the jerry cans again, then stepped into the garden and turned immediately right, following the wall toward the roadside end of the property. Diesel wasn't as combustible as petrol and needed heat to burn, but John had seen something earlier that might solve the problem.

Reaching the section of wall parallel to the end of the bungalow, he put the cans down and shook his arms out, then picked them up again and, moving as fast as he could, he crossed the lawn to reach the corner of the bungalow. He stopped under the security camera on that corner and looked up. He had dealt with the camera feed in the guardroom, but hoped no one in the bungalow was monitoring the cameras. Anyway, it was too late now.

Unscrewing the cap from one of the jerry cans he splashed diesel on the wall then onto the wooden window frames and shutters then, leaving the full can where it was, poured a trail of diesel from the bungalow toward the parking area and the Range Rover he had noticed earlier. By the time he reached the Range Rover, the can was almost empty, and he splashed the remnants over the tyres.

He still had one can left, and he looked around to see what he could do with it.

## 86

She stepped into the room and was immediately struck by the scent of sandalwood and flowers. The door clicked shut and, startled, she turned and glanced behind her. Georges hadn't followed her in and, unlike the outside, the surface of the door was smooth and there was no handle. She frowned momentarily, but excitement got the better of her and she turned her attention back to the room. There was a flute playing somewhere, the soft gentle sound of the Indian *bansuri*, and once again, she was reminded of the Lord Krishna. The only light came from a flickering array of candles in front of the large altar on the right side of the room. There was a beautiful ebony statue of the Lord Krishna playing the flute and Priyanka felt tears of joy filling her eyes. She blinked the tears away and as her eyes adjusted to the dim light of the room, she realised she was alone. A high-backed armchair similar to the one Atman used on stage sat in front of the temple. A thick oriental carpet in reds and golds covered most of the floor and to the left side of the room was an enormous bed, the silk bedcover shimmering in the candlelight.

A door she hadn't noticed opened in the side wall, light from inside filling the room, then Atman appeared in the doorway. He was drying his hands with a hand towel and he then tossed it behind him and smiled.

Her heart did a dance. She had never been alone with the guru before. She looked down at the floor, her nerves getting the better of her.

"Don't be nervous, my child."

She looked up. He was closer now, still smiling. She smiled back, and he gestured toward the altar.

"Come, sit with me."

Priyanka nodded, and gulped, but her legs felt numb, disconnected from her body. Only when he had walked over to his chair and sat down, did they move. He gestured to the floor in front of him, and she stepped forward and sat at his feet.

He smiled down at her, saying nothing, and she looked away, unable to meet his gaze.

"I am delighted with your progress, my child."

"Thank..." the words caught in her throat. "Thank you, Guruji." She whispered.

"Are you afraid?"

She shook her head but still could not look up.

"There is nothing to be afraid of, my child. We have already been together over many lifetimes. We know each other from before."

This time Priyanka looked up, surprised, but... thrilled.

"Yes, you are almost at the end, my dear. This will be your last life in this form. Soon you will ascend to the higher realms. You will no longer have need of this earthly form."

Priyanka couldn't think of what to say. She just stared back at him, now unable to look away. She couldn't believe this was happening to her. Everything she had read in books, the stories she had been told about the great yogis and saints; it had all seemed so unattainable. But now it was happening to her.

"But... I'm..." she struggled to put her thoughts into words.

Atman smiled, leaned forward and placed a hand on her head. She felt a jolt of electricity run down from the crown of her head to the base of her spine, and she shivered.

"Don't think too much about it. Just be."

Priyanka gulped, still feeling the warmth of his hand on her head. She wished Aarthi had been well enough to come with her. She was surely advanced enough to ascend with her. A thought struck her.

"My mother? What about her?"

Atman smiled again and stroked her hair. "When you ascend, your immediate family members ascend with you. That's how it has always been."

A tear trickled from the corner of her eye and ran down her cheek. She was so happy.

Atman wiped the tear from her cheek.

"There is still some work to do, though. Something is holding you back."

"Oh." His words sent a spike through her heart, and she dropped her head, filled with disappointment. She felt his fingertips under her chin as he tilted her head up to look at him.

"It's okay, my child. I will help you."

Priyanka felt a wave of relief rush through her.

"Come closer, let us begin."

She slid closer.

"Closer."

Again she moved forward until she could feel the heat from his legs radiating into her hers.

"Close your eyes, relax."

She did as he instructed, straightened her spine and slowed her breathing down. The room was pin-drop silent and as she breathed in, the sweet smell of incense filled her lungs. She sensed him moving, changing his position, then felt both his hands on her shoulders pulling her forward.

"Keep your eyes closed, and focus on your breath."

She lengthened her inhalation, just as he had instructed during the meditation, and felt her body sink into the floor as the tension melted away from her.

Suddenly, she heard a pounding on the door and the beep of the electronic lock.

## 87

John spotted the motorcycle parked near the gate and he ran over, lifted it off its kickstand, and then wheeled it next to the Range Rover. Removing the wire cutters from his bag, he felt around beneath the fuel tank of the bike until he found the fuel line, then cut it with the wire cutters. Immediately, the smell of petrol hit his nostrils as the tank drained and he directed the stream of petrol onto the tire he had already splashed with diesel. Once it was empty, he let the bike fall to the ground and then stepped back. Removing the cigarette lighter he had taken from the guardroom, he did a quick check to make sure nothing had splashed on him, then lit the cigarette lighter.

"Damn it," he cursed.

As soon as he took his thumb off the lever, the flame went out. He didn't want to risk standing next to the fuel spill, so he looked around for something he could light. There was a leather saddle bag attached to the motorbike, and he pulled open the flap to look inside.

"Bingo."

John removed what looked like a user manual from the bag, fanned the book open, then with the cigarette lighter, set fire to the corners. Using his body to shield it from the breeze, he held it until the pages caught alight, then stepping as close as he dared, tossed it at the Range Rover's tire and stepped back. The manual hit the tire and bounced off, but it was enough, the petrol igniting with a woomph. John stepped back further, waiting for the flames to take hold as they licked the bodywork.

He glanced back toward the bungalow. He still couldn't believe he hadn't been seen on camera.

"Come on, come on," he muttered, turning his attention back toward the fire. The flames grew higher and thick black smoke began to rise as the rubber of the tyre and the diesel fuel caught alight.

"Yes," he exclaimed, and then turned and ran back to the bungalow. Grabbing the other jerry can, he twisted off the cap and splashed diesel up the walls of the bungalow. He looked back over his shoulder at the Range Rover, flames now climbing from the tyre and covering the rear half of the vehicle. Flames were spreading from the SUV toward the diesel trail he had laid, but it wasn't happening fast enough. He ran back toward the vehicle, getting as close as he could, the heat already scorching his face, and he poured more diesel on the ground in a stream leading back toward the bungalow, then tossed the empty can toward the fire.

He moved closer to the bungalow and waited for the flames to get closer, hoping he would be in time. He needed to flush everyone out of the house.

He watched with fascination as the flames spread to the motorbike, which quickly caught alight. The smell of burning diesel and rubber now filled the air, the thick clouds of black smoke visible even in the darkness.

He heard a shout from the house and he ducked down and moved in a crouching run around the side furthest from the ashram toward the sea-facing verandah.

Reaching the corner, he squatted down. John hoped the diversion would be enough to save the girl, at the very least. If he could somehow put a stop to Atman at the same time, then it would be a bonus.

There was a loud bang as something exploded and he heard more shouts from the house, as well as distant shouts from the ashram. Peering around the corner of the building, he saw the cook and a young Indian boy standing on the verandah looking back toward the burning Range Rover, then the imposing form of Georges joined them. Georges took one glance toward the fire, then started barking instructions, pushing the cook and his companion toward the ashram.

John heard a loud curse, then Georges hurried back inside.

## 88

Priyanka opened her eyes and looked up.

Atman sat in front of her with his shirt open and the top button of his pants unfastened. She stared, unable to comprehend what she was seeing as the pounding on the door stopped and the door swung open. A shaft of bright light entered the room, as well as the smell of something burning.

Atman's attention was on the door and he growled in a tone at odds with the man Priyanka had seen over the past few days.

"What is it?"

Georges stepped through the doorway, ignoring Priyanka sitting on the floor, and said, "There's a fire, sir. The Range Rover."

"Then put it out."

Georges' eyes flicked to Priyanka, as if noticing her for the first time, but his expression didn't change, and he looked back at Atman. "The flames are spreading to the bungalow, sir."

Priyanka gasped, Georges' words finally breaking the

spell, and she pushed herself backwards away from Atman's chair. Atman turned to look at her, his shirt still open, his eyes boring through her. His face was different, as if he was someone else, then his lips curled in a predatory smile. "It's okay, my child. There is nothing to be afraid of." His eyes still on Priyanka, he said, "Georges, have Max take her away. You look after the fire."

"Sir, I'm worried about your safety."

"Do as I say, Georges. I will be perfectly safe."

Priyanka looked from Atman to Georges and then over her shoulder at the open door.

"You are free to go, my child. I will call for you again."

Priyanka pushed herself to her feet and then, with a last glance at Atman, ran for the door, pushing past Georges, and out into the internal courtyard. Her mind was numb, as if she was in a trance, even as her legs carried her toward the front door. It was only as she burst out onto the verandah that tears began to run down her face.

A hand grabbed her arm, and she recognised the other young foreigner. His face was lit with a flickering orange light and he said something to her, but her brain didn't register. There were other sounds, voices, shouting, but over it all was a roaring in her ears, a sound that felt like it was coming from inside her head. Shaking off his grip, she jumped off the verandah and onto the lawn then ran into the darkness toward the sea, putting as much distance between her and the bungalow as possible.

## 89

Ashram residents filled the gateway to the ashram, watching the fire and gesticulating, but no-one was coming inside the compound.

John saw a figure running toward them, waving his arms and shouting. Whatever he said, it worked because the onlookers dispersed and he turned and ran back toward the bungalow. John recognised Max, and he dropped lower until his head was about the same level as the verandah, hoping he wouldn't be seen.

Max leaped onto the verandah just as the girl ran out the door. She was still fully clothed but appeared upset, and John hoped he had been in time. Max grabbed her by the arm and shouted something, but the noise from the fire and the residents now running into the compound with buckets of water meant that he couldn't make out what they said. The girl shook his hand off, then jumped off the verandah and ran across the lawn toward the beach, the darkness quickly swallowing her up. John hesitated, wanting to go after her, but Max was still on the verandah watching her run off. Georges too, exited the bungalow. They had what looked to be a heated conversation, then both turned and ran around the corner to deal with the fire.

Atman was still inside.

John looked toward the beach. Should he go after the girl, or should he go into the bungalow? John chewed his lip, then pulled out his phone and sent a quick text. Then he stood, climbed onto the verandah, and made his way toward the front door.

## 90

Rajiv and Mani had found Manoj in his office, looking frustrated and stabbing at the keys on his keyboard. He hadn't even looked up when Rajiv had entered the office, which suited Rajiv. His aim was to give John as much time as he needed.

"I'm busy, Rajiv," Manoj grumbled, forgetting his customary politeness.

"I'm sure," Rajiv replied. Something was troubling Manoj, and Rajiv moved further into the room, stepping sideways to see what was on his screen. Mani stayed in the doorway, holding his hands together, not saying anything. Just before Rajiv could see the screen, Manoj reached up and turned off the monitor, then finally looked at Rajiv. "Is something the matter?"

Rajiv nodded. "It might be nothing, but it seems strange."

Manoj rubbed his face with both hands, then leaned back in his chair and waited for Rajiv to continue.

"Someone has taken some equipment from the guardroom."

Manoj frowned and looked toward the door. "Is this true, Mani?"

Rajiv looked back at Mani, who nodded but did not lift his gaze from the floor.

Rajiv cleared his throat. "It is. I checked myself."

"How could you let this happen, Mani? You are on duty. You are drinking again, aren't you?" Manoj barked.

Mani shook his head.

"What is missing? Have you stolen it? If I find out it was you, I'll beat the..."

"I don't think there is any need for that," Rajiv interrupted. "I've already had a look around. Mani has been very helpful. In fact, he reported it to me, so I think it's highly unlikely that he's taken anything."

Manoj continued glaring at Mani.

"I'll conduct a full investigation in the morning. I'll question all the residents. It could be anyone."

Manoj stopped glowering at Mani, took a deep breath, then turned his attention to Rajiv. "What has been taken? I'd rather not trouble our students unless absolutely necessary."

"Well..." Rajiv heard an explosion, then saw Manoj look toward the window and his eyebrows rise. Rajiv didn't move.

Manoj frowned and then, placing his hands on the desk in front of him, hauled himself out of his chair. He walked toward the window, and Rajiv could see a reflected orange glow on his face.

"Is that a fire?"

Rajiv joined him at the window. The sky above the road end of Atman's compound was orange and even in the darkness, he could see thick black smoke billowing upward.

They heard shouts and then someone screamed, "Fire!"

"Guruji," Manoj gasped, and he pushed past Rajiv and Mani and rushed out the door.

Rajiv waited a moment, then followed after him. Excited residents filled the path, and Manoj pushed them aside as he hurried toward the bungalow, the flames now visible above the wall. Rajiv caught up with him at the entrance to the compound and stepped past him. To his right, the Range Rover was fully alight, the flames reaching high above it; the heat scorching his face despite the distance. A wall of fire ran along the ground toward the bungalow and flames licked at the walls, the wooden window frames and shutters already smouldering.

Rajiv saw Max and Georges moving closer toward the fire, but could see no sign of Atman... or John.

"What do I do? What do I do?" Manoj repeated to himself as he hopped from one foot to the other.

Rajiv felt as indecisive as Manoj. What should he do? Then his phone buzzed in his pocket and he pulled it out and glanced at the screen.

*Find the girl. She's on the beach.*

Rajiv looked up at Manoj, but he wasn't even aware that Rajiv was there. He stepped back, pushing his way through the crowd of onlookers, then ran down the path toward the beach.

## 91

John stepped into the living room and glanced around. It was empty. He walked through and down a short corridor and out into an internal courtyard. Here, the smell of smoke and burning rubber was strong, and the courtyard was bathed in an orange glow from the fire outside. Ahead, at the far end of the courtyard, John could see the large wooden door that Rajiv had described. The one leading into Atman's quarters.

The door was open.

John hurried around the side of the courtyard, passing another open door. He glanced inside as he passed, then stopped, stepped back and entered the room. He could see the fire on the screen, bright white flames with shadowy figures crossing back and forth in front of it. Crossing to the security monitor, he yanked on the cables, ripping them from the connections, turning the monitor dark, then traced them back to where they entered the hard drive underneath the desk. He yanked the power cable from the wall and pulled the cables from the hard drive. He then picked up the hard drive and placed it on the desktop while he looked around the office. There was a locked safe in the corner and what looked like a gun cabinet on the wall. That too, was locked.

There wasn't much else he could do in the room, so he picked up the hard drive and stepped back out into the courtyard.

Loud shouts and the crackling and popping of the fire filled the air, and even though the sea breeze was blowing most of the smoke away toward the road, something in the air stung his eyes and caught in the back of his throat. He lobbed the hard drive up onto the roof, where hopefully it wouldn't be noticed, then turned and headed toward Atman's room.

He paused outside, listening for any sign that someone was inside. Atman had to be in there. But the room appeared to be silent, although it was hard to tell over the background noise of the firefighting. John eased himself inside and looked around. The room smelled of incense and all the light was coming from a candlelit altar to the right of the room. A large high-backed armchair stood in front of the altar and it was only when he heard the voice that he realised it was occupied.

"Come in, John."

## 92

Rajiv moved as quickly as he could through the crowd that was rushing to get a look at the fire in Atman's compound. He spied Manju and grabbed his arm. "Grab the flashlight from the Bolero and meet me at the beach."

"But, sir... the fire."

"I'll explain later. Hurry!"

Rajiv didn't wait and continued on toward the beach. He heard someone calling his name, a woman. Aarthi appeared, a worried look on her face, and he stopped.

"Rajiv, what's happening?"

"Come with me." He took her by the arm, turned her around, and pulled her toward the beach. "Priyanka is on the beach somewhere. We need to find her."

"What's happening Rajiv? Is she ok? There's a fire."

"Don't worry about the fire. It's not important right now." Even in the darkness, he could see Aarthi was confused. So he stopped and turned toward her, holding her by the upper arms and looked straight into her eyes. "Our priority right now is finding Priyanka. She was seen running from Atman's bungalow. We need to find her, make sure she's ok, that she's safe, that she doesn't do anything stupid."

Aarthi's eyes darted around as she struggled to comprehend what was happening. She looked back toward the fire, then her shoulders rose as she took a deep breath. Looking back at Rajiv, she nodded, the confusion gone, replaced by a look of determination. "Okay."

Rajiv smiled, and gave her arms a squeeze. "Let's go. I'll explain as we go."

Once out of earshot of the residents, he filled her in on the events of the past few days. The overheard telephone conversation, the discovery of Trevor's body, his suspicions about Atman and his organisation. Aarthi said nothing, her eyes on the dimly lit path, concentrating on her footing. They reached the gate leading onto the beach and she stopped. "And the fire?"

Rajiv made a face, took a deep breath, and made a decision. He didn't normally involve her in his work, sparing her the details of the grimy, corrupt, and often dangerous world he inhabited. But he knew that whatever he told her would go no further.

"Do you remember that case with the foreign woman? The one who was raped and murdered and left in the grounds of the agricultural college in Bangalore?"

Rajiv could see Aarthi's forehead wrinkle in the moonlight as she frowned.

"The one which Surya Patil and his son were rumoured to be involved in?"

"Exactly. Well..." Rajiv hesitated. How did he explain it? "It's complicated, but the husband is here now, helping me catch Atman."

"What? I don't understand, Rajiv."

Rajiv nodded, then pulled open the gate to the beach

and guided her through. "I told you it's complicated. I'll explain once we find Priyanka. That's the priority right now."

Before Aarthi could say anything, they heard someone running up behind them and Rajiv turned to see Manju with the flashlight.

"Good job. Give it to me." He took the flashlight while the constable bent double, catching his breath. "We are looking for a young lady. Her name is Priyanka. She was seen running toward the beach about five minutes ago. She will be distressed, possibly injured. She may have been... sexually assaulted, so she'll be scared."

Manjunath straightened up, his chest still rising and falling as he got his breath back, a deep frown on his forehead. "Assaulted? Here?"

"Yes. So use her name and identify yourself as police."

Rajiv glanced at Aarthi, then back at Manjunath. "In fact, say you are Madam's friend. That should make her feel safer. Now you go left, Madam, and I will go right. You've got your phone?"

"Yes, sir."

"Good. Phone me if you find her. Off you go."

"Yes, sir."

Manjunath moved past and began walking down the dune onto the harder packed sand below.

"Come on, Aarthi. We need to find her."

Rajiv turned on the flashlight, but it wasn't really needed. The moon was close to full, and the sand reflected the light in a silvery glow.

As they trudged across the sand, their feet sinking into the soft surface, pulling at their flip-flops, Rajiv moved the flashlight beam across the beach looking for any sign of the girl.

"Do you really think she has been... sexually assaulted?"

"I hope not. That's what the fire was for. To get her out of there. I just hope John was in time."

Aarthi didn't say anything for a moment, clearly struggling with the news. Then she said, "But Atman, he's..."

"I told you he's not what you think he is," Rajiv replied, a little too roughly. "That's why I didn't want you to come." Before she could say any more, he called out, "Priyanka. We've come to help. Where are you?"

Aarthi glanced at him, then joined in. "Priyanka, it's Aarthi. You're safe now."

There was no reply, their voices getting lost in the sound of the surf. Rajiv reached the gate from Atman's compound. It was open, and he shone the flashlight beam onto the sand, but there were footprints everywhere.

"Priyanka," he called out again, but doubted she would hear his voice.

Aarthi was looking up the beach, "What's that, Rajiv?" She pointed at a dark object just above the waterline.

Rajiv looked where she was pointing and then sprinted down the beach towards it. The object moved, and he aimed the flashlight beam at it. It was her. She jumped up and started to run... away from him.

"Priyanka," he panted and pushed himself faster. His legs burned with the effort, his lungs unable to suck in enough air. She was getting away from him. Then a wave broke, and the water rushed up the beach, higher than normal, the water catching her ankles and she stumbled, losing her balance and fell to her knees in the surf. Rajiv summoned up one last burst of speed, splashing towards her as the water threatened to trip him. The water receded, the sand firm underfoot, and just as she was about to get up, he reached her, grabbing her shoulder with his free hand.

She screamed and tried to pull away and he gasped, "It's okay, you are safe. Aarthi..." he sucked in air. "I'm Aarthi's husband."

She pulled away again, but looked confused.

He released his grip and held up his hands. "It's okay. Aarthi is coming now. You are safe."

At that moment he heard Aarthi's voice above the waves, "Priyanka, it's me."

Rajiv stepped back and shone the flashlight at his wife as she ran toward them. He heard a sob from Priyanka and then Aarthi fell to her knees beside her and threw her arms around the young woman, even as another wave broke and splashed around them.

Rajiv took another deep breath and said a silent prayer of thanks. She was safe.

## 93

John's surprise quickly turned to anger, and he clenched his jaw and fists as he stepped forward and to the side so he could see the man sitting in the armchair.

Atman smiled back at him, his posture relaxed, as if it was a normal day. "I've been expecting you, John. You are looking well."

"Bullshit," John growled, clenching and unclenching his fists.

Atman chuckled, "I sense a bit of resentment, John. Have you not been doing your practice?" He closed his eyes, held up his right hand, palm facing outwards, and moved his fingertips as if feeling the air. Opening his eyes, he said, "Good, John. You are making progress."

"What did you do to the girl?"

Atman's smile slipped a fraction. "This is your problem, John, always worrying about other people when you should work on yourself. Everyone needs to work through their own spiritual lessons. They need to do the work themselves if they want to progress. You should do the same."

It was all John could do to stay where he was, and he forced down the urge to smash his fist into the smug man's face. "Don't give me this hippy mumbo jumbo. You're a bullshitter and you prey on vulnerable people. What did you do to the girl?"

Atman shook his head. "Absolutely nothing. I was about to remove a block that's halting her advancement, but now she'll be stuck, and that's your fault, John. "

"Oh, fuck off, Atman. If it wasn't for me, you would have raped her and told her it was for her own good. You've done it before, god knows how many times."

Atman cocked his head, still smiling, "You understand very little, John. Which is disappointing. I had hoped that with your practice you would have a better understanding of the inner world and how it affects our outward existence. But it's interesting that you use the term God, so all is not lost."

John shook his head in exasperation and clenched and unclenched his fist. "You are stark raving mad. How on earth do you think that preying on vulnerable women is helping them? You claim to be so evolved but you are still thinking with your dick. You're scum, Atman. You've conned all those people out there," John gestured in the direction of the ashram, "and countless others around the world. You've ruined people's lives. You've had people killed..."

At the last comment Atman blinked. "I've never had anyone killed, John. Now it's you who are delusional."

"Yeah? Nihinsa in Sri Lanka?"

Atman shrugged. "She ran away. Sometimes it happens. Spiritual work can be too much for some people."

John sneered, "Sally Hughes? Mowed down by a truck after she complained about you molesting her. Her brother Trevor killed yesterday. Drugged and then hanged to make it look like suicide. You fucking bastard! He was a good man trying to get justice for his sister," John jabbed his finger at Atman, "who you raped and killed."

Atman frowned and shifted in his chair. He looked genuinely surprised, as if hearing about this for the first time, but John didn't trust him.

"It's about time someone put an end to this," John pointed at his chest, "and that someone is me!"

Atman sighed and looked away. He stared at the idol of Krishna for a moment. When he looked back, he looked sad. "And how do you plan to do that, John?"

John didn't know what to say. He actually didn't know what he was going to do next. He stared back at Atman, his body consumed with anger. He took a step forward and raised his fist, but couldn't go any further. Atman didn't move. Just stayed completely still watching him. John dropped his hand.

"We're connected, John. That's why you have come to me. We go back a long way, lifetimes. "

"I've come to you to save others, you f...."

"You've come to save yourself, John. I can help you. You just need to let go, to surrender. What you see around you... what people are doing... what you think is right or wrong... it's all just part of the cosmic play. None of it matters. It's all karma..."

John had heard enough. "Karma! Here's your karma!" He clenched his fist and took a step forward.

"Stay where you are!"

John recognised the voice. He turned his head and saw Georges standing just inside the room, a Glock in a two-handed grip, pointed straight at him.

## 94

"Perfect timing, Georges. You remember John, I'm sure?"

Georges said nothing, his eyes and the Glock unwavering.

John stared back at him while he did a million calculations in his head. But it was pointless. He didn't have any options. The second he moved, Georges would put a bullet in him. He turned back to look at Atman, who was regarding him with an amused expression.

Georges cleared his throat. "Sir, I need to get you out of here."

"It's okay, Georges. John won't do anything. We are just having a chat."

"It's not that, sir. It's the fire. It's taken hold on the building."

For the first time, John noticed the acrid smell of smoke and burning chemicals had replaced the fragrance of the incense sticks on the altar.

Atman waved a hand in dismissal. "Isn't Max dealing with it?"

"He is, sir, but I'm afraid it won't be enough. I would prefer to move you to safety."

"Hmmm." Atman continued smiling at John, as if nothing was happening. "John has been making some interesting allegations."

Georges stepped closer. "I'm sure he has, sir. But now is not the time."

The room was visibly smokier, and John felt his eyes watering.

"Remove the bag and drop it on the floor," Georges continued.

John turned his attention back to Georges but didn't move. Unusually, he felt no fear, despite having a gun pointed at his chest. He felt strangely calm. There was nothing he could do and whatever happened next was out of his control, anyway.

"Remove the bag," Georges growled again, stepping even closer.

John stayed still, his eyes locked with Georges. For a fleeting moment, he wondered if he could overpower Georges, if he let him get close enough. But he quickly dismissed that idea. Georges was bigger than John and had probably been trained in something like Krav Maga during his time in the Israeli army.

He also had a gun.

John waited. Something would happen. He was sure of it. He took a deep breath, slowing down his breathing... and smiled.

He heard a chuckle from Atman, even as Georges' eyes narrowed and his frown deepened.

"Well done, John. You've made excellent progress. I see you've gained control of your sympathetic nervous system.

The fight-or-flight response. You are no longer reacting to situations. You are responding."

John glanced at Atman— the guy was nuts—and that was all Georges needed.

Time seemed to slow down for John. He sensed Georges moving closer and when he looked back at him, Georges had released his two handed grip on the Glock, raised the weapon in the air, and was bringing the grip in a downward arc towards John's head. Before John could react, his vision starred, then went black and his legs buckled. His knees hit the ground as a blast of pain reverberated around his skull. He blinked his eyes as his sight returned and then felt a boot on his back, forcing him to the ground. The air escaped from his lungs as a knee landed between his shoulder blades and he felt the cold steel of the Glock's muzzle against the back of his head, pressing his face into the rug.

He was not afraid.

The rug was soft against his lips, but smelled musty, as if it hadn't been cleaned in a while.

John noticed all this as if it was happening to someone else. Even the pain in his head seemed separate from the John that was witnessing it.

Was this the end? He didn't think so.

Closing his eyes, he saw Charlotte's face in his mind's eye, clearer than it had been for years. She smiled, her blue eyes twinkling just as he remembered, and then she nodded. Her lips didn't move, and he felt rather than heard her speak. "Everything is going to be okay."

Then he heard another voice, this time in his ears.

"Put the gun down and move away."

## 95

John opened his eyes, but all he could see was the rug and the Glock was still pressed against his skull. The voice spoke again. It was accented, not Indian... something else.

"Put the gun down," it said again.

He felt Georges shift slightly, but the pressure on the back of his head remained.

Then he heard Georges' voice. "What are you doing?"

"I've had enough."

John searched his memory. He had heard the voice before... but where?

"Don't be stupid, Max."

Ahhh, that's why he recognised it. John wanted to turn his head to see what was happening, but daren't move in case Georges pulled the trigger. So he waited, keeping his breath slow and regular, relaxed but ready to move when the opportunity presented itself.

"Put the gun down, Georges."

"Or what? What will you do? I saved your life, remember? You owe me."

"I've repaid that debt many times over. I'm no longer taking orders from you, or you."

John guessed the last was meant for Atman.

Max continued, "You are a fraud, Atman. What you do is not spiritual... that girl was just a kid..."

John felt Georges move. It wasn't much, but the weight shifted ever so slightly, and the pressure on the back of his head eased off a fraction. Something was about to happen.

There was a loud crackle from somewhere in the roof, and a voice in John's head said, "Now!"

## 96

Manjunath picked up almost immediately. "Sir?"

"We've found her. Come up the beach to me. As fast as you can."

"Is she okay, sir?"

Rajiv looked down at the young woman crying in Aarthi's arms.

"I hope so."

Rajiv put the phone away and helped Aarthi move Priyanka above the waterline while he waited for Manjunath to arrive. Tears flowed freely down her face as she clung to Aarthi, who rocked her and murmured in her ear.

Rajiv looked toward the orange glow above Atman's bungalow. The flames were visible above the wall, the fire clearly taking hold of the building. "Come on, Manju," he muttered. John needed his help. Squatting down, he placed a hand on Aarthi's arm. "I have to go. Manjunath is coming. He'll look after you."

"But Rajiv..."

"I'll come as soon as I can." He stood before she could say any more and set off down the beach toward the bungalow. He spotted the dark figure of Manjunath running toward him and he called out, "Manju."

"Sir," Manjunath reached him and bent over, his hands on his knees as he regained his breath.

"They are just past me about another hundred metres. Take Madam and the girl to Madam's room and stay there until you hear from me. Don't allow anyone in or out."

Manjunath straightened up, his breath still ragged. "Where are you going, sir?"

"Don't worry about me. Just look after the two ladies."

"Yes, sir."

Rajiv patted him on the shoulder, then moved past him and ran down the beach, keeping to the packed sand just above the waterline. Once he was parallel to the gate, he headed up the beach, struggling in the soft sand, his thighs burning, then ran through the gate and across the lawn toward the bungalow. There was a human chain ferrying water from the ashram, but most residents stood back near the wall watching the fire as the flames licked the roof of the bungalow. Rajiv ignored them and leaped up onto the verandah and into the living room. The smoke here was thick, and he ducked down while pulling up the end of his shirt and covering his mouth and nostrils. The living room was empty and he kept moving, into the courtyard and around the covered walkway that ran around the edge. There was no sign of anyone, but ahead he could see the open door to Atman's room. John had to be in there. He just hoped he was in time.

As he reached the door, he heard a shout, and he stopped, straining to hear over the crackle and popping of the fire. He heard the voice again, but couldn't make out what was being said. He stepped forward and slowly peered around the edge of the door into the room.

Standing closest to the door, was the young Israeli, legs apart, arms raised, a pistol held in both hands, pointed at the figures further inside the room.

Rajiv ducked back. What the hell was happening? What could he do? He peered around the door frame again, this time looking further into the room. Georges was kneeling on a figure on the floor, a gun pressed to the back of the figure's head. Was that... John?

Rajiv again pulled back, hoping he hadn't been seen. He looked around the courtyard. What the hell should he do? He needed a weapon. Remembering the gun safe, he turned and sprinted back toward the office. Entering the room, he grabbed the front of the gun safe and pulled on the door.

"Dammit," he cursed.

Locked. He ran to the desk and pulled open the drawers, looking for a key, but before he could find anything, he heard a gunshot.

## 97

John rolled sideways, out from under Georges, at the same time feeling a searing hot pain across his cheek and a resounding bang in his ears. Disoriented, he continued rolling, putting as much distance between himself and Georges. There was another loud bang, audible over the ringing in his ears, and he pushed himself on to his butt and scrabbled backwards across the rug, until his back came up against the altar. Jumping to his feet, he grasped the idol of Lord Krishna and hoisted it in the air, ready to defend himself, when his eyes finally registered the scene in front of him.

Georges lay on his back at Atman's feet, his right hand clasping his left shoulder, a dark patch spreading across his white *kurta*. Max was advancing slowly, his Glock still in a two-handed grip, but the weapon was pointed at Georges. John shook his head, clearing his vision, trying to get rid of the ringing in his ears and, above all, trying to make sense of what had just happened.

Max stepped closer to Georges and then, with a sweep of his right foot, kicked an object across the rug toward John.

"Pick it up."

John looked down and then lowered the Krishna idol. He bent down, picked up Georges' Glock and raised it, pointing it in the general direction of the three men in front of him. With his left hand, he touched his cheek and winced. That had been close.

"Have you lost your mind?" Georges grunted through clenched teeth.

"No, I've finally found it." Max jerked the Glock at Atman. "Get on the floor, face down."

Atman looked from him to John and back again. He didn't seem too concerned by the turn of events. Slowly, he slipped out of the armchair and laid face down on the floor with his hands behind his head.

"John, right? You were there in Sri Lanka?"

"That's right." John spoke up for the first time. "Max."

"Yes. See if you can find something to secure these two."

"I've got just the thing." John, keeping the Glock trained on the two men on the floor, flipped up the flap of the sling bag still hanging around his neck and rummaged around the contents until his fingers felt the zip ties. But before he could remove them, a movement in the doorway caught his eye, and he swung the Glock in that direction.

Rajiv stood in the doorway, a table lamp in his hand, his jaw hanging open as he surveyed the scene in the room.

"I don't think we'll be needing that, Rajiv."

Max glanced over his shoulder, then looked back at John with raised eyebrows. "You know each other?"

"You could say that." John lowered the Glock, lifted the end of his long shirt, and slipped the weapon into his waistband. He then stepped forward until he was just out of reach of Georges. "Turn over, Georges."

Georges cursed in a language John didn't understand, but stayed where he was.

Max replied in the same language—John assumed it was Hebrew—and Georges cleared his throat and spat at him. Max repeated what he had said, more forcefully this time. Georges glared, then slowly and wincing with the pain, rolled over onto his stomach. John stepped forward and grabbed the wounded arm, wrenching it up behind Georges, taking pleasure in the cry of pain that escaped his lips. He then grabbed the other hand and quickly fastened the wrists together with zip ties. He then moved over to Atman and did the same.

Rajiv finally spoke up, "What's going on?"

John, still kneeling beside the two prone men, glanced at Max, then replied, "Georges here assaulted me with the weapon that is now in my belt, under the instructions of Atman. He fired his weapon, narrowly missing me." John pointed to what he assumed was a burn on his cheek. "Max came to my rescue, fired his weapon in self defence, and we have now secured both men for our own safety and the safety of others."

"I see," Rajiv said slowly.

John stood up slowly and turned to Max. "Is there anything I have missed out?"

"The girl."

"Ah yes, we believed a sexual assault was in progress and we took steps to rescue the girl who managed to escape." At the last, John looked questioningly at Rajiv.

"The girl is safe and is currently being watched over by my constable."

John breathed a sigh of relief. "Thank God for that. Is she...?"

"Okay? I don't know yet. My wife is with her."

"Your wife?" Max asked, finally lowering his weapon to his side.

"Yes." Rajiv didn't elaborate, and John watched as he walked further into the room and carefully set the table lamp down on the floor. At the same time, Max lifted his shirt and tucked the Glock into his waistband while moving to the side as if wanting to keep a safe distance between himself and Rajiv.

There was a voice from the floor. Atman. "Detective Sampath, need I remind you of your duty to protect me?"

Atman had turned his face to the side so he could see what was happening. Georges, though, lay with his forehead pressed to the rug, his eyes closed, his face screwed up in pain. His shoulder was bleeding profusely, the dark patch now covering most of the side of his shirt.

There was another crashing sound from outside, and John looked up at the ceiling. It was turning black in places and smoke was now leaking in through the joint between the ceiling and the wall. They didn't have much time.

"I..." Rajiv began, but John held up his hand, cutting him short. He needed to take control of the situation. "Max, keep an eye on them. I need to have a quick chat with Rajiv."

Outside in the courtyard, the smoke was thicker and John squatted down next to the wall, pulling Rajiv down beside him.

"Rajiv, listen to me. You need to walk away. Leave the building, make sure the other residents are safe, the girl, your wife."

Rajiv was shaking his head as John spoke. "John, we have to get everyone to safety. Georges needs medical attention. The house is burning…"

"No," John put a lot of force into his answer and Rajiv flinched. "Rajiv, as soon as those two are out of here, there will be a coverup. They will get off scot-free."

"No, no, John. I'll make sure they're prosecuted. I'll pursue the case myself."

"Rajiv, be realistic. They've got away with it before, they're too connected. You know what will happen."

Rajiv was still shaking his head.

"Be honest with yourself, Rajiv. We both know how it works."

"But John, I can't stand by and watch you... do whatever you're going to do..." he trailed off.

"That's why I'm telling you to go now. As far as you're concerned, there was a fire and you've no idea what happened to the people in the house."

"John, no. You can't..."

"Rajiv. Think of Trevor. And he's only one of many. How many others have they killed? How many more if they get away this time? And the girl? What if that had been Aarthi?"

The last point seemed to have an effect. John could see a change in Rajiv's expression... in the set of his shoulders.

"But..."

"Rajiv, leave it to me. You and Max are the only people who know I'm here, or who know that you've been inside the house. Just go. I'll deal with the rest."

Rajiv looked away, and John waited for him to make his decision. He knew how hard it was for him to choose a path that went against everything he represented.

"Okay," he agreed, looking back at John. "What do I do about Max?"

"Ignore him. He saved my life. I'll deal with him. Now go." He gave Rajiv a shove, sending him off balance, and the detective put a hand out to steady himself on the ground, then stood up. He frowned at John, then nodded, and without another word, turned his back and headed for the front door.

John waited until he had disappeared from sight, then stood up and walked back into the room. Max hadn't moved, standing with his arms folded, watching the men on the floor. John beckoned him over, away from Atman and Georges, and lowered his voice so they couldn't hear.

"Rajiv won't give us any trouble."

Max merely nodded.

"Did you have a plan, Max?"

The young man shook his head.

"Okay, here's what you should do. Go into the office, take as much cash as you can carry, and get out of here. Leave the country, never come back. I'll deal with these two."

Max stared back at him, then shook his head. "No."

"No?"

"Not yet."

John frowned, waiting for the young man to elaborate.

"I've stood by and turned a blind eye to what's been going on for too long. I've also been responsible for the harm these two have done. It's time for me to do something about it."

"And what's that?"

Max chewed his lip and looked around the room. "Neither of them should leave this room alive."

John hesitated. Max was right. John had come to the same conclusion himself, but hearing Max say it aloud made it real. John glanced at the men on the floor. He'd killed people before, but never in cold blood. Taking a deep breath, he closed his eyes for a moment and remembered the young girl Nihinsa, in Sri Lanka, and Priyanka running from the bungalow that evening. It had to be done.

"Are you sure? This will stay with you for the rest of your life."

Max looked at John and narrowed his eyes. "I've done a lot of things I regret, John. In Israel, in the Territories, here... I'll just add it to the list." He looked over at Atman and Georges. "But actually... this I won't regret."

## 99

"We'll have to move fast," John said as a crack appeared in the ceiling in the corner closest to the road and smoke began seeping in.

"You go." Max replied. "I'll handle it."

John shook his head. He planned to finish what he had started.

"We need to make it look like an accident. They were trapped in here and the fire got the better of them." He jerked his head toward the door. "Is there any other way out of here?"

"No."

"Okay." John thought fast. The room was filling fast with smoke, and the crack in the ceiling had widened. He couldn't see outside but hoped the fire had spread enough that by the time the fire brigade arrived, if there was one, it would be too late.

"Let's help the fire along in here. Grab anything flammable and pile it up against the altar. We'll set it alight with the candles."

Max nodded, and he hurried across the room to the

bookshelf and began pulling books off and tossing them on the floor near the altar.

"You can't leave us here," Georges called out from the floor, but John ignored him. He grabbed the bedcover and felt the fabric between his fingers. It felt like silk. He wasn't sure if it would burn or not, but he bundled it up anyway and tossed it onto the pile of books.

"There's money in the safe, I'll give you the combination, you can take it, just let us go," Georges continued.

"I know the combination," Max called out from the other side of the room.

Georges cursed, then tried again. "Max, we're brothers. We've been through so much together. Don't throw it all away."

John walked over to the open door in the side wall and looked inside. It was a small bathroom, and he spotted a bottle of aftershave on the vanity unit. Picking it up, he walked back outside, pulled off the top, and emptied the contents onto the growing pile.

"That's enough, Max, let's go."

Atman spoke for the first time, "John, I have one request. Just put me in my chair."

John thought for a moment, then stepped closer and grabbed Atman under the arms and hauled him up, dragging him over to his armchair. He sat him down, then stepped back.

"I forgive you, John." Atman gazed back at him, his face calm, the hint of a smile at the corners of his mouth.

John was struck with doubt. Was he doing the right thing? Who was he to decide who lived or died?

There was a loud crash as a piece of the ceiling broke free and hit the floor. John flinched and pushed the doubt away. This man had ruined a lot of lives and would continue to do so until he was stopped. "Do you think I care?" he replied

Atman shrugged as much as he could with his hands bound behind him. "Perhaps not. Only you will know that. But you must do what you have to do." He smiled. "In the end, it's all part of the Supreme Being's grand play." He chuckled, "None of this is real."

John frowned. He hadn't expected that. Had he got it all wrong?

Flames were now visible through the hole in the ceiling and they began to lick at the interior of the bungalow. John looked back at Atman, who had closed his eyes, his lips were moving in prayer. John stood stock still transfixed until Max spoke.

"John, it's time."

He turned and saw Max standing above Georges, his weapon drawn and pointing at the back of George's head.

"No!" John raised his hand. "I told you it needs to look like an accident."

"I'll be long gone by then."

John shook his head. "Don't underestimate the Indian police. They'll track you down if they suspect foul play. Don't do it."

Max hesitated. "It's the least I can do for him. Spare him some pain. He saved my life once. Anyway, he has a bullet in his shoulder."

John shook his head, his hand still raised. "Don't do it, Max."

Max hesitated a moment longer, then slipped the Glock back into his waistband. He knelt down and pulled Georges into a seated position. Georges glared at him, still defiant. Max placed a hand on each shoulder and looked into his eyes. "This one last thing I will do for you." He then moved around behind him, put his right arm around Georges' neck, wedging his forearm under his chin then anchored it with his left. He squeezed while pushing Georges' head forward, restricting the blood flow to his brain. Georges began to struggle, but there was little he could do from a seated position with both hands secured behind him. He soon went limp, but Max maintained the pressure for what, to John, seemed like an eternity, before finally letting go. Georges slumped to the floor, and Max pushed himself to his feet and looked at John.

"He's dead?" John asked.

Max bent down and placed his fingertips on the side of Georges' neck. After a moment, he straightened up and nodded.

John said nothing. It wasn't the first time he'd seen someone die, and Georges deserved it. He looked back at Atman, who had opened his eyes and was looking at Georges' body, his lips still moving.

"Give me your Glock," John commanded.

And Max raised his eyebrows, "Why?"

"The bullet wound. Let's make it look like Atman did it."

Max frowned, then pulled out his weapon and, reversing it, handed it over to John. John gave it a wipe with the end of his shirt, then placed it on the ground near Atman's feet. He looked up at Atman, but he had closed his eyes again and was leaning back against the back of the chair.

Another piece fell from the ceiling, sending a shower of sparks into the room.

"Let's go," John hurried over to the altar, picked up a candle, stepped back, then tossed it onto the pile of fabric and books. The candle spluttered, then the flame caught alight on the aftershave and with a whoosh of blue flame, the fabric caught alight. He turned and rushed toward the door where Max was waiting. Pulling out the wrench from his sling bag, he smashed the digital keypad on the inside of the room, pushed Max through the door, and then pulled the door behind him. It clicked shut, and he gave it a push to make sure it was secure, then moved past Max toward the office. "What's the combination to the safe?"

"I'll show you."

## 100

Max squatted in front of the safe and twirled the dial while John looked around the office. He opened the filing cabinets. "Is there anything here I should take? Anything incriminating?"

There was a click as the safe opened and Max looked back over his shoulder. He shook his head. "No. Nothing in there. It's all on the computer, but you'll need the passwords and I don't have those. Georges never told me."

John nodded and turned his attention to the desktop computer. Bending down, he looked under the desk and grabbed the CPU and pulled the cables from the back, then dragged it out and hoisted it onto the desktop. Looking over at Max, he saw the young man had removed several large bundles of cash in various currencies and dumped them on the floor. He'd also pulled out a bundle of passports and was leafing through them, removing two and tossing the rest back into the safe.

John grabbed the wastepaper bin and emptied the contents onto the floor, then removed the bin liner and handed it to Max. "Here you go. Take what you need."

"You don't want any?"

John shook his head. "Nope."

Max stuffed the cash into the black plastic bin liner, then stood up and slipped the passports into his back pocket. He saw John watching and shrugged. "We've always had more than one."

John nodded and replied, "Whose are those?" He jerked his head toward the discarded passports in the safe.

"Georges' and Atman's"

"Give them to me."

Max hesitated for a moment, then bent down, removed them and tossed them to John.

John caught them in midair and then dropped them into his sling bag without looking at them. Time for that later. He picked up the CPU, hoisted it under his arm, and moved toward the door. "Let's go. We're not safe yet."

John stepped out into the courtyard and immediately flinched back as a wave of heat scorched his face. "Go, go, go!" he shouted and ran down the corridor toward the living area. Once in the relative safety of the living room, he paused and looked back. Atman's end of the bungalow was now fully alight, and the fire was spreading forward toward the office they had just been in. The roar and crackle of flames, and shouting from outside, filled the air as the ashram residents tried in vain to douse the fire. It had to be obvious now they were wasting their time.

John heard a siren, getting louder, and he glanced at Max. "Sounds like the fire brigade is finally here."

Max nodded and looked back toward Atman's room. "Too late for them, I think."

John nodded. He didn't want to think too much about it.

The lights flickered and then went out.

"Come on, we aren't home free yet." John moved toward

the front door and slowly poked his head out, looking toward the left and the ashram. A crowd still filled the ashram entrance, all their attention on the fire, but the chain of residents ferrying water seemed to have given up.

He ducked back inside. "Keep close to the wall. We'll go right then, head for the beach."

Max nodded and John stepped out, turned right and sidled along the wall to the end of the verandah, then jumped off onto the grass. He waited for Max to join him, then bent double and ran toward the boundary wall. Reaching the wall, he paused to regain his breath. The CPU was heavier than he thought. Max joined him, hardly breathing, and John made a mental note to train even harder if he got out of this alive. "Ready?"

He saw Max nod in the darkness, then he took a deep breath and set off along the wall toward the beach. Only when he reached the end wall did he slow and, panting heavily, walked along the wall until he found the gate. It was open, swinging slowly in the breeze, and John stepped through and out onto the beach. Max joined him and they stood silently, gazing down the long expanse of sand glowing in the moonlight. The sea rippled in the moonlight like quicksilver. There was no-one to be seen, and apart from the crash of the waves and the breeze rippling through the fronds of the coconut palms above their heads, it was silent.

John broke the silence. "What will you do now?"

Max looked down at the sand and dug a hole with the toe of his shoe. "I don't know." He looked up. "I'm sorry, John." He shook his head. "I turned a blind eye for too long, telling myself I was only doing my job." He sighed loudly, the sound audible even over the sound of the waves. "That girl was the last straw. So innocent." He shook his head again. "Bastards."

"Yeah."

Max looked directly at John. "You're a better man than me, John. You saw bad things happen, and you did something about it. There were so many things I could have stopped, but I didn't."

John reached out with his spare hand and gripped Max's shoulder. "It's never too late. You did something this time."

Max said nothing and couldn't hold John's gaze. He looked away.

John gave his shoulder a squeeze and let go. "Come, let's move away from here. Tell me everything you know, and I'll make sure the story gets out."

Max looked back at John, his forehead creased with a deep frown, then his face relaxed. "Okay."

## 101

Rajiv covered his mouth with a handkerchief as he stepped carefully through the still smouldering wreckage of the bungalow. The walls were still standing, but the interior was gutted and the roof was open to the sky, just a few charred rafters sticking out like blackened claws.

By the time the fire engine had arrived, the blaze had been fierce and there had been little they could do to put it out. They instead focused their efforts on ensuring the flames fuelled by the sea breeze would not spread to the neighbouring properties. Now, in the early morning, the fire was finally out, but smoke and steam still rose from the wreckage.

Expecting a contingent of local police, Rajiv had changed out of his ashram clothing and into his uniform, and as he walked through the wreckage, a fireman nodded at him.

"Be careful, sir. It's still hot in here."

Rajiv nodded in reply, but continued on through the living room and out into what was the internal courtyard.

The polished wooden pillars that supported the roof covering the walkway around the outside of the courtyard were reduced to blackened stumps, and broken tiles and ash littered the floor. Rajiv ignored it all, his eyes only on the room at the end. Atman's room.

Another fireman stood beside the half-open door and he held up his hand. "Sir, there's... a body inside."

Rajiv frowned. He'd known it was a possibility. He studied the man for a moment. Soot and grime filled the deep lines on his face, the whites of his eyes red from the smoke and exhaustion, and his khaki uniform was stained with black.

"Just one?"

"Looks like it, sir."

"Do we know who?"

The fireman shook his head. "Sir... I just put out fires. I've no idea who was here."

Rajiv nodded and placed a hand on his shoulder. "Thank you. Get some rest. I'll take a look inside."

The fireman hesitated. "Sir... it's still not safe."

"It's okay." Rajiv gave the man a smile. "I've done this before. I'll be careful."

The man looked unsure, then exhaustion got the better of him and he stepped back from the doorway, took one last look at Rajiv, then made his way out toward the front of the building.

Rajiv watched him go, then turned his attention back to the door. He had seen dead bodies before, but was nervous about what he would find inside. John hadn't answered any of his calls and now his phone was switched off. One body, the man had said. He just hoped it wasn't John's.

The door was charred but mainly intact and Rajiv pushed it wide with the toe of his shoe, then stepped into the space that had been Atman's quarters. He stopped as soon as he was in and looked around. There was nothing left. The room was open to the sky, and the floor was strewn with black, smoking wreckage. To his left were the remains of the bed, and directly ahead in the far wall was the open doorway that led to the bathroom.

Rajiv looked to the right, and he stiffened. There was a smell too, a pungent, sweet smell that caught in the back of his throat. His gut told him what it was, but his eyes refused to confirm it. He slowly moved closer, mindful of his footing, and then crouched down beside a pile of burnt debris. His stomach churned.

A charred hand poked out from beneath a pile of ash. He stifled the urge to retch and examined the scene more closely. The body was too burnt for him to identify who it was. He prayed it wasn't John. He stood up and stepped back, almost losing his balance, his foot connecting against an object on the floor. Looking down, he spotted the Glock.

Rajiv stared at it, wondering what he should do. As a policeman, he knew what he was supposed to do, but... while there was a chance John was still alive he didn't want to complicate things. He glanced at the body again. "Damn it, John," he whispered, then pulled out his phone and once more dialled John's number. He waited for it to connect, then groaned when he heard the message, *'the number you are calling is currently switched off.'*

"Detective Sampath."

Rajiv spun around with a start.

"Is everything okay?"

Rajiv took a deep breath, then nodded at Prakash, who was standing in the doorway. "Yes, sorry. I was ah...," he trailed off.

Prakash made his way into the room, two uniformed constables following after him.

"What happened here?"

Rajiv looked around the room, giving himself time to compose an answer. "Well... a fire broke out last night in the carpark. It then spread to the bungalow and took hold before the fire department could get here."

Prakash was shaking his head, while he too looked around the room. "What a mess." He looked back at Rajiv. "No-one hurt, I hope."

Rajiv grimaced and then gestured at the body on the floor.

Prakash's eyes widened, and he moved forward until he was next to Rajiv. "Shit. Who?"

Rajiv shook his head. "I don't know."

"Guruji?"

Rajiv shrugged. "It was his room."

Prakash turned and called out to one of the constables. "Find out if anyone is missing. Atmanji, his bodyguards, ah...," he looked back at Rajiv.

"Georges and Max."

"Georges and Max," Prakash repeated. "Anyone else. Quickly!"

"Sir."

The constable left and Prakash looked back at the body. "If it's Guruji, the press will be all over us." He looked sideways at Rajiv, "And the CM."

Rajiv nodded. He didn't want to think about that. His primary concern right now was to find John. He noticed Prakash staring down at his feet.

"Is that a...?"

"Glock."

Prakash looked back at him with wide eyes. "Why would there be a Glock in the ashram?"

Rajiv shook his head. The less he said, the better, and besides, he had just spotted something else.

Walking forward, he crouched down, removed a pen from his breast pocket and with the end of it, moved some debris aside. There was another body.

## 102

It was another hour before Rajiv could slip away from the crime scene, because it could no longer be passed off as an accident. The discovery of the two bodies and the weapon prompted Inspector Prakash Rao to look harder at the cause of the fire, and his men had already found the remains of two jerry cans near the burnt out Range Rover.

Rajiv had stepped back, allowing Prakash and his men to take over. It wasn't Rajiv's jurisdiction and besides, he had no desire to solve the case. He knew who had started the fire and why. He just didn't know if John had survived it.

The constable had come back and reported that Atman, his two bodyguards, and the manager, Manoj Shetty, were all missing. Two bodies but four people missing. Five if you counted John.

As soon as Rajiv could make his excuses, he rushed over to the ashram, jumped in his vehicle and headed toward the guesthouse where John was staying. He pulled up outside the gate and was about to get out when his phone rang. He pulled the phone from his pocket and, without looking at the screen, held it to his ear. "J..."

"Detective Sampath. What's going on down there?"

Rajiv grimaced. How the hell had he found out so quickly? "Sir."

"Well?" SP Muniappa barked down the phone.

Rajiv rubbed his eyes with his left hand. He suddenly felt very tired. "There's been a fire, sir."

"I know there's been a fire. Where is Atmanji?"

"I..." Rajiv took a deep breath. "We don't know, sir. He's missing. We are still investigating."

"You're supposed to be protecting him and you don't know where he is?"

"I..."

"Find him and find him quickly. Need I remind you that the CM has a personal interest in this Rajiv?"

"Yes, sir. No, sir."

"I want an update in an hour."

The phone went dead before Rajiv could reply. His grip tightened around the phone, his knuckles turning white, then he tossed the phone onto the seat beside him. Taking a deep breath, he opened the car door and stepped out. Inside the guesthouse compound, he could see the fisherman owner watching him from beside his house.

"Your guest. He's here?" Rajiv called out.

The fisherman shook his head.

"What?"

"He's gone...sir."

Rajiv pushed open the gate and stepped inside. "What do you mean, he's gone?"

The fisherman shrugged. "See for yourself. I went down to the beach early this morning and saw his door was open. He's gone. The room is empty."

Rajiv glowered at him, then pushed past and ran down the pathway toward the room John had been staying in. He leaped up the steps onto the verandah and pushed the door open. The room was indeed empty. The bed looked as though it hadn't been slept in and John's bag was missing. Rajiv hurried across the room to the bathroom. It too, was empty. Not even a toothbrush remained, but there was a piece of paper wedged between the plastic frame of the mirror and the wall. Rajiv saw his name written on it. He pulled it from the frame and opened it up. Just two words were written inside. *Thank you.*

Rajiv frowned, then gradually relaxed. John was safe. He had to be. He stepped back out of the bathroom and turned to see the fisherman standing in the doorway.

"You didn't see him leave?"

The man shook his head. "No."

"When did you last see him?"

The man shrugged. "Yesterday evening."

Rajiv nodded slowly, casting his eyes around the room again.

The fisherman cleared his throat. "My boat is missing too."

Rajiv looked up.

"Someone took it during the night."

"Your boat?"

"Yes."

"Stolen?"

"Well..." the man looked away, down toward the beach. "Whoever took it left some money in a bag."

Rajiv's mouth twitched. "Some money? Enough to pay for the boat?"

The fisherman looked back at Rajiv. He stared at him for a while, not saying anything, then eventually replied, "Two boats."

Rajiv struggled to keep the smile from his face. "So... do

you wish to report it?"

The fisherman chewed his lip. "No."

Rajiv nodded. "Good."

# 103

John turned on his phone as he waited for his bag and it immediately vibrated with incoming messages. Despite the long flight, he felt well rested, the lie-flat business class seat allowing him to sleep for most of the fifteen hour journey from Dubai to Sydney.

He scrolled through the messages as the luggage belt started up and nodded with satisfaction. Adriana and Ramesh had been busy.

When news first broke, the headlines had been all about the tragic accident that may have killed one of the world's most popular and charismatic spiritual teachers.

Three days later, things had changed drastically and for the first time, John appreciated the sensationalism of popular media.

*'Fraudulent guru dies in fire after murdering bodyguard.'*
*'Popular ashram a front for money laundering.'*
*'Whistleblowers murdered by fake guru.'*

The last one made John chuckle. *'Chief Minister orders thorough investigation.'*

"Yeah, that won't go far."

"I'm sorry?"

John looked with surprise at the lady standing next to him. "Oh, sorry, I was just thinking out loud." He gave her a friendly smile and then stepped forward to grab his bag from the luggage belt. He dumped it on the trolley and then wheeled it away while checking the remaining messages. There was one from Ramesh, the subject line a winking emoji. John opened it up and read the article attached. *'Ashram manager on the run after pornography found on office computer.'*

"Well done, Ramesh," John muttered, then looked over his shoulder to check the lady hadn't heard him.

John slipped the phone into his pocket, then looked around for the exit signs. Atman and his legacy had been destroyed, and hopefully with all the negative publicity in the world press, people would think twice before having blind faith in these so-called spiritual leaders.

John spotted the exit and made his way out of the terminal. He had one more task to complete before he could consider his work done.

Two hours later, John turned off the engine of the rental car and gazed out the side window at the modest two-storey house in Sydney's western suburbs. He double checked the address against the one on his phone, then took a deep breath and opened the door. It wouldn't be easy, but it had to be done.

He walked around the car, down the path toward the front door, and rang the doorbell. There was no response for a while and he had just raised his hand to ring it again when he heard a sound from inside.

Stepping back, he waited, and then the door opened halfway. Despite the age difference and the dark shadows under his reddened eyes, the resemblance was noticeable.

"Mr Hughes?"

"Yes?" the man frowned and looked past John over his shoulder, as if expecting someone else.

John stepped forward and held out his hand. "I was a friend of your son. In India."

The man's face crumpled, but with a visible effort, he composed himself and took John's hand in a firm grip. "Why don't you come inside?"

# 104

John set the teacup down and smiled across the table at Trevor's mother. She had said little since John arrived, her eyes moist and her face lined with strain.

"He was a good man, Mrs Hughes. Honest, strong, and determined to get justice for your daughter."

Mrs Hughes sniffed, and her lips trembled. Mr Hughes placed a comforting hand on her shoulder.

John looked down at the table and thought about what he wanted to say. They had lost both children in a short space of time and there was nothing he could say or do that could bring their children back, but he wanted to give them some comfort.

"I know you've suffered an unimaginable loss," he said, looking up. "And nothing I can say will ease your pain. But..." he took a breath. "Their deaths weren't in vain and if you believe in..." John shrugged, and looked around, words suddenly failing him.

"God?"

John looked at Mr Hughes for a moment, then nodded.

"Yes... whatever you believe in... I... I believe it won't have gone unnoticed."

At this, Mrs Hughes looked up, a glimmer of light in her eyes.

"What do you mean?"

"Well..." John pursed his lips. "I..." he sighed. "Look, I personally don't believe in a traditional god..." Mr Hughes frowned as John continued, "but I believe the innate goodness of humanity will always prevail. Your daughter's bravery in telling someone about her experience, your son's courage and determination to put an end to it... well, that must have larger repercussions. It was a victory of light over darkness. Good over evil. The man your daughter followed... Atman... he and his organisation have been destroyed. He was not a good man. He abused his position and took advantage of vulnerable young women. People were murdered. But he'll never do that again. Your children's sacrifice has saved countless other lives, and maybe it will serve as a warning to others. I know it doesn't bring them back, but you should be proud of them."

Mrs Hughes sniffed and wept silently as Mr Hughes shuffled closer in his chair and pulled her to him, pressing her head against his chest.

John paused and took another deep breath. He understood internally what he was trying to convey, but putting it into words without sounding like a loony was harder than he thought.

"At the risk of sounding too ahh... new age... um... like a hippy... I do believe that on another level, perhaps in the next life, if you believe in reincarnation, they will also benefit from the good deeds they have done," John trailed off. It had sounded good in his head, but now he had said it out loud, he wouldn't be surprised if they kicked him out of the house.

He felt a hand on his arm. He looked up to see Mrs Hughes smiling at him with wet eyes. "Thank you. That means a lot to me..." She looked at her husband, "To us."

Mr Hughes was nodding slowly. "I travelled through India myself when I was their age." He looked up at John. "That's why they went there, I think. Because of the stories I told them when they were growing up." He paused for a moment and gave his wife a sad smile. Looking back at John, he continued, "I understand what you are saying. Thank you."

John gave a faint smile and looked away. He wished there was more he could say or do.

"Are your parents still alive?"

John looked up in surprise.

"Yes."

"Are you close to them?"

"Ahh... no. Not really."

"Can you do something for us?"

John straightened up. "Of course."

"When you leave here, go and see your parents. Spend some time with them. Whatever your equation is with them... I don't want to know, but spend time with them." Mr Hughes looked at his wife, took his hand off her shoulder and wiped a tear from her cheek. "Because when they have gone, you'll regret not spending more time with them."

John looked away. He hadn't seen his parents since Charlotte's funeral.

"Promise me that."

John swallowed and felt a lump in his throat. He nodded. "I promise."

He pushed back his chair and stood up. "I must go now." He gestured at the table. "Thank you for the tea."

"You never told us your name."

John smiled and reached out his hand. "Hayes. John Hayes."

**John Hayes will return in The Neighbor.
Pre-order your copy on Amazon**

# ALSO BY MARK DAVID ABBOTT

**The John Hayes Series**

Vengeance: John Hayes #1

A Million Reasons: John Hayes #2

A New Beginning: John Hayes #3

No Escape: John Hayes #4

Reprisal: John Hayes #5

Payback: John Hayes #6

The Guru: John Hayes #7

Faith: John Hayes #8

The Neighbour: John Hayes #9

**The John Hayes Box Sets**

The John Hayes Thrillers Boxset : Books 1-3

The John Hayes Thrillers Boxset : Books 4-6 (Save 33 % )

**The Hong Kong Series**

Disruption: Hong Kong #1

Conflict: Hong Kong #2

Freedom: Hong Kong #3

The Hong Kong Series Boxset :Books 1-3 (Save 33%)

**The Devil Inside**

The Devil Inside

Flipped

The Devil Inside : Boxset (Save 33%)

**As M D Abbott**

Once Upon A Time In Sri Lanka

# READY FOR THE NEXT ADVENTURE?

The next book is currently being written, but if you sign up for my VIP newsletter I will let you know as soon as it is released.

Your email will be kept 100% private and you can unsubscribe at any time.

If you are interested, please join here:

**www.markdavidabbott.com**
(No Spam. Ever.)

## ENJOYED THIS BOOK? YOU CAN MAKE A BIG DIFFERENCE.

First of all thank you so much for taking the time to read my work. If you enjoyed it, then I would be extremely grateful if you would consider leaving a short review for me on the store where you purchased the book. A good review means so much to every writer but especially to self-published writers like myself. It helps new readers discover my books and allows me more time to create stories for you to enjoy.

# ABOUT THE AUTHOR

Mark can be found online at:
www.markdavidabbott.com

on Facebook
www.facebook.com/markdavidabbottauthor

on Instagram
www.instagram.com/markdavidabbottauthor

or on email at:
www.markdavidabbott.com/contact

Printed in Great Britain
by Amazon